DIRTY ROTTEN HIPPIES

and Other Stories

I0681113

GRINDHOUSE
PRESS

BRYAN SMITH

Dirty Rotten Hippies and Other Stories copyright © 2019 by Bryan Smith. All rights reserved.

Grindhouse Press
PO BOX 521
Dayton, Ohio 45401

Grindhouse Press logo and all related artwork copyright © 2019 by Brandon Duncan. All rights reserved.

Cover art by Matthew Revert © 2019. All rights reserved.

Grindhouse Press #051
ISBN-10: 1-941918-48-4
ISBN-13: 978-1-941918-48-7

This is a work of fiction. All characters and events portrayed in this book are fictitious and any resemblance to real people or events is purely coincidental.

No part of this book may be reproduced, stored in a retrieval system, or transmitted in any form or by any means, including mechanical, electric, photocopying, recording, or otherwise, without the prior written permission of the publisher or author.

Other titles by Bryan Smith

"Fuck peace, let's jam."
    —Matthew Shannon Turbeville, circa about 1990

You left this world too soon. RIP (Rock in peace).

Seven Deadly Tales of Terror

DIRTY ROTTEN HIPPIES

ONE

IN GREAT NUMBERS, THEY CAME from far and wide to congregate in the southern countryside for a long weekend of peace, love, and groovy jams. For days in advance, a long parade of vehicles wound its way through the narrow and rutted back lanes, backing up on the interstate and causing traffic delays that dragged on for hours on end. In normal backed-up city traffic, horns would honk endlessly until the logjam cleared, but out here there were few outward displays of impatience or cantankerousness. The hordes on their way to the big outdoor music festival were blissed-out and happy to be there, away from the noise and filth of urban life and away from the vast array of concerns that make so much of modern life such a dreary drag.

The massive festival featured dozens of acts performing each day across multiple stages on six-hundred and fifty acres of farmland. Thousands of tents dotted the land. Attendees without tents spent the nights outdoors in sleeping bags or simply on the muddy ground itself. Conditions for the weekend were clear, but there'd been rain for several days beforehand. As expected, the drugs that had long been standard at such events circulated widely. Molly, marijuana, LSD, shrooms, etc. All the feel-good drugs. The ones that enhanced pleasure and expanded the senses. Recreational psychoactive substances that connected with the vibe of the event. Drugs that fueled aggression and negative feelings, such as meth and cocaine, were present only in minimal quantities and consumed only by that element not truly in tune with what the festival was all about.

As the festival got underway, however, something new began to circulate among the gathered masses. This new thing was called "Delight", and it came in a pill form, delivering sensations of euphoria and intense empathy that initially mirrored the effects of MDMA, aka Molly. Indeed, most who tried the new drug that weekend at first assumed it was MDMA under yet another new name.

That this was not the case began to become apparent deep into the first night of the festival, in the wee hours of the morning after the last notes of live music performed across the various stages had finished resounding through the countryside. The temporary cessation of performances did not mean the party had come to an end for everyone in attendance. Masses of people stayed up until dawn and even beyond, singing and dancing around bonfires and making even more of a mess of the muddy ground. Scores of people with acoustic guitars led group singalongs. Many present that night experienced a sense of bonding with like-minded human beings so intense it was unparalleled by anything they'd ever experienced. Instead of slowly fading as the hours passed, however, the effect intensified steadily. People clung to each other and wept with joy as their minds were assailed with what felt like fresh revelations about the nature of existence and the true origin of the cosmos. A celebratory sense of all things wondrous and magical held sway over all of it.

This lasted until the transcendent feelings peaked with a sense of almost unbearable euphoria, at which point the experience began to transform and take a darker turn. Some who'd taken the drug early that day began to perceive an ugly, screaming blackness lurking just beyond the illusory veil of light and love. An endless void seething with horrors almost beyond fathoming, hungry and horribly sentient entities howling madness and rage from the edge of the universe. Beings aching to surge forward and consume them all, consume the entire world.

Tears of the purest joy became the anguished wailing of the hopeless and the damned. Laughter got louder and louder and finally gave way to screaming. Hundreds and then thousands of people dropped to their knees or flopped to the ground and rolled around in the mud while giving agonized voice to the rot taking root in their souls. Some attendees immediately killed themselves instead of trying to ride out the effects of Delight. Perhaps because they were intensely troubled human beings to begin with and didn't need much to push them over the edge. This was undoubtedly true in some cases, but others who took this route had been perfectly happy and well-adjusted. The drug broke them, overwhelmed previously strong psyches and twisted them into unrecognizable shapes.

As dawn neared, most in attendance began to recognize the new and strangely prevalent drug as the likely culprit behind the crushing wave of bad vibes. Not everyone had tried Delight, but the supply was so plentiful the opportunity had been there for virtually all attendees. The unaffected soon found themselves engulfed in a frantic effort to start bringing things under control. The general consensus was that roughly half the festivalgoers had tried Delight at various points throughout the day, some early on and some as recently as just before the drug's dark side began to reveal itself. The long onset of the worst symptoms filled them with foreboding. Getting a handle on the situation was looking more and more like an impossibility. Like it or not—and most of them didn't—the authorities would have to be brought in. Calls were made. The wait for help started.

And went on until well after sunrise.

Other symptoms began to manifest, starting with a vile odor emanating from the orifices of all who'd taken Delight. A stench of rot and death. A graveyard smell originating from within. At the same time, the skin of the affected began to take on a yellow hue that darkened and became purplish within an hour. The sickened complained of unbearably bad headaches that caused them to moan at a high volume. Many of the unaffected had the eerie sense of being surrounded by thousands upon thousands of walking corpses. Speculation ran rampant. The odor of death and ugly external transformations meant the victims were rapidly rotting from the inside out. This in turn had to mean Delight had been deliberately circulated among the festival attendees by an unknown person or group with evil intent. The purported happy party drug was the ultimate Trojan Horse—a disguised delivery system for a powerful and possibly lethal toxin.

Suspicion turned to certainty shortly afterward as many of the early partakers began to fall over dead in the fields. At that point, it finally dawned on everyone that a tragedy of historic proportions was underway. While many continued their increasingly futile efforts to help the affected, many others gave up and began the process of fleeing the scene. A number of factors complicated things for those taking flight. In many cases, their cars were parked miles from the concert stages. Others trying to leave had their cars boxed in by vehicles belonging to the dead and dying. Still others remained impaired from various substances and had difficulty remembering where they'd parked. As the hopelessness of the situation became increasingly obvious, many opted to abandon their inaccessible vehicles and flee on foot, running as fast as they could in the direction of a little country town not far from the big patch of farmland.

Even in the midst of panic, many others chose to stay and continue trying to help. To these people, it didn't matter how hopeless it looked. These were the diehards, the old school hippies (young and actually old) who believed in community and duty to their fellow man.

They were the first to be devoured when the dead began to rise and walk. And after that first feast, the rotting dead began to follow the living out of the fields and toward the little country town.

The risen dead moved with surprising swiftness, chasing down and tearing into those trying to flee. It was a bloodbath so vicious and devastating it turned the mud red. By the time it was over, only a lucky few survived, perhaps less than one percent of those attending the festival.

But they knew they were not safe.

They ran as fast as they could toward the town.

Driven by an insatiable, painful hunger and a burning, primitive hatred for the living, the dead followed.

TWO

DAN FERGUSON WAS JUST SITTING down to his usual Saturday morning light breakfast when he heard the disturbance from his backyard. The breakfast consisted of a single slice of bacon and a single slice of lightly buttered toast. This was a far cry from the heartier breakfasts he'd enjoyed most of his life, but he was getting up there in years now and he had to think about his health first. Or so the doctor and Helen, his wife of almost forty years, kept telling him. He supposed they were right. Knew it, in fact. Knowing it didn't stop him from missing the hell out of that daily stack of butter-slathered pancakes and the accompanying piles of bacon and scrambled eggs.

He savored that once-daily slice of bacon the way he imagined a Russian oligarch might savor a portion of the finest caviar, drawing the process out as long as possible by taking little bites and chewing them slowly. He'd been looking forward to today's first taste of glorious bacon since almost immediately after awakening, but it was looking like that almost orgasmic experience would have to be delayed a bit because the dog was barking up a storm.

"Helen!"

His wife had retreated to the bathroom in their bedroom after setting the plate bearing his breakfast in front of him. She probably had the fan running in there, too, to cover the sounds of her dainty old lady farts and dumps. It was therefore extremely unlikely she

5

could hear him, but he tried summoning her anyway in hopes of not having to check on the commotion out back himself. He called out for her again when she didn't respond within a few seconds.

Still nothing.

Sighing and grumbling, he pushed his chair back from the rickety old breakfast nook table and got shakily to his feet, wincing at the way his knees strained and his old bones creaked. There was a lot he didn't like about getting old. The slow and inexorable deterioration of the body was probably the worst of it, though. Things that used to come so easily to him were now a struggle. It was the natural order of things. He knew that. Didn't stop him from being bitter about it, though. In his youth, he'd been a strong man. Tough and imposing. Nobody messed with him back then, not if they were smart.

Those days were gone.

He couldn't just race outside and face down any threat that happened to wander onto his property, whether by accident or intent. Caution was called for in any potentially dicey situation. He grumbled again as he shuffled his way over to the back door and took a peek outside through the window slats.

He frowned. "What the hell?"

Tojo, their six-year-old black-and-white border collie mix was straining at the end of his ten-foot lead, which was tethered to a spike planted in the approximate center of the yard. The dog was only "chained up" when they wanted to give him a bit of outside time, but he was mostly an indoor dog, preferring to curl up with them in their living room rather than chase squirrels and rabbits. It was necessary because they didn't have a fenced-in yard and they didn't want him running off. They lived off a lightly-traveled road in a rural area, so there was little chance of anything bad happening to him, but better safe than sorry was their motto. Tojo usually spent about an hour outside in the mornings, when Dan and Helen were having their breakfast. Sometimes he barked to let them know he was tired of being outdoors and wanted to come in with them. But his barking in those situations always sounded excited and happy.

This was different.

Tojo was in a ferocious frenzy, mixing in a lot of growling with the loudest barks Dan had ever heard out of him. At first Dan was confused as to the source of the dog's ire, but after a moment of scanning the area around the back of their property, he was able to identify the likely reason. Someone had come out of the expanse of woods some fifty yards distant from the back of their house and was wandering in this direction. Dan had missed the guy at first because he'd been hidden by the toolshed out back.

Now that he could see him, Dan understood why Tojo had his hackles up. Something was off about the man slowly weaving his way across their yard. He looked drunk or otherwise impaired, wobbling and nearly falling over with every other step. He looked dirty and unkempt in general, with muddy clothes and long, greasy hair that spilled well past his shoulders. The man's T-shirt was a loud swirl of multiple bright colors. There was a word for that kind of shirt, one he hadn't heard in a long time and at first he had a hard time summoning it from the recesses of his mind. Memory was another on the long list of things that got trickier to deal with as age advanced. For a moment, he was sure he wouldn't be able to think of it, but then it came to him.

The shirt was a tie-dye.

Another revelation followed shortly on the heels of this one. The scrawny young man in the tie-dye was a hippie who'd wandered over from the music festival. The festival grounds were several miles distant, but this was the only explanation. It was well-known the festival was a hive for illegal drug activity, particularly of the kind that deranged the mind and caused hallucinations. A lot of the locals hated the hippie element that invaded their community for several days every summer for this very reason, but it was tolerated because these people brought so many dollars into an otherwise stagnant local economy.

Dan had always viewed the festival with a kind of passive ambivalence. He didn't much care for the hippies or their music, but he also didn't harbor unreserved hatred for them the way some of his neighbors did. He had friends who used a lot of hateful and bigoted language when talking about them. Shameful stuff, some of it. Dan was old enough to remember the first wave of beatniks and hippies, along with the quagmire that was the Vietnam War. He hadn't cared for the extremism on either side of things back then and still felt pretty much the same way now. As long as the peace and love types kept to themselves and didn't bother him or intrude on his property, he didn't have a real problem with them.

This one was now ten feet from Tojo, who was being driven to new levels of frothing frenzy with each step closer the man came. Dan didn't think the man would hurt his dog, but as always when it

7

came to his buddy, erring on the side of caution was the way to go. The idea of confronting a man so much younger than himself filled him with anxiety and dread, but not coming to the defense of his dog wasn't an option. He wouldn't be able to live with himself if something bad did happen.

He opened the door and stepped out onto the back stoop. "Hey, you out there! You need to get away from my dog and get off my damn property!"

The young man's unkempt long hair stirred in the stiffening breeze as he took another wobbling step toward Tojo. He gave no indication of having heard Dan's shouted warning. The dog's loud barks became higher-pitched, like the yips of a much smaller dog. He was scared and was shrinking away from the advancing stranger now instead of straining at his lead.

Dan sighed.

Goddammit.

He stepped down from the porch and knelt to grab the old rake he'd left on the ground yesterday. He winced again as his knees made creaking and cracking sounds, but he gritted his teeth and forced himself to stand up straight again faster than he normally would. A creature he loved was in trouble and he didn't have the luxury of taking it easy on his weathered old body.

Forcing himself to move with a quickness he hadn't attempted in years, he closed the wide gap between himself and the wobbly intruder to something more manageable within just a few moments. He felt a degree of relief at knowing he'd likely be able to put himself between Tojo and the slowly advancing stranger before anything bad could happen. Sweat was pouring from his temples and he was breathing hard, but he didn't seem in imminent danger of keeling over, which felt like a minor miracle.

He raised the old rake and gripped the wooden handle securely in both hands, positioning the rake's rusted metal prongs at an angle that would allow him to drive it hard into the stranger's chest should that become necessary. In the event that happened, he just might be able to summon up enough of his dwindling strength to give the man a shove hard enough to send him tumbling to the ground.

Still hoping he could head off a physical confrontation, Dan raised his voice again and fought to keep the rake steady in his grip as he said, "One last chance, asshole. Take your scraggly ass off my property or get knocked over. You won't get another warning."

The long-haired stranger raised his head and groaned loudly as he came yet another step closer.

This was Dan's first good look at the man's face and it was not a pleasant one. Until just now, he'd been lumbering closer with his head drooping forward and that dirty hair hanging in his eyes. Only a small sliver of his face had been visible through the dangling strands, but now it was mostly unobscured. There was something wrong with the man's skin, purplish and yellow hues that wouldn't ordinarily be seen in the flesh of the living. There was a strong odor coming off him, too, something Dan couldn't attribute to the filth the man had evidently been wallowing in since arriving at the festival. It was a smell of rot and death, a smell so intense it made his eyes water and triggered a feeling of queasiness from deep in his stomach.

The stranger was like a walking dead man.

Tojo had taken up a position at Dan's heels and was barking louder again now that his human companion had arrived. The noise wasn't doing much to calm his nerves. It was apparent now Tojo's wariness of the stranger had been well-founded. Whatever was off about this person couldn't be attributed merely to drug or alcohol impairment.

There was something unnatural about it.

Something fundamentally *wrong*.

The intruder came another groaning step closer and Dan finally decided he'd been patient enough. Tightening his grip on the rake's handle, he summoned up what strength he could and charged forward, intending to ram the head of the rake into the man's chest with hopefully enough force to knock him down. He would then grab Tojo and retreat to the house. After locking the house down, he'd call the sheriff and have them send some men out to cart this asshole off to jail.

This plan went astray when the toe of one of his shoes snagged in a dip in the ground and caused him to pitch forward in ungainly fashion. He let go of the rake in an effort to get his hands under him in time to break his fall. Unfortunately, his right arm came down at a bad angle. His forearm snapped as it hit the hard ground. He screamed as he rolled onto his back and saw a bloody bit of bone protruding through a hole in his flesh.

He screamed again when he looked up and saw the foul-smelling stranger looming above him. The man had stopped advancing and was staring down at him. Dan felt a jolt of fear as he looked into the man's badly bloodshot eyes. Eyes without a spark of life in them.

Tojo's barking frenzy reached new heights. The dog sounded like he was straining harder than ever at his lead. In another moment, Dan saw a blur of movement in his peripheral vision and realized Tojo had pulled the spike out of the ground and was running away. Seconds later, he heard a desperate scratching sound and knew the dog had gone to the back door and was trying his best to alert Helen to their predicament.

Dan felt tears in his eyes.

Good boy.

He had a choice here. He could either stay right where he was and leave himself at the mercy of this malign stranger or he could make an effort to push through the pain and get off the damn ground. If he could just get back on his feet, he'd still have a fighting chance of getting back inside the house safe and sound with his beloved dog.

Sucking in a breath and steeling himself for the jolt of severe agony sure to come, Dan again tapped reserves of dwindling strength and rolled toward his good side. He meant to get his good hand braced on the ground so he could push himself up. Tojo was still scratching and yammering at the back door as he got himself into a sitting position. Hope flared anew inside him as he began to think he might have a real chance here.

That hope died as the stranger fell upon him, driving him back to the ground and pinning him there. The groaning sounds issuing from the man's mouth were louder than ever as his jaw opened wide and dropped toward him. That ripe breath was like a direct blast of rancid air from the foulest sewer on earth. Then the man's teeth were on him, biting and tearing into his flesh. Dan whimpered as he felt a spurt of warm blood jet from a hole in his throat.

The last thing he saw before he died was the stranger chewing on his flesh.

He was *eating* him.

Dan had long made a habit of envisioning all the many ways he might one day shuffle off this mortal coil. It was a natural thing for an old man to do. But he'd never seen anything like this coming.

Aw, fuck it.

The world faded away and the last thing he heard was Tojo, still barking like crazy.

THREE

TRAVIS KINCAID HAD NEVER RUN so hard in his life. Running was never an activity he engaged in voluntarily, nor was it one he'd done with any regularity since graduating high school several years ago. Back then he'd often been forced to run laps around the track in PE class. Though he hadn't enjoyed it, he'd been fortunate in a way a lot of other kids who weren't athletically minded were not. He'd been blessed with good genes that kept him skinny and fit no matter how much junk food he ate. And he ate a lot of junk food. Being made to do laps was often torture for the overweight kids, but not for him. He could glide around the track with ease numerous times when made to do so. His PE teachers often told him he should try out for the track team, advice he always ignored.

For Travis, the issue wasn't whether he was physically capable.

He was.

He just didn't *want* to do it, nor did he much care for being forced to do anything against his will. From early in his life, he'd been contrarian and anti-authoritarian by nature. For this reason, he found much that spoke to him when reading up on the counter-culture of the 1960s. He naturally gravitated to participation in activist groups upon entering college. His interest in protesting things eventually waned somewhat, but he nonetheless became immersed in stoner culture and later took to following around various jam bands on tour.

The politics still spoke to him, but it turned out his bigger interest was in getting high and staying that way as much as possible. He became part of a tight group of friends who essentially lived on the road, making money by selling drugs and doing odd jobs here and there. It wasn't a bad way of life as far as he was concerned. He got to spend all his time with people he genuinely liked and he wasn't beholden to anyone for anything, especially not authority figures.

Now all his friends were dead and for the first time in years he was being forced to run, only this time his very survival depended on it. He'd been going full-tilt nearly nonstop for what felt like at least an hour. The strain of it was just starting to get to him. He felt like he could keep going for a while yet, but not forever. His stamina had limits. If he wanted to live, though, he'd have to push those limits to their absolute furthest reaches.

A horde of ravenous dead was still hot on his heels. Mostly he kept his focus on the way ahead, on digging down deep and forcing his muscles to work at peak capacity, but now and then he glanced over his shoulder to gauge the severity of the threat behind him. At the least he had to keep them from gaining ground, but he kept hoping he'd eventually start to put some real distance between them. Thus far the latter had not happened, but he'd been successful at maintaining the status quo.

The rural road was lined on both sides with the parked cars and campers of festival attendees. He'd passed the old VW bus in which he and his friends traversed the country some miles back. The keys to the vehicle were in his pocket, but he'd made no attempt to drive away in it. The dead would've swarmed over him and devoured him if he'd slowed down enough to try. They were that fast and that relentless. He'd be a pile of shredded, bloody meat in no time if he let up for even a few seconds.

A helpless whimper came to his lips as that basic fact took up front and center residence in his consciousness for the first time in a while. He was mostly able to keep that terrifying reality at bay by staying focused on the physical act of running, but soon there'd be no getting away from it. His lungs and muscles would begin to betray him. He'd slow down, maybe stumble and fall.

And then it'd be all over.

He sniffled as tears misted the corners of his eyes. Maybe he should just give up and let it happen. Get it over with rather than continue to endure this tortuous contemplation of the inevitable. He still wanted to live more than anything, but the hopelessness of the situation was apparent. The end of his time on earth was going to happen on this stretch of dusty road regardless of what he wanted. There was no solution. No way out.

No escape.

The slowing of his pace initially happened at an almost unconscious level. He was still running at a good pace, but no longer at full-tilt. His muscles were relaxing. He was breathing more easily now that his lungs weren't straining so hard. Sweat streamed down his face and got in his eyes. He wiped it away and sniffled again, thinking of his dead friends. Caitlin and Sierra. Opie and Sage. They'd shared so many good times during their travels. He'd been closer to them than he'd ever been with his family. In many ways, they'd become his real family, the only one that really mattered to him, the one that embraced and accepted him as he truly was rather than forcing him to live a normal, conformist life.

He'd watched in slowly mounting horror as Caitlin, Opie, and Sage first became ill and then got progressively sicker. He and Sierra were the only ones of their group who hadn't tried the new party drug making the rounds that first day. They'd tried in vain to help their friends, but nothing was working. Their friends just got sicker and sicker and finally succumbed to the devastating effects of the drug. Only when it became clear that it was hopeless did they decide the time had come to flee the festival grounds without their ailing friends.

Travis took Sierra by the hand and tried his best to lead them back in the direction of the VW bus, which was parked on the main access road leading to the festival grounds. By then some of the dead were already rising and attacking the living. Many of the living were flailing about in a blind panic, unable to comprehend what was happening or know what to do about it. Threading their way through the throngs of the living and undead was hazardous in the extreme. Travis worked hard to dodge the risen dead and, on occasion, ward them off when necessary. In between shoving the transformed creatures out of their way, he watched dead people tear into the flesh of the living and rip apart their bodies. He saw puddles of blood and piles of fresh organs steaming in the sun seemingly everywhere he looked.

Progress was maddeningly slow. Sierra was in her bare feet and wearing a long, frilly dress that hampered her ability to move with quickness and efficiency. The homemade dress was patterned after a kind typically worn by women living on the American frontier in the

19th century. Aside from a few comfy T-shirts, Sierra made almost all her own clothes. The grasping fingers of the hungry dead snagged and tore at the fabric, ripping it apart and exposing her vulnerable flesh. Fingernails scraped her skin and drew forth streams of blood. All the while, Travis kept pulling her out of the reach of the dead just in time to avert disaster. For a brief time, he was able to allow himself the delusion they'd make it to the road together safe and sound.

That lasted until the dead went into berserker mode. They went from plodding and clumsy to fast and deadly in an instant, as if a switch had been flipped inside their fevered brains. Large packs of energized dead things swarmed over those who'd fought and survived to that point and slaughtered most of them within minutes. They came at Travis and Sierra from all directions, and he was forced to relinquish his grip on her hand without making a conscious decision to do so. He desperately fought off multiple attackers long enough to see more of them tear the front of his friend's homemade dress wide open and then rip open her belly. She was screaming as long loops of intestines spilled out to the ground. The dead things were feasting on her guts within seconds. Then they rode her to the ground and it was all over.

That was when Travis started running.

In the time since then, he'd covered miles of ground, but it wasn't going to be nearly enough. Like all his friends, he wouldn't be able to outrun death.

Now his pace continued to slow and soon he was down to a lazy jog that was barely more than a fast walk. In just a few more seconds, he *was* walking, exhaustion sweeping over him as he slipped firmly into acceptance mode. He came to a full stop in the middle of the road and heaved a tired breath. For another moment, he only stood there, staring off into the unreachable distance. He'd left the open farmland behind a while ago and was now on a winding stretch of rural road flanked by tall trees on each side. The normal world was still somewhere out there, miles beyond that next bend in the road, but he'd never see it again. And maybe that was okay. Without his friends, did he really want to see it again, anyway?

He closed his eyes and waited for the end, which he expected to happen within a few seconds. When several moments elapsed without the dead swarming over him, he opened his eyes again as a look of deep puzzlement twisted his features. He turned slowly around and saw what he expected. The hordes of dead were still after him. They clogged the road, there were so many of them.

What he hadn't expected was the gaping distance he'd put between himself and them. The leading edge of the horde was about the length of a football field away now. This was astonishing. The last time he'd risked a glance over his shoulder to assess the threat level, the vanguard of the dead had been no more than twenty feet to his rear. At first this confused him, but he soon understood why the dead were lagging behind him now. The berserker mode that had transformed them into such a ferocious and formidable killing force was no longer in effect. Though the dead still pursued him, now they lumbered and shambled slowly forward instead of running full-tilt like undead Usain Bolts.

Something about either the drug they'd taken or the transformation they'd undergone ignited the propulsive fury that gripped them, but it seemed there were limits to their unearthly energy. Travis figured he could easily outpace the slowed-down horde by resuming a brisk walking pace. And the sooner he got going again, the better. Against all odds, it seemed he might survive the day after all, but he was under no illusions. Berserker mode was no longer engaged, but the dead were still dangerous. Survival still depended on getting as far away from them as possible.

Travis turned away from them and started off down the road again.

At first he walked until his lungs no longer felt on the verge of collapse, but then he started running again. Salvation lay somewhere up ahead. And with a renewed flicker of hope burning inside him came a new determination to do whatever it took to get there.

FOUR

THE FIRST THING HELEN FERGUSON heard when she came out of the bathroom and shut off the fan was Tojo's manic barking and scratching at the back door. She frowned as she stepped out into the hallway and moved toward the kitchen. It wasn't like Tojo to get so wound up. He was an easygoing dog. Besides that, they lived in a sparsely populated area, on a patch of land well removed from the road and surrounded by woods. Sometimes Tojo would bark at deer or other animals that wandered out of the forest, but even then he never sounded like this.

He sounded terrified.

Helen stopped in her tracks in the hallway and called out to her husband. She waited a beat and, when Dan didn't respond, called out again. When he again failed to respond, Helen decided to detour into the den where she went to Dan's gun rack and opened it, taking out a pump shotgun. She loaded it with some shells from a box on the lower shelf.

Then she went into the kitchen.

Tojo's yapping had grown even shriller by then. She could almost see the deep grooves his claws were etching in the other side of the door. By now she understood that something really wrong was happening. Her first guess was that something had happened to Dan. He'd fallen down and broken a leg or had a heart attack, and now his faithful canine pal was trying to raise the alarm.

Yes, those were the most likely possibilities. They lived in a place city people would think of as the middle of nowhere. In all their years of living out here, not once had their property been intruded on by strangers. During the daytime, they mostly left their doors unlocked precisely because the threats city dwellers had to worry about every day simply didn't exist out here.

Except now Helen was wondering whether they'd been wrong to think that way. This was a world full of vultures and predators. Sure, you were far more likely to encounter the loathsome dregs of society in more populated areas, but that didn't mean such creatures might not one day stray into their territory, perhaps in an effort to lose themselves in rural anonymity and thus avoid the long reach of the law. Helen watched a lot of true crime shows on TV. It wasn't hard to imagine when you really thought about it.

Tojo almost sounded like he was screaming now.

She loved the dog almost as much as Dan did. Forcing him to endure even another second of terror wasn't an option. Letting out a stabilizing breath, she unlocked the door and pulled it open. Tojo nearly knocked her off her feet as he came barreling in with the spike still attached to his lead. She heard his claws scrambling across the kitchen tiles for a moment before he disappeared somewhere deeper inside the house. The spike made loud thumping sounds as it bounced off walls and doorjambs.

Helen stepped out onto the stoop and felt her heart skip a few beats when she saw her beloved husband on the ground some twenty feet away from the toolshed. He was lying on his back and staring blankly up at the clear blue sky. Even from here, she could see the bloody, shredded mess that had been made of his throat. A natural impulse to deny the reality of what she was seeing came and went. There was no time for that.

Not with her husband's killer coming straight toward her.

That this scraggly, long-haired man was responsible for the death of the love of her life was not in doubt. The man's face was smeared with Dan's blood and bits of bloody flesh were visible at the corners of his mouth. The front of his tie-dyed shirt was also sticky with a copious amount of blood. He stared at Helen with eyes so bloodshot they looked like the pulsing alien orbs of some nightmare creature. There was something wrong with the man's skin and a smell so rotten it nearly made her swoon emanated from his orifices. As he came another lurching step closer, a loud farting sound ripped out of his backside. The gaseous eruption was so forceful it propelled the hideous man another step forward and nearly made him tumble to the ground.

But he did not fall over.

He kept coming.

And the closer he got to Helen, the hungrier that groaning noise issuing from his rotting throat sounded. The edges of his mouth twitched and his jaw began to unhinge as he reached out to her with grasping, shaking fingers.

Helen stepped down from the stoop and raised the shotgun, bracing the stock against her shoulder. "You stop right there, you bastard! Come one step closer and I'll blow your dadblamed head off."

The man's cracked and bleeding lips peeled back from his teeth, revealing blackened gums and a lump of swollen, putrid flesh Helen needed a moment to recognize as his tongue. She recoiled in disgust as another gust of foul-smelling air wafted out of his open mouth, causing her to loosen her grip on the shotgun as she took a helpless step backward. At the same time, another fart so loud it was like a gunshot blasted out of his backside and propelled him another wobbly step closer. His grasping fingers were now less than ten feet away.

Helen got the shotgun's stock braced against her shoulder again and called out to the man again. "Last warning, you son of a bitch. Back off or I'm blasting a hole right through your belly."

Her words appeared not to register as the man came yet another step closer. Helen's grip tightened on the shotgun as she curled a finger around the trigger and tried to gird herself for a moment of shocking violence that seemed inevitable. Being a country girl all her life, she knew her way around firearms, but until today she'd never aimed a gun at another living creature, either animal or human. She didn't doubt her ability to shoot this deranged and obviously diseased stranger, but she didn't relish having to do it either, even knowing he'd savagely murdered her husband.

Still another step closer.

And another.

That guttural groaning now sounded more like a hungry growl.

Helen sneered. "Goddamn you."

She squeezed the trigger and the shotgun roared, rocking her backward a step. In her youth, she would've been strong enough to fully absorb the recoil, but she was an old lady and it'd been decades since she'd last fired a big gun like this one. The last time she'd done it to scare a bear away, firing the weapon over the beast's head. That time the warning shot worked. The animal retreated into the woods and, as far as Helen knew, never strayed onto their property again.

This time the warning shot did not work.

The stranger shambled another step closer. He didn't appear the slightest bit rattled by the close-range blast of the shotgun. He hadn't even flinched. The reaction wasn't natural. It was as if he didn't understand the threat the shotgun represented. That something was wrong with him had been clear from the beginning, but now Helen realized she'd underestimated the extent of that wrongness. His brain was functioning on only the most primitive level. He cared only about getting to her and tearing into her flesh, just as he'd done to Dan.

He was five feet away now and still advancing.

Helen's terror of being killed in so horrendous a fashion finally overrode her reluctance to kill. She adjusted her aim and squeezed the trigger again. This time the blast hit the man full-on in the belly, knocking him backward and causing him to topple to the ground. She let out a gasping cry of relief and lowered the gun as tears began to stream down her face. Shooting a human being, even one as monstrous as this one, felt as awful as she'd imagined. It was a feeling she hoped she'd never have to experience again.

Her body shook with her sobbing as she worked to rub the tears from her eyes. She felt queasy and on the verge of puking her guts up when she realized she was still hearing that guttural groaning. Her tears quickly dried up as she again focused on the man she'd shot. Her vision was still slightly blurry from crying, but she perceived movement on the ground. After grinding the heel of a palm into her eyes to clear away the excess moisture, she gaped in disbelief upon seeing that the man was sitting up and attempting to get to his feet.

Helen frowned, shaking her head. "No. No, no, no. That's not possible. You stay down."

Except she was wrong about it not being possible, because within another few moments the groaning, lurching stranger was upright again. He wobbled around precariously in place for a moment and Helen was sure he'd soon fall over again, probably for good this time. She could see bits of shredded organs through the hole in his belly. He should be screaming in unbearable agony, but now that he was standing again, he appeared as unfazed by the wound as he'd been by the warning shot. He should be bleeding out on the ground, already dead or close to it.

The weird thing about that was how he'd already looked and smelled like a dead man even before she'd shot him. Her brow furrowed as she processed this information and made a correlation with bits of popular culture she'd absorbed over the years. She soon arrived at an obvious conclusion, albeit one she found difficult to believe even with this visceral proof right in front of her.

"Oh," she said, grimacing as she raised the shotgun again. "You're one of them. And I guess there's only one way to deal with the likes of you."

She squeezed the trigger and the shotgun roared a third time. This time the blast blew apart the top of the man's head, sending a spray of blood, brains, and bone fragments all over the yard. He fell over again and this time he stayed down. She observed him closely for signs of movement a few moments longer, but he remained absolutely still.

She'd killed the walking dead man.

This time the feeling didn't hit her so hard. He'd been dead already, anyway, so it wasn't like she'd committed murder. Not really. All she'd done was to correct a wrong. The dead weren't meant to walk around in the world like living folk. It was an abomination. What she'd done could even be seen as an act of mercy. She wasn't sure the sheriff would see it that way. He likely wouldn't even believe her tale of a reanimated dead man, but did it really matter? She'd been defending her property and her own safety and had acted within her rights. The sheriff would look past the abnormalities of the situation and find a way to explain it all away, absolving her of any responsibility for the man's death. It was the way things worked around here. Locals looked out for each other. And there was no doubt whatsoever this man was *not* local.

She was about to go inside to phone the sheriff when she caught a glimpse of something at the edge of her vision. Putting a hand to her brow to cut the glare of the sun, she squinted into the distance and saw something that brought back that queasy feeling.

Two more shambling dead things had stepped out of the trees and were moving in the direction of her house.

"Goddammit."

Helen supposed this shouldn't have come as a surprise. On the TV shows and in the movies, there was never just one of these things. Sometimes there were just a few to deal with, but often they moved in great numbers. In packs or herds, whatever you wanted to call them.

Indeed, even as she tracked their slow progress from the bottom of the gently sloping hill, she saw two more of the creatures amble out of the woods. Then came another. And another.

Helen shook her head. "The hell with this."

A couple more she maybe could've dealt with on her own, but there was no telling how many more of these things might come out of the woods. She wasn't a one-woman army, unlike some of the ladies on the TV shows.

She needed help.

Helen went back inside the house.

After closing and locking the back door, she went over to the phone mounted on the wall by the refrigerator and began punching in the sheriff's number. Tojo came back into the kitchen as she listened to the phone ring.

He sat down at the back door and stared at it, growling.

TRAVIS KEPT RUNNING FOR ANOTHER twenty minutes before again slowing his pace, recognizing the need to conserve his energy. He could no longer see the dead behind him, the leading edge of the horde having disappeared behind one of the bends in the looping stretch of road. They were still back there, though, and still dangerous. Pushing himself beyond the brink of exhaustion before he reached safety would be foolish. For all he knew, the dead might be capable of a level of rejuvenation after a period of rest, just like living humans. They might even be able to go back into berserker mode at some point. He didn't think that would happen, but dismissing the possibility entirely wouldn't be smart.

He tried to guess how far he'd come since fleeing the festival grounds, but that was impossible to know with anything approaching certainty. Several miles at the least was the closest he could get to pinpointing it. Though he wasn't carrying much in the way of extra weight, he wasn't a trained runner and was feeling the strain of the unusual physical effort deep in his bones. If he managed to make it out of here alive, he'd be hurting for the next several days. It'd be nice to relieve his body of this burden and find a ride back to civilization, but so far no cars had come down the road from the direction of town. This struck him as deeply strange. There should be at least a few late-arriving festival attendees. There were always second-day stragglers at these things. Unless word of the massive calamity had gotten out to the larger world, that is, and that didn't seem likely based on everything he'd witnessed as the situation had worsened through the morning.

As things had deteriorated, he'd noticed people trying to call 911 or directly contact authorities. A few people claimed to have gotten through on the emergency line early on, but something happened after that and suddenly no one was able to reach anyone anywhere or even get a signal. Travis had no idea what the explanation for that could be, but it seemed ominous, as if access to the outside world was somehow deliberately being prevented. He also couldn't imagine who would do such a thing or why, but that didn't mean anything. There were always people or groups out there looking to hurt other people on a mass scale, maybe more so than ever these days. As crazy as the idea seemed on the surface, it was possible he was the sole survivor of the strangest terror attack in history.

Whatever the case, help had never arrived and probably never would. Living to see another day was entirely up to him. He could keep pushing forward or give in to mounting exhaustion and surrender. Just lie down and die or wait to be rescued, though the odds of the latter happening seemed remote at best. For now he was still opting for pushing forward, but that was subject to change at any time.

Another indicator of how far he'd come was that the cars and trucks of festival attendees were no longer lining both sides of the road. He estimated he'd seen the last of them slightly less than a mile back. Until now he'd been too focused on outrunning the dead things to bother with attempting to break into any of the vehicles, but now he was wondering whether he should turn back and try to get into one of those cars while he still could. He thought he'd left the dead far enough behind that backtracking a relatively short distance might still be a viable option.

The deciding factor against this idea was the practical reality of what stealing a car entailed. Though he'd lived the free-spirited life of a group of hippie kids traveling the highways and byways of the land for a while now, he had no experience whatsoever in real criminal endeavors. The same went for his friends. Apart from their penchant for selling and indulging in various illegal substances, they'd all been conscientious law-abiders. In theory, he could knock out the window of somebody's car, but what then? Unless someone had helpfully left a spare key in a place where he could easily find it (unlikely), he wouldn't be able to start it. Any way he looked at it, the effort would be a waste of time and he'd lose ground for no good reason.

It wasn't a real option at all.

He kept moving forward instead.

About another half mile down the road, he began to hear a faint sound of music emanating from somewhere out in the woods off to his right. He stopped in his tracks and frowned as he turned to stare at the line of trees. The sound was so faint he first thought he must be imagining it, an auditory hallucination produced by his traumatized psyche. In those first few seconds after he stopped, he was almost certain this was correct, because he was no longer hearing the music. Then it started again, still faint but definitely there. He couldn't quite identify what the music was, but something at the back of his mind detected something familiar in the sound.

Still frowning, he moved closer to the edge of the road and the line of trees and perked up his ears, straining hard to better make out what he was hearing. What he knew was that it wasn't aggressive hard rock, nor was it EDM or some other form of modern pop. No, this music was too soft and mellow for that. It was meandering guitar-based music. Sounded like a jam band, actually, similar to many such bands that had been set to play the festival over the weekend.

A lot of hippies were back-to-nature types. They liked to camp out in the woods or live off the grid. Maybe what he was hearing was a small gathering of like-minded souls who'd come out to the country for the festival, but had opted to spend the night camped out among the trees instead of on the festival grounds. It was a theory based on not much, but it felt plausible to Travis. These people out in the woods might even be some of the second-day stragglers he'd been expecting to see all along but had somehow never materialized. He craned his head around, searching the road for signs of a parked vehicle. If he was right, there had to be one somewhere, but he wasn't seeing it. Didn't mean much, though. Though this was his third time attending this particular festival, this was still basically foreign territory. He knew the way out to the festival grounds from the interstate and the way back again. The lay of the land beyond that was a mystery, so the campers might well have parked on some other secondary road.

He stood at the edge of the road a while longer, fidgeting and uncertain about what to do. The stretch of road he could see back in the direction of the festival grounds was still clear of dead things. He might have time to venture into the woods and attempt to make contact with whoever was playing the music. Or he might not. Thanks to the winding nature of the road, however, that visible part of it was not very long. Less than a hundred feet, probably. Made it hard to judge his safety level with any real certainty. Based on how slowly the dead things had been moving the last time he glimpsed them, he still believed he'd created a substantial buffer zone. Unless the creatures started accelerating again, he felt he could easily spend up to a half hour investigating the source of the music without unnecessarily endangering himself.

Another thing to consider was his basic responsibility as a decent human being. There was a strong chance these theoretical campers were unaware of the carnage that had overtaken the festival. He had no doubt many of the walking dead things would stray into the woods rather than stay on the road. At the very least, it was his duty to warn these people. With any luck, they'd be able to take him to wherever their car was parked. It wasn't just the humane and compassionate thing to do, it might be his best means out of here.

His decision made, Travis stepped down into the shallow ditch at the side of the road and in another few seconds entered the line of trees beyond. Maintaining his focus on the music, which was still faint at that point, he worked at moving in the hopefully right direction. Progress was slow at first, because he occasionally had to stop and listen for a moment to better home in on the correct way to go before continuing. He was about fifteen minutes removed from the road when he was finally able to identify what he was hearing. He smiled when he realized it was the Grateful Dead, some live album rather than the more typical greatest hits collection. The song playing at that moment was "Casey Jones".

The realization further cemented his belief he was doing the right thing. These were his people. They'd never met, most likely, but they were kindred. Like many of their tribe, they were tuned in to the same spiritual wavelengths. These people would help him, he had no doubt.

In another few minutes, he was hearing the music clear as day. The trees were less densely grouped together and he soon realized he was nearing the edge of a clearing. Soon he was able to glimpse a part of the clearing and saw the back of a tent erected there. As he reached the edge of the clearing, he saw two more tents. The tents were grouped around a campfire that appeared to have been doused a short while ago. Some embers were still smoldering a bright red in the pile of gray ashes.

Rather than proceeding directly into the clearing, he hesitated, lurking behind a tree as he scanned the area for signs of the campers. He still believed he was likely to find these people welcoming and friendly, but it was probably smart to proceed with a bit of caution. The music was coming from an old-fashioned boombox placed within a few feet of the smoldering campfire. It made sense that a bunch of traveling hippies would listen to their music on such an archaic device. In Travis's experience, his people were often not up-to-date on the latest technology and gadgets. Such things were expensive and hippies rarely had the money to spend on them. What money they had was mostly spent on gasoline, food, and weed.

As he continued to observe, however, he began to feel slightly wary. He'd been standing there a few minutes without catching sight of any of the campers. Either they were in their tents or they were out walking around in the woods. Which begged the question of why music was playing on the boombox with no one around. He guessed it was possible most of them were still asleep in their tents while the one person who'd been jamming the tunes had wandered off into the woods for a few minutes to take a leak or a shit.

A plausible explanation, for sure. The best course of action might be to wait around until that person returned before stepping into the clearing and announcing his presence. Otherwise he'd risk startling the people in the tents. So he stayed behind the tree and waited a while longer.

Maybe ten more minutes passed before he started getting antsy. There was still no sign of anyone in the vicinity. He was starting to think about how much time had passed since he'd left the road. It was getting close to a solid half-hour. Maybe not enough time yet for the dead to catch up with him, but enough to close the distance significantly. If these people didn't show up soon, he might be forced to head back to the road. Otherwise he ran the risk of having that avenue of escape cut off, trapping him out here in the woods with no idea of an alternate way out.

He waited a couple minutes longer, his frustration mounting until an impulse caused him to step out from behind the tree and tentatively enter the clearing. Out in the open now, he craned his head around, still scanning the area for signs of anyone at all. Once again, he saw nothing but the surrounding trees and the stillness of the seemingly empty clearing. He was less concerned now with the possibility of disturbing anyone who might be in the tents. The time for being considerate had come and gone. Waking them up and alerting them to what was happening was for their benefit as much as his own.

He was within several feet of the campfire by the time he was able to get a look inside one of the open tent flaps. His brow furrowed in confusion when he saw it was completely empty. No sleeping bags or other camping supplies whatsoever. This initially struck him as only slightly odd, but then he moved on to the other tents and found them empty as well.

After staring into the last of the empty tents for nearly a full minute, he retreated to the center of the clearing, where he stopped and took another look around. By then the truth was impossible to deny. No one else was here. He began to feel deeply unsettled. The music playing in the middle of nowhere with no one around to listen to it felt off and wrong.

It felt fucking *strange*.

The eeriness of the situation made him think of the stories he'd heard of large groups of people who went mysteriously missing with no explanation. The lost colony of Roanoke and the vanished crew of the Mary Celeste. In the case of the latter, the ship was found adrift with its cargo intact and the crew's belongings still on board and undisturbed. Neither mystery had ever been definitively solved as far as Travis knew.

Could this be a similar situation?

He thought about it a moment and decided it wasn't likely. There was a real threat out there, but it had nothing to do with ancient mysteries or other flights of the imagination. He had no clue where these people had gone, but there was a rational explanation, he was sure of that. He decided to take one last stab at establishing contact. If nothing came of it inside of about a minute, he'd hurry back out to the road and pray he hadn't lingered here too long.

He knelt and hit the stop button on the boombox, cutting off "Friend of the Devil" mid-song. After taking a moment to clear his throat, he cupped his hands around his mouth and called out to the unseen campers. *"Hello! Is there anyone out there?"*

Some moments passed.

Travis again craned his head around and scanned the entire perimeter of the clearing. Yet again, he saw nothing. And no response came from the missing campers. He was ready to give up, but he decided to give it one more try.

"Hello! If you're out there, please show yourself. Something terrible happened at the music festival and we all need to evacuate the area as soon as possible. I'm fucking serious here. This is a life and death situation."

He fell silent and waited a beat.

Just when he was sure he'd have to give up and head back for the road, he heard a crunching sound. Someone out there in the woods, just beyond the line of trees from the sound of it, had stepped on a stick. He held his breath a moment, waiting for someone to appear.

When someone finally did emerge from the woods and enter the clearing, his mouth dropped open in surprise, because this person was not at all what he'd been expecting. Pretty much the exact opposite, in fact.

The man who approached him was a tall and bearded beast with bushy brown hair. In addition to being tall, he was hugely fat. He wore dirty denim overalls, and a Miller High Life baseball cap sat perched atop his head at a crooked angle. His beard was not the well-kempt and groomed type associated with hipsters. It was scraggly and there were bits of what might be food in it. A toothpick was wedged into a corner of his mouth. Most disconcertingly of all, a double-barreled shotgun was propped over his right shoulder. His eyes had the dead-eyed look of a dedicated meth user and his smile was not at all friendly.

Every instinct Travis had told him to immediately turn tail and flee back into the woods before this walking redneck cliché forced him into some act of horrifying backwoods perversity. It was what he wanted more than anything just then, but he felt rooted to the spot, unable to move, barely able to think.

His mind tried to rationalize the situation as the man came closer. He told himself the fear he was feeling was a product of unfair and shameful stereotypes. This man didn't *really* mean him any harm. What he had to do here was stay calm and try to warn the man about the approaching dead horde.

He'd just opened his mouth to attempt that very thing when more people stepped out of the woods and came into the clearing. There were three more of them now. Two more men and a young woman. The other men were dressed almost identically in flannel shirts, dirty jeans, and boots. Both flannel shirt guys carried bolt-action rifles.

The woman was smaller and much skinnier than her male

counterparts. Her tight jeans were ripped and frayed in numerous places, allowing for what would've been tantalizing glimpses of creamy smooth flesh under other circumstances. She wore a dark blue mechanic's work shirt with the name Darlene stitched on a patch above her left breast. Black hair framed a pale, almost pretty face devoid of makeup. The black ballcap she wore was adorned with a confederate battle flag patch. The smile she showed Travis when he looked at her revealed multiple missing teeth. He guessed she was in her early twenties, younger than her friends by several years at least. Unlike the others, she was not carrying a gun.

Travis trembled as he realized they'd formed a circle around him. The circle was slowly tightening as they moved steadily closer. It hit him with sudden, undeniable clarity that these people would absolutely kill him if he didn't somehow get away. And they might well do a lot worse than just kill him first.

The woman laughed. "Got another one to take a bait."

The others laughed, too.

The man in the overalls sneered and reached down to scratch his balls through the denim.

One of the flannel shirt guys said, "Works every time. Ain't a hippie alive can resist the Grateful Dead."

The other flannel shirt guy said, "This keeps up, we'll have enough meat stored away to last us the rest of the year."

Overalls guy made a deep, rumbling sound that might have been a kind of guttural laughter. He was still fiddling with his balls in a way that was increasingly seeming less like the scratching of an itch and more like something far more sinister and upsetting. "Gonna have to tenderize that shit first, though. Tenderize it real *good*."

Darlene was closer than the rest of them, just a few feet away now. She smirked and looked Travis up and down. "Look how bad the sumbitch is shaking. We're gonna have some fun with this one."

Travis felt on the verge of fainting.

Then he felt a flicker of anger and a new resolve.

Goddammit, he hadn't spent the morning outrunning a horde of fucking zombies just to wind up getting gang-violated by a bunch of hillbilly freaks. He turned in the general direction of the road and bolted, but before he could get beyond the circle of rednecks, the stock of a rifle cracked against the side of his head and knocked him to the ground.

He felt woozy as he looked up and saw Darlene standing directly over him. "You ain't goin' anywhere, you dirty fuckin' hippie. This party's just getting started."

She hocked up a wad of saliva and spat it in his face.

Then she stomped a boot down on his head, causing the world to first go gray and then turn black.

SIX

BACKSTAGE PERSONNEL AND BANDS PLAYING the festival that weekend were not spared the ravages of Delight, with the drug circulating as widely behind the scenes as it did among attendees. Members of nearly all bands present that first day tried the drug, along with many members of their road crews and entourages. A positive initial buzz led to a high level of interest. It was reputed to be a feelgood party drug that wouldn't inhibit the ability of musicians to play or crew members to do their jobs. In the early stages, this description struck most indulging as accurate, but the detrimental effects of Delight did not begin to take hold until after the last band finished playing that night.

Inside a fenced-off compound housing dozens of trailers and buses, access was limited only to those with the proper credentials. This was where artists and assorted hangers-on were able to relax and hang out without being hassled by fans. The party vibe in the compound was just as wild as the debauched indulgences of festival attendees. In the first few hours of the festival, Oscar Perez personally witnessed no fewer than a dozen sex acts being performed right out in the open, with no one at all batting an eye. Hot girls in hot pants glided around on roller skates carrying trays with piles of cocaine and plastic bowls filled with various pills. The whole scene was like something straight out of the decadent 70s. It could not have been more at odds with the peace and love and progressive hippie message the festival endorsed in all its public marketing, but virtually no one in the compound appeared to have any qualms with this apparent contradiction.

The contrast was interesting, to say the least. The young people who'd come from all around to see this thing were all about weed. A lot of them also loved ecstasy and consciousness-expanding psychedelics. From what Oscar had observed at past jam band festivals, they were decidedly not into things like cocaine and meth. These were the drugs of aggression and toxic behavior. They were not viewed favorably by most in attendance. Behind the scenes, however, so many of the musicians they admired appeared to love coke above all other substances. He wondered how disillusioned the attendees would be if they could see what was happening backstage.

About that, he was not sure. He'd covered a number of similar events in recent years and what he was seeing here wasn't common. Oh, you always saw a few people doing little bumps of coke at these things, but nothing on this scale. It struck him as being something unique to this particular event. He couldn't help wondering if perhaps the organizers were also drug traffickers on the side. Or maybe the drugs were the main thing and the festival was nothing more than a gigantic money-laundering endeavor.

Or maybe he was just getting really cynical the closer he got to turning thirty.

Oscar was not a musician and was not here as part of anyone's crew or entourage. He was a journalist covering the festival for Pitchfork. On countless occasions since arriving at the festival and getting his compound pass, he was offered the opportunity to sample the various substances going around. Sometimes it was the roller skate girls offering him a taste. Other times members of the bands would do it right in the middle of an interview. Numerous other reporters at the festival enthusiastically accepted these offers, but Oscar declined every time. He wasn't above having a good time now and then, but he took his job seriously. He was here to gather substantial material for a nuanced and in-depth piece about all aspects of the festival and he meant to do precisely that.

Of course, the piece would need a fair amount of sugarcoating to be publishable. He could tell the general truth about the backstage decadence, but not the full truth. Some of the more famous band members would have to be referred to anonymously, with the exception of those who gave him express permission to use their names. Not that it mattered, because most reasonably astute readers would be able to infer identities from certain telling details the article would include. His phone was packed with outrageous photos of stars engaged in all manner of illicit activities. Some of the more interesting ones would surely stir massive levels of controversy if ever released to the public, which wasn't going to happen. He had too much integrity for that. Nor would his publisher allow it, in the highly unlikely event he submitted them for publication. It wasn't like he was working for TMZ, after all.

He was sitting at a table in the compound nursing a beer while reviewing the hundreds of festival photos he'd taken when he first noted indications of things going wrong on a widescale level. It took longer than it probably should've, but for a time he was too deeply engrossed in the process of deciding which photos to delete and which ones to transfer to a password-protected album online later on. He'd deleted somewhere around one-hundred photos when he began to perceive sounds of people in distress.

Frowning as he looked up from his phone, he took a look around and saw people huddled together and crying at various locations throughout the compound. Some were wailing on their knees in a way that made him think of extreme displays of bereavement at funerals. He'd never seen such a thing in real life, but he'd seen portrayals of it often in movies. These were displays of grief of some kind, he had no doubt.

That it was happening on such a widespread level got his journalistic instincts buzzing. He didn't yet know what this was in response to, but he could think of some obvious possible reasons. Right up at the top of this list was the possibility that someone at the festival had died. And to provoke an outpouring like this, it'd probably have to be someone important or famous. There were a lot of big bands at the festival. Maybe a singer or some other musician had OD'd. With the abundant supply of potent drugs floating around, this certainly wasn't out of the realm of possibility.

Gears in his mind were turning fast as he began to envision a very different kind of article from the one he'd originally planned. The reconfigured article would be more in the vein of a devastating expose. If this thing turned into a debacle on the scale of the Fyre festival—or even close to that—he could have his hands on something big here. Something that could make him famous or even lead to a high-profile gig with a major media TV outlet.

He decided he was done deleting photos. There would be no deferring to celebrity anonymity in the kind of blistering expose he was beginning to compose in his head. Nothing would be off the table, including even the most outrageous of all the photos he'd taken. Even the ones he'd deleted weren't irretrievably lost. They were sitting in his "recently deleted" folder. Thinking fast, he went to that folder and immediately restored all the deleted ones to the main photo album.

Next he opened his news app and scrolled through the headlines to see if any early word of the apparent festival tragedy had leaked out to the media. A big grin spread across his face when he saw nothing about the festival. A quick search of Google also failed to yield results. His grin got bigger. He was right on top of this thing, but he needed to start shifting into investigative mode right now because he had a lot of colleagues here who were probably all thinking the same thing.

He just needed to try one last online search before he got up and started asking questions. There was information he needed that might not be easily accessible via Google. He decided to hit up LexisNexis to see if he could quickly dredge up any legal dirt on the festival's organizers, but there was a problem—he was no longer getting a signal.

That was weird.

New cell towers had been erected nearby prior to the first year of the festival precisely for this reason, to facilitate better service and connections to the outside world. This was the middle of nowhere, basically, at least as close as you could get to that in the heart of America. With the amount of people converging on the place over the weekend, the ability to communicate with the larger world in the event of an emergency was crucial. And until now he'd had no service problems at all. His phone had shown four bars of strong signal strength from the moment he'd arrived, but now all he was getting was a "no service" message.

He stood up and moved away from the table, holding his phone up in the air and turning it this way and that in an increasingly frantic effort to get a signal. Even one weak bar would suffice, but nothing he tried worked. In desperation, he found a ladder, climbed atop a trailer, and again held his phone aloft, once again to no avail. By then he'd noticed other people trying similar tactics. Judging from their reactions, no one else was having any luck either.

After climbing back down, he threaded his way through a sea of worried faces until he reached a pop-up bar under a canopy tent that was no longer being manned. Ducking behind the bar, he grabbed a cold bottle of Stella from a cooler and popped off the cap with an opener. He chugged it down fast and immediately grabbed another bottle. This one he drank more slowly as he remained behind the bar and observed as the situation inside the compound continued to deteriorate. Things weren't quite fully out of control yet, but he had a bad feeling, even though he still had no idea what had so many people in such a state of distress.

On a professional level, he was kind of falling down on the job. He should be out there talking to people, asking questions and trying to ascertain the exact nature of the problem. The thing holding him back was the sense of dread taking root deep in his gut. Like so many of his journalistic heroes, Oscar Perez believed in doing whatever it took to get to the real heart of a story. Sometimes that meant putting himself in some iffy settings and situations. He'd even been threatened with bodily harm a time or two in pursuit of a scoop. But he was a music correspondent, not a war reporter. The job came with no expectation of getting killed in the line of duty, and though he still had no inkling of what was going wrong here, that bad feeling was getting stronger by the minute. He feared it might get to a point soon where he'd have to start thinking about self-preservation first and the story second.

The main question on his mind was simple—*how the hell am I getting out of here?*

His employer had flown him out to a nearby city, where he'd stayed for a night in a three-star hotel before taking a rental car out to a small town closer to the festival grounds. After spending the next night in a decidedly less swanky hotel, he was flown out to the festival via helicopter. He was currently set to depart again by helicopter late tomorrow night, after the closing night's headliner played its set.

That would simply not do, the way things were going. He needed to get on top of things and arrange a way out of here *now*. Only that wasn't possible at the moment because he couldn't get a goddamn signal. He checked his phone again to confirm this was still the case and muttered a curse when he saw it was.

He gasped when he saw one of the many people moaning and staggering around suddenly drop like a sack of bricks over by a champagne fountain. One second he was upright, the next he was two hundred pounds of deadweight flopping to the ground. To Oscar's great surprise, no one rushed over to attend to him. Everyone was too consumed with their own problems. That told him all he needed to know. He couldn't continue to wait around hoping to finally get a signal. By the time it finally happened, it might be too late.

He'd have to try to get out on foot.

Shit.

It'd be a long, long walk. And it would mean having to push his way through the tens of thousands of festivalgoers camped out for the duration. Another thing he didn't know yet was conditions out there. He had to assume they were at least as bad on the festival grounds, maybe even worse. In that case, many who'd come planning to stay the weekend would also be looking to make an early exit. There'd be a logjam of people trying to get out by the only available route. The whole endeavor would almost certainly be unpleasant in the extreme.

A young woman clad only in tiny gold booty shorts and a matching bikini top came wobbling by the canopy tent. Despite the grim developments, Oscar couldn't help but smile and shake his head. She was yet another of the many contradictions in play here. Out there in the mud and grass, thousands of hippie kids were wearing the same shit hippies had been wearing for generations—tie-dyed shirts and loose and flowery boho dresses. Not all of them dressed like throwbacks, of course, but a heavy percentage did. This woman in no way resembled any kind of hippie chick, stereotypical or otherwise. She looked more like an urban party girl, one who'd rather be grinding on the dance floor at a club than hanging out with a bunch of Phish fans.

His smile slipped when she wobbled over to a trash can right outside the tent, bent over to grip the edges of the can with both hands, and began to violently puke into it. He considered approaching her to ask if she was okay, but the urge faltered when he caught a whiff of the foul odor wafting over from her general vicinity. She paused in the regurgitation process long enough to turn a sweaty face his way and weakly utter a pitiful plea: "Help . . . me."

Oscar had been content to hang back and watch things unfold until now, but he wasn't a monster. He couldn't ignore a direct request for help from a woman in distress, even if he had no clue what he could possibly do for her.

"Hold on, I'll be right there."

After knocking back a big gulp of Stella, he set the bottle on the bar and heaved a big breath, psyching himself up to get closer to that horrible stench. The poor thing smelled like she'd crawled out of a sewer. Even from this distance, it made his stomach clench. He couldn't imagine what could cause an odor that horrendous to emanate from a beautiful young lady, unless she'd ingested something apocalyptically toxic.

"Please . . ."

Her face looked sweatier now. Darker in color.

He forced a tight smile. "Coming."

Before he could slide out from behind the bar, however, the woman abruptly collapsed, banging her chin against the edge of the trash can before flopping over onto her back.

Oscar gaped at her in disbelief a moment before saying, "*Fuck!*"

He hurried out from behind the bar and approached, holding a hand over his face as he stood over her and felt his stomach clench tighter. At such close proximity, the awful smell was close to overpowering. He wanted nothing more than to get away from her as fast as possible, but his sense of basic human decency kept him where he was for the moment. At the very least, he needed to determine whether she was still alive. She'd done a deadweight drop just like that guy by the champagne fountain and the way she'd banged her chin on the edge of the can had looked pretty bad.

Grimacing, he knelt next to her and took hold of a slender wrist to feel for a pulse. He kept his fingers there as long as he could bear it, nearly a full minute, but he detected nothing. While he wasn't anything close to a medical professional, he thought the woman was clearly dead. He didn't understand it. She was young and looked like she'd been in the prime of health prior to succumbing to whatever malady had overtaken her.

He spent the next few moments wondering what he should do next. Maybe attempt to administer CPR? It seemed possible it wasn't too late for her if typical life-saving efforts were applied. Maybe she could be resuscitated. He tried to imagine pressing his mouth over hers and knew he wouldn't be able to do it without becoming violently ill himself and what good would that do? This woman needed the help of a professional.

There was a medical tent somewhere inside the compound. He'd seen it several times while wandering around throughout the day. The question was whether he'd be able to get this woman there in time. He knew her chances decreased with every second that went by. He saw no immediate sign of the medical tent when he looked up to scan the vicinity. What he needed was one of the golf carts he'd occasionally seen zipping around during the day. If he had to scoop up this woman in his arms and go around looking for the medics, he'd never get to them in time.

Another quick scan of his immediate surroundings revealed no sign of any of the golf carts. Of course not. This was obviously one of those situations where the only luck in abundant supply was the bad kind. Something told him no matter what he tried he'd run into nothing but roadblock after roadblock.

He was about to pick her up anyway when another gust of hot, malodorous air assailed his nostrils, making him cough and gag. Looking down, he saw that in the brief time his attention had been diverted, her flesh had turned a deep shade of bruised purple. Also, her jaw had come unhinged, letting out that last big gaseous waft of putrid air. Even without knowing exactly what had happened to her, he immediately understood it was not the result of anything of mundane origin. And it seemed to be happening to many other people as well.

A belated thought came to him then, causing him to spring to his feet and reel backward in shock and terror.

Oh shit, is this contagious?

He continued to move backward in numb, open-mouthed horror until his back was against the bar. Tremors racked his body as he stood on the brink of nuclear meltdown-level panic for several minutes. Sweat beaded on his brow and dampened his armpits. The main thing on his mind during that time was how completely fucked he was if what he was seeing was the result of some kind of rampant, fast-spreading viral contagion. Something airborne. He'd never seen or heard of anything like the symptoms he'd observed, which meant the likelihood of there being some kind of vaccine for this was somewhere near zero percent.

His terror of the situation kept increasing until he reminded himself his chances of getting out of here unscathed were also extremely low unless he could calm down and start thinking straight. For right now, he was physically unaffected, having manifested nothing remotely like the appalling symptoms the afflicted were exhibiting. Other than the natural queasiness he was feeling, he was okay. More or less in perfect health, in fact. After allowing this essential fact a few moments of residing in the forefront of his consciousness, he let out a big breath and felt the tremors gripping him begin to subside. There was a lot still to figure out, but he no longer felt on the edge of a total breakdown.

He took his glasses off to wipe away the sweat that had dripped into his eyes. When he put them on again, he saw someone else coming into the pop-up bar. He was taken aback when he realized who it was.

"What the hell are you doing here?"

Kyle Bile chuckled as he went behind the bar and took a tall can of Boddingtons Pub Ale out of the cooler. He cracked the can open and a bit of foam gushed out of the opening. "Same thing you are, I reckon." After blowing the foam away, he chugged down a few big gulps of beer, then gestured with the can. "Watching the shit-show unfold and having a cold one."

Oscar had forgotten about the open bottle of Stella he'd left sitting on the bar until that moment. Now he grabbed it and followed the singer's lead by gulping down most of it in one go.

Then he shook his head and said, "That's not what I meant. What I meant is, what's a sleaze metal relic like you doing at a jam band festival?"

Even as he asked the question, Oscar realized Kyle being here wasn't really so odd at all, not in context with the many other things he'd seen inside the compound that ran counter to the vibe and supposed message of the festival.

Kyle shrugged and took another gulp of beer. "I'm good friends with one of the organizers. He invited me down for the weekend to hang out and party."

The heavily-tattooed old rocker looked in better shape than a lot of his peers from back in the day, many of whom had gone badly to seed in the years and decades that'd passed since their time in the limelight ended. He was somehow able to wear tight black leather pants and a black vest over an otherwise bare torso without looking completely ridiculous. Oscar was reasonably fit, but the singer's chiseled build nonetheless made him feel a touch self-conscious about his appearance, mainly because the old bastard was more than a quarter-century his senior.

If I ever get out of this, I seriously need to start hitting the gym again.

His gaze flicked back in the direction of the woman lying on her back just outside the tent. Still no detectable signs of life there. He didn't need to feel for her pulse a second time to know her heart hadn't spontaneously started beating again. Not only that, but the time he'd spent in the grip of panic had sealed her fate. There could be no bringing her back now, surely. The knowledge brought with it a twinge of guilt and regret. In his fear, he'd failed to render any kind of substantive aid to the woman. Taking her to the medical tent, wherever the goddamn thing was, was the very least he could've done, but he hadn't even been able to do that. He knew he wasn't entirely to blame for her death. That was the fault of whatever had sickened her. But his inaction had been a contributing factor.

Or had it?

For all he knew, the woman had been beyond help. The visual evidence strongly suggested this might be the case, which should've been at least mildly comforting, but it was not.

I should've at least fucking tried, damn it.

Kyle had come out from behind the bar and was squinting at him as he popped open a second tall can of Boddingtons. "You look troubled, young scribe. What about?"

Oscar grunted and glanced again at the dead woman before focusing on the singer. "You mean aside from the shit-show out there?"

Kyle smiled and sipped from his beer. "Yeah. Aside from that."

Oscar sighed and told him about failing the woman.

Kyle craned his head about and tilted his chin in the general direction of the corpse. "You mean that lady over there?"

"Yeah."

Kyle snorted and waved his beer can around in a dismissive gesture. "Not a damn thing you could've done for her, man. You know the prevailing theory about what's happening here, right? About Delight?"

Oscar frowned. "Delight? What is that?"

"A new party drug. Kind of like ecstasy, but more intense. A hardcore empathy experience. Made a big splash as the big show was getting underway. Shit was everywhere." Kyle rolled his eyes and shook his head. "Not really my thing. I'm more of an old school cocaine and amphetamines kind of guy. You know, the rock and roll drugs. I was offered this Delight shit so many fuckin' times I lost count. Turned it down every time. Good thing, too, from the looks of it."

Oscar grunted. "I'm not really into drugs at all. Kind of hate them, actually. Drinking a beer or two is about as far as I go."

Kyle gulped down more beer. "Normally I'd say that makes you kind of square, but today it makes you one of the lucky ones."

Oscar's frown deepened as he thought about it a moment. "Huh. I don't get it, though. What's the connection to Delight? Wait . . . the only people getting sick are the ones who tried it. Right?'

Kyle tipped his beer can at Oscar. "Bingo."

Oscar shook his head. "Jesus. We need to do something. Get help for these people somehow. Is your phone working?"

"Cell phone? No. Nobody's cell phone is working. Something's blocking them."

The possibility that the lack of service was the result of a deliberate action by some nefarious group had crossed Oscar's mind more than once. This carried with it an even more sinister implication, that the sick people staggering around and collapsing inside (and probably outside) the compound were all victims of a mass-poisoning attempt. A terrorist attack.

His panic level began to elevate significantly again.

"Fuck!"

Kyle nodded. "Yeah, I know. It's some dire shit. But I'll let you in on a secret. I've got—"

Before Kyle could let Oscar in on the so-called "secret" he was harboring, both men were distracted by a loud hacking and coughing sound. The coughing soon ceased and was replaced by a steady moan. The men made eye contact for a moment, then their heads turned slowly in the direction of the moaning.

Oscar gasped and actually jumped back a step. "Holy shit!"

Kyle grunted, nodding again. "About sums it up."

The woman Oscar had assumed was dead was sitting up again. The whites of her eyes had turned a bright blood-red and she was looking right at him. Her skin had continued to change in color and texture. She looked like a corpse rapidly and unnaturally progressing through the stages of decomposition, only that couldn't be because she was up and miraculously alive again. As she awkwardly flailed about in what resembled a toddler's uncoordinated attempt to stand, the moaning sound she was making got louder and louder.

Kyle's beer can slipped from his fingers. "Goddamn, man. Chick is a fucking zombie now."

The z-word took Oscar by surprise. His initial instinct was to scoff, but that passed as he watched the woman continue to struggle to her feet. The herky-jerky movements of her head and the way she snarled and hissed when she looked at him was enough to convince him. That shit wasn't natural. That she'd been dead seemed an incontrovertible fact, based on what he knew, yet now she was up and moving around again. That, too, was not open for debate. It was happening right in front of him right fucking now. He didn't know how to explain it, but seeing was believing. He also felt certain the woman's mortality status wasn't as simple as dead versus not dead. She was dead. She'd *died*. In death, however, something had transformed and animated her corpse, making her into this . . . thing.

This *zombie*.

Screams rang out throughout the compound as others who'd recently succumbed to the lethal latter-stage effects of Delight began to rise. Some of what they were hearing was a result of shock and terror, but there was a different, more distressing quality to some of those screams. It was the kind of shrill, nerve-shredding sound made only by people in excruciating physical pain.

At first Oscar found this puzzling, but then the woman who died outside the tent regained her feet and came sprinting toward him. He shrieked in surprise and fright and stumbled backward, tripping over his own feet and toppling to the ground. Then she was on top of him and he felt her hot, foul-smelling breath on his face. He braced his hands against her shoulders and tried with all his might to shove her off him, but death had transformed her in another way, investing her animated corpse with an unnatural degree of strength. Her teeth repeatedly snapped at him in a way that made it clear she wanted to take bites out of his flesh. The muscles in his arms strained close to the breaking point as he struggled to keep that from happening.

He was on the brink of despair when he heard a loud clang as something smashed against the side of the dead woman's head. The sound repeated mere seconds later and the dead woman rolled away from him. She was on her feet again almost immediately, still hissing and snarling as her attention shifted to Kyle. She ran at him like something shot from a cannon, so swiftly she was almost a blur as she blazed across the space between them. Fortunately for Kyle, he was able to get the fire extinguisher he'd found somewhere up in time to slam its bottom end straight into her face. The impact occurred with enough force to stagger Kyle backward a few steps, but he managed to stay on his feet.

The dead woman was on the ground, but she was already trying to get up again. Kyle wasted no time. He pounced on her immediately and raised the fire extinguisher high above his head, bringing it down again as hard as he could, his teeth bared and the muscles in his neck standing out in stark relief as he smashed it against her head again and again. At first she continued to struggle and claw at him, but in a few more moments her arms flopped to the ground and she ceased moving. Kyle nonetheless continued to drive the blunt bottom end of the extinguisher into what remained of her head, doing it numerous more times until he finally stopped.

Oscar was sitting up again by then. He thought he was going to be sick when he saw the pulpy mess the extinguisher had made of the woman's head. She'd been so pretty before this sickness gripped her, but the lovely face he remembered from those scant few minutes before her flesh began to darken and bloat essentially no longer existed. She was just a smear of red on the ground, her head reduced to lumpy bits of brains, tissue and collapsed bone fragments. Kyle remained atop her another couple moments, sweating and panting with his stringy hair hanging in his face as he worked to catch his breath.

Then he got to his feet and glanced at Oscar. "Shit. That was intense. You want to get out of here?"

Oscar stood up and nodded. "Yeah. But how?"

He could hear more of those agonized screams now. Many more. He heard crashes and other loud noises. People were running around in a blind panic to get away from the reanimated dead things. He looked past Kyle and saw one of the creatures tackle a woman from behind and drive her to the ground. In another moment, the creature had torn out her throat and was devouring her flesh. And all the dead things were moving so goddamn fast. He couldn't imagine how anyone could hope to avoid them for long.

Escape seemed hopeless and all but certain.

But for some reason Kyle was smiling. "I've got a satellite phone in my trailer. Don't know if it'll get through whatever's blocking the cell phones, but it might. It's our only real shot."

Still clutching the blood-smeared fire extinguisher, he walked out into the chaos and Oscar followed.

What other choice did he have?

SEVEN

TRAVIS DRIFTED IN AND OUT of consciousness as the rednecks took him deeper into the woods. The big guy in the overalls
had hold of one of his ankles and was dragging him along like a bag
of trash. He felt twigs and undergrowth scratch against his flesh and
open numerous cuts that leaked blood onto the ground. The back of
his head bounced off more than a few rocks of various sizes, causing
him to cry out in pain multiple times and, during his more lucid moments, beg for mercy. His pleas only made them laugh.

Just as the journey through the woods seemed as if it would go on
forever, they arrived at a clearing larger than the one where they'd set
up their trap. By then Travis was close to fully awake. He was able to
lift his head enough to glimpse a ramshackle cabin. The cabin had a
long porch with rickety-looking wooden rails and some rocking chairs
arranged at either end. Off to a side of the cabin was a large old shed
that looked on the verge of falling over. The door to the shed was
standing open. As they moved closer to the cabin, Travis glimpsed
something through the opening that ignited a sick sense of despair.
The nude body of another young man was hanging upside down from
a rafter. He'd been gutted just recently, judging from the pile of guts
and organs on the shed's earthen floor. His blood-matted hair was so
long it nearly reached the ground. A multi-colored peace symbol was
tattooed on one of the dead man's limp arms.

When they arrived at the porch, the guy in the overalls let go of his ankle and gave him a kick. "On your feet, boy."

Travis hurt too much to make an immediate attempt to get up. He moaned and looked up at them through eyes brimming with fresh tears. "Please . . ."

A corner of the big man's mouth twitched. "*I said, get on your got-damn feet!*" He gave Travis a much harder second kick in the side, one delivered with enough force to make him scream and twist in agony. Then the twin barrels of the big man's shotgun were in his face, the big open ends maybe an inch away from grazing the tip of his nose. "You got five damn seconds to do as you're told 'fore I blow your brains out all over the ground."

The one called Darlene moved into his field of vision, smirking as she peered down at him and said, "Reckon you might ought do as the man says. Jasper don't make no false promises. One of his favorite things in the whole wide world is watching some poor motherfucker's head blow open like a melon when he unloads both them barrels. You really want that to happen to you?"

Travis whimpered and said, "N-n-noooo . . ."

The toothpick wedged into a corner of her mouth moved around some as she chuckled. She took it out and held it pinched between her thumb and forefinger as she said, "Didn't think so. Most folks prefer to keep their thinkin' goo inside their noggins. You look kind of out of it. Maybe this'll wake your sorry ass up."

She inserted the toothpick inside one of his nostrils and gave it a hard upward shove, making him screech in pain. That got them all to laughing again as she wiggled the end of the toothpick around some, making him cry out again as well as do some more begging. She removed the toothpick from his nostril and licked the little bead of blood off the end before again wedging it into that same corner of her mouth.

Her grin faded and her tone hardened as she said, "Get off your ass right now, boy. Else I'll start sticking things in your dickhole instead of up your nose."

She slapped him hard across the face and got to her feet.

The double barrels of the shotgun kissed his forehead as the one called Jasper started counting. "Five, four, three—"

Travis held a shaky hand up in a gesture of acquiescence. "I'm getting up."

He groaned through gritted teeth as he heaved himself into a sitting position, an effort that required nearly every remaining bit of his depleted strength. He felt lightheaded and ached to flop back to the ground, but the shotgun still hovering inches from his face was all the motivation he needed to not let that happen. His head wobbled around some as his vision blurred, but he gave it a hard shake to regain focus. The rednecks were yelling at him again. Their threats included more references to "thinkin' goo" ejection and various ways they might abuse all of his orifices. They told him if he wasn't on his feet in another five seconds they'd tear his pecker off and feed it to their coonhound. The sadistic hillbillies had a particular fixation on five-second countdowns, it seemed. Maybe they couldn't count any higher than that. Travis didn't see a dog around, but he had to assume this wasn't an idle threat. The beast was probably out roaming around in the woods somewhere. Almost as if one cue, he heard a faint sound of canine yowling from somewhere off in the distance.

Jasper had nearly reached the end of another countdown when Travis finally managed to propel himself to his feet. He felt lightheaded and ready to fall over again, but in another instant he realized no one had a hand on him. His best chance at getting out of this might be to make a run for it and hope to get back into the woods before they could gun him down. Knowing the lightheadedness would almost certainly cause him to tumble to the ground after just a few steps was the only thing that kept him from trying it.

One of the flannel shirt guys seized him by an arm, got him turned around, and pushed him toward the cabin's porch. Someone else gave him a kick in the ass, making them all laugh again. Only the flannel shirt guy's iron grip on his arm prevented him from pitching forward and bouncing the tip of his chin off the edge of the porch's bottom step. In another couple seconds, he was up on the porch, wobbling unsteadily in place. The other flannel shirt guy got the door open and went on into the cabin. Travis and the man holding onto him followed him inside. Darlene and Jasper came in after them and shut the door.

The rundown old cabin had a wide-open main room with a recessed little kitchen nook in one of the back corners. Travis saw a couple of cots with rumpled bedding and some sleeping bags on the floor. A boxy old TV with rabbit-ear antennas sat atop a produce crate that was pushed up against one of the walls. Another corner of the room was hidden by some wicker fold-out panels, the kind he'd sometimes seen in old movies. He supposed these were in place in the event any of his redneck captors ever felt in need of a moment of privacy. The surface of a decrepit-looking wooden table in the center of the room was littered with bottles and empty cans of Milwaukee's Best. Also on the table was a large, old-style boombox. It looked like the bigger older cousin of the one they'd left behind in the woods. Darlene pulled a chair away from the table and the flannel shirt guy promptly dumped Travis into it.

Jasper put the shotgun right up against his face again. "Don't you move, boy. I mean it. You so much as twitch, I'll make a mess outta that purty face."

Travis frowned.

Purty face?

Those words did not bode well on any level whatsoever.

He heaved a sigh and slumped down in the chair, feeling the physical strain of his desperate flight from the festival grounds in every bone in his body. "You don't have to keep threatening me. I doubt I could get to the door without fainting dead away anyway."

Darlene was pacing about the cabin in a way that conveyed a high level of pent-up aggression. She paused to grab a meth pipe from the table's crowded surface while her male friends opened a cooler and plucked out dripping-wet cans of beer. After holding the flame from a cheap plastic lighter to the bowl for the requisite amount of time, she put the end of the pipe between her lips and inhaled deeply. The men cracked open their beers while Darlene pressed a button on the boombox and began to dance wildly around the room to "Purple Haze". One of the flannel shirt guys began to play air guitar with his rifle, while the other flannel shirt guy dropped his rifle on one of the cots. The second one then unbuckled his belt, lowered his pants, and began to flick at his clit as he sat on the edge of the cot and stared intensely at Darlene.

Travis did a cartoon-like doubletake.

Now hold on just a goddamn minute! What the hell is happening here!?

Then it came to him. Flannel shirt guy number two was actually a flannel shirt gal. Never in a million years would he have guessed. Now his gaze flicked over to the one playing air guitar. He squinted at him, trying hard to discern subtle indications of a hidden femininity, but he then realized how pointless that was. The two weren't twins. They looked nothing alike. He'd only grouped them together in his mind because of their similar attire. His gaze went again to the one with the vagina. She smirked and licked her lips when she saw him looking at her, causing him to quickly look away.

God help me, what have I gotten myself into?

The strangest part of this overall deeply strange situation was how little he feared the zombie threat now. Barring any unlikely and miraculous developments, the massive horde of undead had not neutralized. They were still out there and some of them—perhaps quite a few of them—would eventually stray into this part of the woods, but it no longer mattered because he knew there was no chance he was getting out of this cabin alive. These sadistic backwoods weirdos were going to have their fun with him and then they'd kill him. He'd end up strung-up in the shed with that other unfortunate bastard. Tears started spilling down his face again as "Purple Haze" gave way to a Die Antwoord track. Despite his terror, Travis almost laughed. For a bunch of crazy hillbillies, these people sure had some eclectic taste in music.

Jasper had been watching Travis this whole time, keeping the shotgun trained on him while occasionally chugging from his beer. When the can was empty, he crushed it and tossed it on the table, making Travis flinch. He then yelled at Darlene loud enough to be heard over the music. She kept on dancing and he raised his voice even higher, almost to eardrum-shattering levels.

She came to an abrupt stop and glared at him. Her face was red and dripping sweat. "What, motherfucker?"

He shoved the shotgun into her hands. "Keep an eye on the new meat. I need a minute to get ready."

She rolled her eyes, cradling the shotgun in her arms while she also fiddled with the meth pipe and her lighter. "Whatever, ho-beast. Make it quick, though."

He sneered and adjusted the Miller High Life hat atop his head. "You ain't the boss of me, you skinny bitch, so shut yer piehole."

Before she could retort, Jasper retreated to the corner of the room hidden by the wicker panels, disappearing behind them seconds later.

Darlene managed the impressive juggling act of holding on to the shotgun while also getting the meth pipe lit again. After another deep inhalation, she surprised Travis by offering him the pipe. "Want a hit?"

Travis actually gave it a moment's consideration. Meth wasn't his thing. He liked weed and mellow good times, not chemically-induced mental derangement. The prospect of one day winding up on one of those "faces of meth" posters also wasn't exactly an enticing one, at least not under normal circumstances. There wasn't a damn thing normal about the circumstances facing him today, though. Maybe a bit of mental derangement was exactly what he needed to face the torturous remaining moments of his life.

Just as he was about to accept the offer, she laughed and snatched the pipe away. "What a fuckin' dumb piece of shit you are," she said, shaking her head. "You think I'm actually gonna waste good meth on a worthless fuckin' hippie?"

Travis sniffled. "Please . . ."

She put the pipe and lighter away and raised the shotgun as she moved closer. "Open your mouth wide as you can."

What she had in mind was immediately obvious. Travis was sniffling and trembling almost uncontrollably by now. "P-p-p-please . . ."

She poked at his mouth with the barrels of the shotgun. "No! No you don't, bitch! No begging allowed. Just do as you're fuckin' told. Open that goddamn mouth right now. If you don't, I'll shoot your dick off. How's that sound?"

Tears streamed nonstop down Travis's face. He blubbered unintelligibly for a few moments, completely unable to form coherent words or sentences.

Darlene poked his mouth with the shotgun again. "Aw, hell, it's five-second countdown time again. Five, four, three, two—"

Travis opened his mouth, straining his jaw muscles to accommodate both barrels of the shotgun as she slid them in.

She smiled. "That's real good, hippie. Just in time, too. Now make like you're sucking a metal dick."

It wasn't an easy thing to do with that much steel in his mouth, but Travis did his best to mimic the act of fellatio.

Darlene laughed. "Yeah, that's hot, ooh baby." She laughed again. "But you can still do better. Let me hear you sound like you're having a real good time."

His tears fell on the shotgun's barrels as Travis did his best to fake a moan of sexual ecstasy. In the next instant, his simulated sound of arousal was echoed by the real thing. His eyes flicked over to flannel shirt gal, who was masturbating frantically on the edge of the cot and still staring at Darlene with that disconcerting level of intensity. Her flannel shirt-clad male counterpart dropped to his knees in front of her and tried to go down on her, but she shoved him away. On the boombox, a second Die Antwoord track gave way to "The Time Warp" from the *Rocky Horror Picture Show* soundtrack.

Travis glanced at the boombox while still feigning sounds of ecstasy.

What the actual fuck is the deal with these people?

Over in the hidden corner of the room, a big hand appeared at the top of one of the wicker panels and turned it aside. Travis eyed the open space between the wall and the folded-back panel with mounting anxiety, not having a clue what level of madness to expect next but fearing it anyway.

Then Jasper stepped through that space and back into the main room.

Travis sighed around the barrels of the shotgun.

Of fucking course.

Atop Jasper's head was an ill-fitting platinum blonde wig, the tresses of which reached his hairy and almost impossibly broad shoulders. His face was garishly painted with badly-applied mascara, eyeshadow, and lipstick. He was wearing an obscenely small blue dress with spaghetti straps, the hem of which was not nearly low enough to hide his semi-erect penis. He made eye contact with Travis, smiled, and started moving in his direction.

Travis looked at Darlene and tried to say something around the barrels.

She took the shotgun out of his mouth and giggled. "I'm sorry, I couldn't hear you. What did you say?"

Travis cleared his throat and tried to speak loudly enough to be heard over the music. "Please shoot me now. I mean it. I'm ready."

Darlene cackled and shook her head. "No fuckin' way, hippie. We're just starting to have our fun with you. This is gonna go on all fuckin' day."

They were all crowding around him now. All of them eyeing him with almost identical hungry looks on their faces. Flannel shirt girl was now devoid of flannel, as well as all other garments. She glanced back and forth from him and Darlene as she bit her bottom lip and squeezed one of her tiny breasts. Flannel shirt guy, now the one and only, began to unzip his pants. Jasper was grinding his sizeable hips like a stripper. His cock was fully erect now. Even Darlene was getting in on the act, beginning to undo the buttons of her mechanic's shirt with one hand while holding the shotgun with the other.

She laughed and said, "What we're about to do now, hippie, is have ourselves a good old-fashioned gang rape. Then, just as soon as we've all gotten off good and proper, we're gonna start in with the torture. I'm talkin' nails and hammers, pliers, and knives. I'm talkin' amputations and smashed-in bones. At some point we'll break out the acetylene torch."

Flannel shirt guy grinned. "Mmm, that's always my favorite part. Favorite part of the torture, I mean. My real favorite part is the fuckin'."

Jasper had his hand on his cock now. He smiled and said, "Me, too."

The circle of depraved humanity around Travis drew tighter and tighter. He considered making a grab for the shotgun. What did he have to lose at this point?

Darlene had the front of her shirt all the way open now, allowing him a glimpse of creamy pale flesh and a lacy black bra. "Reckon my favorite part is later, when we eat them. Always work up a hell of an appetite when we go all freaky-deaky on a motherfucker." She grinned broadly, exposing her meth-decimated teeth. "Don't mind the fuckin', though. Not one bit. Especially once Eunice and me break out the strap-ons and start plundering that ass until it fuckin' bleeds."

They all laughed maniacally at that.

Travis looked around at their leering faces and despaired. Eyeing the shotgun, he scooted his ass closer to the edge of the chair and psyched himself up to make his last-ditch desperation move. Before he could do that, however, they all heard the creaking sounds from the porch during a lull between songs from the boombox.

Flannel shirt guy leaned over to stab the stop button, silencing "When Doves Cry" by Prince mid-song. "Did you hear that?"

Their heads all turned toward the front of the cabin. The creaking sounds could be heard much more clearly now. From the sound of it, there were several people out there on the porch. There was another sound, too, a low moaning and groaning. And there was that ripe odor Travis knew so well.

Darlene said, "We all heard it."

Jasper looked scared as his cock began to wilt. "Who do y'all think it is? The law, maybe?"

Darlene grimaced as she gripped the shotgun with both hands again. "Raunchiest-smelling po-lice ever, if it is. Whoever it is, we ain't goin' out easy. Get your guns, bitches."

Travis started laughing softly as the rest of them began to gather their weapons. The sound grew steadily in volume until he was almost braying wild laughter.

Darlene turned back toward him and leveled the shotgun at his face again. "Shut it, hippie. What's so goddamn funny anyway?"

She was trying hard to maintain her outward veneer of scary toughness, but he sensed the fear lurking beneath her gruff tone. The worry lines on her face were more pronounced now, too, making Travis realize his original estimate about her age might be off by several years. He guessed she was closer to thirty than twenty, but the extra years only became obvious when she was scared.

Like right now.

The rest of them looked uneasy, too.

Travis at last managed to get his laughter under control. He chuckled softly and was still smiling when he said, "It's not the law at the door."

Darlene sneered. "Oh, yeah? Well, who is it then?"

He chuckled again. "It's just a bunch of dirty rotten hippies. They've wandered over from the festival, just like me."

Darlene made a sound of disbelief. "Bullshit."

Still smiling, Travis shrugged. "It's not, though. But don't take my word for it. Open the door and see for yourself."

He was in no hurry to go to his grave at the hands of a bunch of reanimated dead things, but he preferred it over being sexually violated and brutalized by a gang of demented, meth-addicted hillbillies.

The moaning from outside was getting louder.

So was the creaking of the wooden porch planks.

The naked lady he now knew was called Eunice went to one of the covered windows at the front of the cabin, peeled back an edge of the blackout shade covering the window, and peeked outside. Almost instantly, she gasped and jumped back from the window. The look she showed them when she turned around was abject horror mixed with despair.

"What's out there?" Darlene asked.

The fear in her tone had deepened yet again.

Travis began to laugh softly again.

Eunice shook her head. "You'll never believe it."

"*Spit it the fuck out!*" Darlene screeched, her voice suddenly laced with more anger than fear.

Eunice shivered visibly and hugged herself before glancing briefly at Travis. "He's right," she said, nodding at him. "It's a bunch of hippies, but there's something really wrong with them. I think . . . I think

. . ." She paused and shivered again, grimacing as she gathered her nerve. "I think they're dead. Walking dead people."

Jasper guffawed. "Aw, hell. Come on. Y'all pullin' my leg, right? There cain't be zombies out there. That's TV show bullshit. That resurrectin' and walkin' around nonsense don't happen none in real life." He glanced around at each of them in turn, even at Travis, smiling nervously the whole time. "Right?"

Darlene made a huffing sound and brushed by Eunice on the way to the window, making the other woman grunt in dismay and stagger sideways. She peeled back the edge of the shade and took a look for herself. Unlike Eunice, she didn't immediately flinch and retreat from what she saw. Instead, she stood perfectly still for a prolonged period of time before reacting, perhaps as long as a full minute.

Then she turned slowly around and sighed heavily. "Shit. She's right."

She moved away from the window as the rest of them took turns peeking out at the situation on the porch. Soon enough, they were all convinced. There were zombies out there. A shitload of them.

Jasper pulled off the platinum-blonde wig and started pacing manically around the cabin, crying and running his stubby fingers through his real hair. "What're we gone do now? We're fuckin' fucked. Oh my lord, how the hail we gettin' outta this mess?"

Travis tilted his head back and laughed a little louder.

"Don't know, brother," Darlene said, addressing Jasper while glaring at Travis. "But we're gonna start by getting rid of this piece of hippie scum-shit."

Travis gasped and leaned back in the chair, his eyes widening in alarm as she came at him and raised the shotgun, again aiming it at his head. "Wait, no! Hold up! I can help. I can—"

Darlene smirked. "Shut the fuck up. You're done."

She squeezed the trigger.

EIGHT

THEY HAD TO FIGHT HARD to make their way across the compound to Kyle's trailer. By the time they got there, the compound was engulfed in bloody chaos. The living still slightly outnumbered the risen dead, but Oscar estimated the ratio would swing the other way within an alarmingly short span. The resurrected were fast and ferocious, overwhelming their mortal counterparts with shocking ease in most cases.

The only reason Oscar made it to the trailer alive was because he stayed as close to Kyle as possible without actually gluing himself to him. Kyle fought like a man possessed, swinging the fire extinguisher about and warding off the many threats that came at them in a frenzied way that belied his years. He remained unscathed while countless people half his age fell victim to the rampaging dead things. The blunt end of the fire extinguisher smashed into and pulped the heads of seemingly dozens of them. There were numerous times when he had to abruptly wheel about and rescue Oscar from certain death with another viciously devastating swing of the only weapon they had at hand.

Oscar was drenched in blood spatter as he followed Kyle up a short set of steps and into the trailer. Only once he was inside did he realize how close the pursuing dead things had come to taking him down. The door to the trailer was still standing open as the nearest zombie reached the steps and began to climb. Kyle grabbed Oscar and heaved him aside just in time to swing the door shut in the creature's face. It'd reached the top of the steps by then, and when the door closed, the thing immediately began clawing frantically at it from the other side.

Kyle locked the door and put his back against it to hold the creatures back. They were piling up on the steps and trying to batter their way inside. He pointed to a couch against the opposite wall at the far end of the trailer. The couch faced a wall-mounted television. An all-girl porn movie was playing on the screen. On the couch was a busty young woman wearing only a tiny pair of black panties. Her eyes were closed and she didn't react to either their arrival or the clawing and pounding of the zombies outside the trailer. Oscar guessed she was either unconscious or dead. Another victim of Delight, perhaps?

A chill rippled through him at the thought.

He frowned. "What? You want me to wake her up?"

Kyle scowled. "No time for that. She's on the nod. See the syringe on the floor?"

Oscar glanced that way again. This time he saw the syringe and also noted the length of plastic tubing wrapped around her right bicep. "Oh." He looked at Kyle. "What do you want me to do then?"

"Roll her ass off the fucking couch and drag the fucking thing over here. We need to block the door. I can't hold them back forever."

Oscar scratched the back of his head, his frown deepening at the thought of manhandling the woman in the suggested way. Putting his hands on a woman without being invited to do so was something he'd normally never even dream of doing. This was an emergency situation, but it was nonetheless difficult to rebel against his instincts and ingrained civility. "I don't know . . ."

"Fuck!"

Kyle launched himself away from the door, grabbed hold of Oscar's shirt, and spun him around, pushing him up against the door. "I'll do it, goddammit. Just hold the fucking door. If you can't do that, we're fucked."

Oscar felt the pressure from the other side of the door the instant Kyle let go of him. He'd known it would be considerable, but he hadn't expected it to be quite this intense. He had to brace his feet on the carpeted floor and put his back into it. The pounding made his whole body vibrate and it was all he could do not to break down and collapse into a blubbering, helpless mess on the floor.

Kyle stomped his way over to the couch and brusquely rolled the woman to the floor, doing it with enough force to send her rolling all the way to the opposite wall. She remained unconscious even then, oblivious to both the rough treatment and the worsening situation outside.

Kyle grabbed hold of the nearest end of the couch and dragged it closer to the door. Displaying a level of strength that was less surprising after his one-man wrecking crew performance out there in the compound, he stood the couch on end, turned it about, and flipped it over so the back side was facing the door. With that accomplished, he gestured for Oscar to get out of the way.

Oscar didn't need to be told twice.

He scurried sideways and out of the way as Kyle shoved the couch forward and braced its back against the door, which was still shaking violently in its frame. Instead of taking a moment to catch his breath, he raced back down toward the far end of the trailer, soon disappearing through a door into another room. In a few moments, he reemerged gripping a device of some kind in his right hand. At first glance, Oscar took it for a standard-looking smartphone, but on closer examination he saw it featured a more rugged casing. An antenna stub protruded from the top. As he watched, Kyle pulled the antenna out to its fullest extension, punched in a number, and put the phone to his ear. By then Oscar was feeling resigned to his apparent fate. Pessimism colored his every thought and he had zero hope of Kyle's satellite phone getting through whatever was blocking everything else.

That abruptly changed when Kyle started talking, apparently to someone on the opposite end of a connected off-site call. Oscar was so astounded by this seemingly miraculous development the actual content of Kyle's conversation with the mystery person at first failed to register. Then he heard the word "helicopter" and things snapped back into focus. He gathered the singer was initially having some trouble conveying the gravity and nature of the situation to the person on the other end. Some yelling and palpable anger on Kyle's part soon changed this state of affairs, however, and within just a few minutes he ended the call.

He flipped long locks away from his sweaty face and showed Oscar a cockeyed grin. "Cavalry's on the way."

Oscar gaped at him in disbelief for a moment. Part of him almost didn't want to trust in what the old heavy metal dude was telling him out of fear of the news being revealed as a cruel prank in the next instant. There was no reason to think anything like that would happen. The singer had fought like a madman to save his life, after all. This was just lingering paranoia, left over from his earlier musings on who or what was behind this unfolding tragedy.

He heaved a sigh and shook his head. "I don't believe it."

Kyle chuckled. "Believe it, man. All we have to do is hold out here for maybe an hour. That's about how long it'll take my people to get a chopper out here."

"A chopper?"

"Helicopter."

Oscar made a sound of dawning awareness. "Oh. Yeah. Right." Then his frown returned as he glanced at the door before again turning his gaze on Kyle. "But we're trapped in here. Surrounded. How are we supposed to get out and rendezvous with the helicopter?"

Still grinning, Kyle raised an index finger and pointed up. "We go out that way."

Oscar looked up and saw a skylight in the roof of the trailer. He then noted the latch on the window and understood it could be opened. The rest of it became obvious at that point. They were supposed to climb up on the roof and await rescue there. He imagined the copter hovering above the trailer, its spinning rotors louder than a thousand buzzsaws revving all at once while a ladder was lowered for them to climb to safety. The whole process would be nerve-wracking as hell, but it wasn't like there were any other viable options. If he wanted to survive this nightmare—and he definitely did—this was the only way out.

First, though, they would have to survive another hour inside the trailer. The dead had not ceased in their assault on the door. They continued to bang on it and claw at it, their fingernails scraping loudly against the metal. The middle of the door was bulging inward in several places. As they watched, the legs of the couch skidded a couple inches in their direction. It became clear the couch alone would not suffice as a barrier, not for an entire hour, so they set about fortifying the barricade by piling on everything in the trailer that wasn't nailed down, as well as some things that had to be removed from their moorings, including a heavy mini-fridge and the wall-mounted television. Other additions to the barricade included chairs and a mattress from the bedroom along with a matching box-spring.

After close to a half-hour of frantic work, some of Oscar's worst concerns began to recede. They were still in a difficult and dangerous situation, but, against all odds, they seemed close to having it under control. At least as far as their personal safety was concerned, that is. Nearly everyone else in the compound and on the festival grounds was almost certainly doomed. That was a terrible, shitty thing. A tragedy of unprecedented proportions in the world of music. Oscar felt more than a smidge of guilt at the likelihood of being one of the few to survive, but deep in his heart he knew he'd never hand the opportunity over to someone else to go in his place. He wanted out of this catastrophic horror show more than he'd ever wanted anything else in his life.

Kyle had taken some beers from the mini-fridge prior to helping Oscar heave it atop the couch. Now he opened two of them and offered one to Oscar, who at first waved it off and said, "No. I should try to keep my wits about me."

But Kyle was not to be dissuaded. "Come on, man. Drink up. It'll help with your nerves when it's time to climb up out of here."

Oscar didn't need much more convincing than that. He felt steadier than he had at any point since the beginning of the outbreak, but he was still trembling and his heart was still racing. Adrenaline had burned off the effects of the beers he'd had earlier. A few more as an additional calming method couldn't hurt. He accepted the beer and took a sip.

"Hey, do you think I could use that for a minute?"

He gestured at the satellite phone, tucked away now in Kyle's vest pocket.

Kyle shook his head sadly as he gave the phone a protective pat. "You can use it to call whoever you want as soon as we're safely away. Until then, I want to keep the line open in case our ride out of here arrives sooner than anticipated."

Oscar supposed he could see the wisdom in that.

They leaned against the wall where the couch had been and drank their beers mostly without talking over the next approximately half-hour, listening as the moaning of the dead continued to grow louder and more eerie-sounding. There was a sense of being adrift at sea in a lifeboat with hungry sharks circling endlessly in bloody waters. Oscar was mildly curious about the unconscious woman on the floor, but not as much as he would've been under less dire circumstances. He nonetheless was about to ask Kyle about it when the satellite phone buzzed.

Kyle put the phone to his ear. "Yeah?"

Oscar could faintly hear another voice emanating from the phone while the singer listened and occasionally nodded his head.

Kyle grunted. "Ten minutes. Gotcha."

He tucked the phone in his vest pocket again, chugged the last of his current beer down, and tossed the empty on the floor. "Be right back."

Oscar shrugged. "Not going anywhere."

Kyle again disappeared into the room at the back of the trailer. He came back out with a loaded syringe a few moments later, knelt over the unconscious woman, and raised the hypodermic high over his head.

Oscar frowned. "What are you doing?"

"Giving her a jolt."

Oscar winced as Kyle slammed the syringe down and pressed the plunger as soon as the needle pierced the woman's skin. Barely more than a heartbeat later, the woman sat bolt upright, gasping for breath.

Kyle chuckled, glancing at Oscar as he stood up again. "Shades of *Pulp Fiction*, right? Not the first time I've had to do this. Come on, help me grab that fridge again. It's about time to catch our ride."

Working together, they extracted the fridge from where it was wedged into the barricade and dragged it across the floor until it was positioned directly beneath the skylight. Kyle then climbed atop it and reached for the skylight. After fiddling with a latch that initially seemed stuck for longer than was comfortable, he was finally able to get the skylight unlatched and open. He then hopped down and invited Oscar to climb up on the fridge and be the first out on the roof.

Oscar frowned. "Why me?"

Kyle hooked a thumb in the direction of the recently revived woman, who was just now woozily getting to her feet. "Because I'm gonna have to lift her up and have you pull her up onto the roof. I'll be the one doing the heavy lifting. I just need your help getting her up there for me. Can you do that?"

Oscar shrugged. "Sure. Of course. Who is she, by the way?"

"Wife number six. Carla, I think her name is."

"You *think?*"

Kyle laughed. "Yeah, man, I'm pretty sure. All right, let's make this shit happen."

After shrugging again, Oscar climbed up on the fridge and stood there precariously a moment while getting his balance, holding his arms out to either side to help keep him from falling over. As soon as he felt he was steady enough, he reached up and gripped the edge of the opening. Grunting with the effort, he began to haul himself up. Kyle helped by gripping him hard by the ankles and giving him an upward shove. In another moment, he was through the opening and on the roof. His heart was hammering in his chest as he took a look around and saw the massed hordes of the dead. They were everywhere he looked, with nary a living person left anywhere. Strangely, many were now much less frantic than earlier. They were shuffling and shambling about, swaying on their feet and sometimes falling awkwardly over. Whatever strange energy was animating them had its limits, apparently.

Kyle was yelling at him from inside the trailer.

Snapping out of his momentary trance, Oscar knelt at the edge of the open skylight and took hold of Kyle's wife under her arms as she was lifted through the opening. Once he had a secure hold on her, he scooted carefully backward, moving slowly in fear of knocking into something that'd put him off-balance. He didn't want to fuck up and go rolling over the side of the trailer with deliverance from this nightmare so close at hand. In another couple moments, however, he had her safely out on the roof. Before he could even finish heaving a sigh of relief, Kyle had hauled himself up through the opening, joining them.

The three of them spent the next few minutes sitting there and observing the shambling sea of dead things. The woman whose name was maybe Carla rested her head against her famous husband's shoulder. At the same time, she reached for Oscar, putting a hand on his crotch. He gasped softly in surprise and moved her hand away. She immediately put it in the same spot again.

And squeezed.

Oscar again moved her hand and scooted out of range.

Kyle laughed. "That's Kari for you. Oh, wait. That's her name. Kari, not Carla." He laughed again. "Anyway, she'll fuck anything at any time under any circumstances. You gotta love her for that."

Oscar frowned, glancing at him. "You do?"

Kyle shrugged. "Yeah. Whatever, man. Someday she'll be an ex, too, just like the rest of 'em, with yet another tell-all book to peddle. So what does it really matter?"

Despite everything, Oscar was able to laugh at this. "Wow. You're

60

such a romantic."

"Don't I know it. Fuck. Wish I'd brought along a couple more of those beers."

With that sentiment, Oscar could wholeheartedly agree.

It wasn't much longer before they began to hear the rotors of the approaching copter. As soon as the craft appeared as a speck on the distant horizon, the three of them got to their feet. Oscar's excitement soared as it rapidly drew closer. Not so long ago, he'd firmly believed all hope was lost. He'd never see any of his colleagues, friends, or family again. And now here he was, mere minutes from being transported away from this catastrophe.

"Hey, Oscar?"

Oscar glanced over at Kyle while still keeping a hand to his brow to reduce the glare of the bright morning sun. "Yeah?"

Kyle smiled. "You remember that bad review you gave our comeback album a few years ago?"

Oscar glanced at him again, confusion pulling at his features. "Um, yeah. I wouldn't call it bad. It was more mixed than anything. Um . . . why bring that up now?"

By now the copter was close enough they had to shout at each other to be heard over the buzzing rotors. In another couple moments, it would be directly overhead.

Kyle leaned close and shouted his parting words, "*Because fuck you, that's why!*"

Oscar tried flinching away when he realized what was about to happen, but by then it was too late. The singer had a solid grip on his arm and was spinning about, preparing to launch him over the side of the trailer. He tried planting his feet to halt the momentum, but it was no good. The old singer was just too strong. He went over the side of the trailer and for an all-too-brief moment was airborne above the seething zombie masses. In that last moment before his inevitable earthward descent, he imagined being magically gifted with the ability of flight. He imagined flying away into a golden sunset, safe from any threat of harm and forever far away from anything like the horrors he'd witnessed over the last couple hours or so.

Then he fell and hit the ground.

The last thing he saw as the dead fell upon him and began tearing and ripping at his flesh was the copter flying away—and Kyle Bile leaning out the side of the craft and waggling an extended middle finger.

nine

THE TOP OF THE HIPPIE kid's head blew apart as Darlene unloaded both barrels on him, spraying blood and brains everywhere. With the booming report of the weapon still ringing in her ears, she gave the chair a kick and sent his corpse tumbling to the floor. The others were still cringing at the blast of the shotgun as she hurriedly retrieved Purvis's rifle from where he'd dropped it on the cot. She needed to act fast and didn't have time to reload the antique shotgun. Once she had hold of the rifle, she drew a bead on Purvis and shot him in the side of the head.

Jasper squawked in surprise and was slow to react as she worked the bolt lever to chamber another round and shifted her aim in his direction. He was blinking slowly and his mouth was hanging open as he watched Purvis drop and begin to bleed out on the floor. Then he looked at Darlene with a squinting expression of confusion, as if completely unable to comprehend the sight of his sister aiming a weapon at him.

Darlene had learned long ago to be ruthless and unforgiving in situations like this. You didn't want to hesitate or have second thoughts, because the person on the other side of the equation wasn't about to forget you'd just pointed a gun at them, especially if that person was someone who'd loved or trusted you.

She squeezed the trigger and a nickel-sized hole appeared dead-center in Jasper's forehead. Blood and brains jumped from the bigger hole at the back of his head, depositing her brother's essence on the already heavily blood-spattered floor. He toppled over, sprawling across the dead hippie's corpse with the hem of the frilly blue dress riding up over his flabby thighs.

Eunice watched her warily for a moment before saying, "You done now?"

Darlene hocked up a loogie and spat it on her brother's face. "Reckon I am. At least until it's time to start shooting zombies."

Eunice shook her head. "Zombies. Goddamn. That's really what those fuckers are, huh?"

Darlene grunted. "Looks that way."

She lowered the rifle and approached Eunice, pulling her into a tight embrace and then kissing her hungrily for a moment. The other woman's arms went around her waist and settled on her ass, clutching at it tightly while Darlene probed her mouth with her tongue. She slid a hand between her naked lover's legs and inserted a finger in her vagina.

Eunice gasped. "Oh, god . . ."

Darlene smiled and broke the clinch, pulling gently away from her. "Ain't got time for that. We've gotta get ourselves out of this cluster-fuck first."

Eunice took a pointed look around at all the bloody carnage. Her expression conveyed a level of surprise that fell short of actual shock. She'd witnessed her share of bloodletting and abominable acts over the last few years, probably dozens of them since that summer day when Darlene and her brothers had snatched her from the festival grounds. Back then she'd been an ardent LGBTQ activist who at times found herself associating with elements of hippie culture. She liked the music, and tagging along with friends for a weekend of partying and positive vibes sounded like a great time. Now she barely resembled the person she'd been in those days, having been transformed by a period of relentlessly brutal slavery. She was constantly threatened with death or worse if she ever failed to do as she was told. This meant she sometimes had to maim and kill other people not much different from the person she'd been. In time, she even became a semi-willing participant in the vile deeds perpetrated by the unhinged siblings, acquiring a taste for it that would've appalled her former self. Murders galore and epic torture and rape sessions that sometimes went on for days before the victims finally expired.

Experiencing anything akin to genuine shock was a rare thing these days. It almost never happened anymore.

But this . . . this came close.

She shook her head and looked at Darlene. "Mind explaining why you did this at this particular point in time?"

Darlene shrugged. "This is what we were always gonna do someday. We talked about it, remember?"

Eunice wasn't sure what Darlene was talking about at first, but then a dim memory of a night the two of them spent in a sleeping bag outdoors came back to her. This was several months back, at least. The memory returned in wispy, hard-to-grasp fragments. Not surprising, given how drunk they'd been that night. Other substances had been involved, too, of course. It was just the two of them, holding each other in the clearing and staring up at the stars. The brothers had been off somewhere else, probably prowling the countryside in their pickup truck looking for victims. Darlene told her she wished it could always be this way. Just the two of them. She vowed to make it happen someday.

Well, "someday" was today, apparently.

The youngest of the murderous siblings had always displayed reckless and impulsive tendencies. Eunice long ago lost count of the number of batshit crazy things Darlene had done over the last three to four years. The girl never went into explicit detail about it, but she occasionally dropped hints about a background of abuse at the hands of her siblings and deceased parents that went back to early childhood. Even knowing this, the abrupt gunning down of her brothers was about the last thing Eunice had been expecting.

Processing it mentally required a few moments.

Darlene smirked. "Yeah, guess you were pretty fucked up that night and maybe don't remember it so well. Let this be a lesson. I mean what the fuck I say, by god."

The comment elicited a small smile from Eunice. "Yeah, I guess you fucking do." She sighed. "Well, what now?"

Darlene's smirk became a smile. "I'll show you what now. Hold this."

She handed Eunice the rifle, grabbed hold of an edge of the rickety old table, and pulled it clear of the threadbare rug beneath it, dislodging many of the empty bottles and cans crowding its surface and causing them to clatter to the floor. Next she pulled away the rug and tossed it aside, revealing the hidden trap door beneath.

Eunice had been under the impression the siblings no longer had much in the way of things they kept from her, but it appeared she'd been wrong about that. She guessed there was a cellar under that door. She'd never had a clue it was there. How they'd kept its existence from her all this time was a mystery, seeing how she'd been in the company of one or more of them at all times, but she guessed they had their ways. You didn't survive in the serial-killing game as long as they did without having a gift for trickery.

Darlene plucked the rusted iron ring opener out of the recessed plate at the edge of the door and hauled the door up, the old hinges creaking loudly. Once she had the door fully upright, she stood at the edge of the opening and glanced at Eunice. "Wait here. I'll be right back."

She began to slowly and carefully descend the steps into the dark cellar. As soon as she'd disappeared into the darkness, Eunice did an impulsive thing of her own. She hurriedly circled around to the other side of the trap door and kicked at it from behind. It maddeningly stayed where it was despite how hard she'd kicked it with her bare foot. She immediately tried again, but the result was the same. The door wouldn't budge. Instead of kicking it again, she grabbed hold of the top edge of the door and began rocking it back and forth in a desperate effort to disengage the mechanism holding it up.

"What the hell's going on up there?" Darlene yelled at her from the cellar.

Her heart hammering, Eunice abruptly ceased her effort to lower the door and trap Darlene in the cellar. The last thing she wanted was Darlene coming back up those steps in time to see what she was trying to do, because she definitely feared her more than the encroaching horde of dead things.

"Nothing," she called back, raising her voice enough to be heard from up here. "Just those things making a racket."

"Well, hold tight," came Darlene's reply. "I'm about to come up there with something that'll take care of those fuckers once and for goddamn all."

Eunice sighed heavily. "Okay."

She wasn't sure why she'd picked this moment of impending doom to finally rebel against her sole surviving captor. In all her time with Darlene and her brothers, she hadn't attempted anything of the sort. Not even once. Her absolute terror of them and the potential of their sadistic wrath kept her from even considering it. Until this morning. Then suddenly the opportunity to imprison the last of them was right in front of her and she simply couldn't resist.

It just happened. And now it was over and done.

A failed gesture of resistance.

And now she was once again resigned to spending what little remained of her life under Darlene's thumb. She'd been coerced into becoming the girl's lover through a process of years of brutalization and terror tactics, but the truth was Eunice hated her every bit as much as her far stupider brothers. Maybe more so, because of the false emotional intimacy she'd been forced to feign throughout their time together. The moments of pleasure she'd derived from the things they'd done together had only been possible via an exhausting process of psychological compartmentalization. Essentially, there were two versions of her living inside her head at the same time. Sometimes the lines between her two selves blurred to the point of indistinguishability, but other times the delineation abruptly became clear again. The latter was happening right now.

Feeling tired and suddenly unwilling to devote much more mental energy to worrying about the threat lurking outside the cabin, she leaned against the upright door, bracing her arms over the top edge and closing her eyes as she began to weep. She cried not for the grisly fate she was undoubtedly about to meet, but belatedly for the loss of the person she'd once been.

In the next moment, however, two things happened almost simultaneously. The pounding hand of one of the dead things broke through a window pane at the front of the cabin. And Eunice heard a click from somewhere near the base of the trap door's opposite side. She gasped and jerked away from it as it fell away from her, slamming back into place with a loud thud. Darlene immediately called out to her again, but the sound was fainter now, her words unintelligible.

Eunice knew she had to act fast, without taking the time to think about what she was doing. She flipped the table over, sending more bottles and cans scattering across the floor as she dragged it back into place over the trap door, only now the table's surface was braced against the door. Whether the table was heavy enough to prevent Darlene from pushing the door up and open again, she did not know. She was considering what else she might pile atop it to make it heavier when she heard a series of loud, rapid pops from somewhere beneath her. Then she saw the holes appearing in the floor and realized Darlene was firing some kind of automatic weapon up through the roof of the cellar in hopes of hitting her. She'd finally realized what Eunice was really up to and now she was trying to kill her.

In the same moment she realized this, she heard another clatter of breaking glass from the front of the cabin and one of the zombies finally came tumbling through the shattered window. It got awkwardly to its feet and began to stagger slowly in her direction. The thing's flesh was a dark shade of purple. It looked rotten. In life, the reanimated dead thing had been a tall and skinny hippie kid, with long, blood-flecked hair hanging in his face. He wore bell-bottom jeans and a torn and bloodied Widespread Panic shirt. The hair and attire made him look a lot like the other hippie kid Darlene had murdered just minutes ago.

Another zombie spilled through the broken window.

And then another.

Soon enough, they'd overwhelm her.

She had to try to get out of here. Going out the front door was impossible. She'd never be able to push her way through the mass of them crowding the porch. The only other option was the back door. Maybe there were more of them back there, maybe a lot of them, but she had to try. She was turning in that direction when she felt a bullet penetrate the bottom of her right foot, causing her to cry out and pitch backward. More bullets punched through her flesh in multiple places as she crashed to the floor. The popping sounds from the cellar continued. Still more bullets ripped through her torso and continued their upward trajectory, making holes in the ceiling.

The shuffling, groaning zombies were closer now. She hoped consciousness would fade and disappear before they reached her.

That did not happen.

She was still cognizant a few moments longer as they tore into her with their hands and ripped into her flesh with their teeth. She screamed one last time, but did not struggle, having no strength left for that. The last thing she saw was a rotting corpse face lowering itself to her, filling the entirety of her field of vision in the instant before the thing tore loose a scrap of her cheek and gobbled it down.

Then she was gone.

Darlene could tell by the sound of the slow, shambling footsteps above her the dead things had filled the cabin by now. And judging by the pitiful sound of Eunice's final wail of pain and despair, she was now one of them. She imagined the girl going completely still for a moment before tentatively and awkwardly beginning to reanimate, the way it always happened in those old movies they used to watch back in the days when they still had power out here.

Those days were long gone now, just like her momma and daddy. She smiled as she glanced toward the back of the large cellar. The body pit was back there. It was filled with the liquefied remains of most of the victims she and her brothers had taken over the years.

Including Momma and Daddy.

An ammonia-like odor was ever-present down here. That was the lye they used for dissolving the bodies. Most people hated the smell, but she'd grown to love it over the years. It was the odor most inextricably tied to what her life had always been about. Hurting people. Killing them.

She'd always loved it. Killing her brothers hadn't been an act of vengeance for being forced into a life of murder and terror. The intent hadn't been to rescue Eunice and escape together to a less insane life somewhere else. The abuse stories she'd fed the former hippie bitch had largely been lies to garner sympathy. Only one person in her life had touched her without her consent and that had been her daddy. And, well, she'd taken care of that sorry-ass motherfucker, hadn't she?

No, she killed Jasper and Purvis for the simple reason that she wanted Eunice to herself.

It was sheer selfishness, nothing else.

Only now the bitch had betrayed her and she was trapped down here in the cellar with what sounded like dozens of those dead things tromping around on the floor above. She could keep firing rounds up through the roof with her AR-15, but she couldn't be sure of getting them all. Besides, if movie rules applied here, she'd have to get head shots on all of them to put them down. Pretty much impossible without being able to see what she was shooting at. No, there was only one viable course of action.

She'd have to wait them out.

Without anyone else left alive to feast on inside the cabin, they'd have to leave eventually?

Right?

She didn't have a definitive answer to that question, of course. That hope was all she had, though. She could survive down here a long time without having to come out of the cellar, which was well-provisioned for riding out apocalyptic scenarios of all kinds. There were cases and cases of bottled water and enough canned food to last a year or longer. She could piss and shit in a bucket and dump the waste in the lye pit.

She smiled.

Nah. I ain't in any hurry.

She felt a bit miffed at Eunice's betrayal, but other than that she was okay. Sooner or later, she'd get out of here, and by the time that happened, she was sure this whole zombie thing would've blown over. And, hey, if not, she'd get to live the post-apocalypse dream of roaming the land and blowing away walking dead fucks with all the firepower at her disposal.

Which was a lot of fucking firepower.

Chuckling at the thought, she laid the AR-15 down atop a crate of hand grenades and took a seat on the floor, folding her legs beneath her as she stared off toward the lye pit. There was a radio around here somewhere. She'd have to find it at some point. It'd alleviate boredom and help her keep abreast of the situation in the outside world.

She thought of the other hippie kid they'd taken overnight, another quick snatch job from just outside the festival grounds. Before they started in with the torture and other fun stuff, the dumb fuck briefly believed he could win them over by offering them drugs. Consciousness-expanding hippie shit.

What had he called it?

Delish? Delight?

Something along those lines.

She dug one of the pills she'd taken off him out of her pocket and stared at its neon-green coating a moment. Smiling at the memory of how he'd screamed as they strung him up from the rafter of the shed, she shrugged and popped the pill in her mouth. Normally she wasn't into this ecstasy-type shit. She loved her meth above all else, but there wasn't any goddamn meth down here.

She smiled again and got ready to enjoy the trip.

TEN

STANDING ON THE SECOND-FLOOR balcony at the back of their house, Helen Ferguson was engaged in what was looking like an increasingly hopeless battle to drive the reanimated invaders away from her property. More and more of the shambling, mud and blood-encrusted, straggly-haired dead things kept coming out of the woods and climbing the gently sloping hill toward the home she'd shared with her dead husband for so many years. There were dozens and dozens of them now. Barely a second went by without another one or two emerging from the distant tree line.

She'd locked all the doors and bolted all the windows on the bottom floor, lowering all the heavy wooden privacy shutters as an extra barrier in case the creatures were able to batter their way through the windows. Going by how they struggled to weave and stagger their way up the hill, she doubted any single one of them would have the strength to do that. The danger would lie in an overwhelming number of them piling up against the house from all sides. Even then, she doubted their combined efforts would be sufficient to force their way in, but doubt wasn't certainty. She had to allow for the dismaying possibility that it might happen.

Which meant she had to kill as many of them as she could before they could even reach the house. To that end, she again braced the stock of her late husband's rifle against her shoulder, took aim through the attached scope at a wobbling dead thing about fifty feet distant, and squeezed the trigger. There was a gratifying spray of blood from the back of its head as the round drilled through the thing's temple. It fell over and did not move. She shifted the rifle over, sighting down on another of the nearby shamblers. The satisfaction she felt at dropping them was not exactly pleasure. It was more a sense of righteous accomplishment. These creatures had been living people not long ago. They had people who loved them and would grieve for them. But Helen couldn't concern herself for that. Not now. Maybe later, when this was all over. *If* it was ever all over. The only thing she had room for in her mind at the moment was defending her home. She would not lose it to some sinister, mysterious force, whatever was behind this madness, not if she could help it.

She'd raided Dan's gun cabinet after retreating to the house and battening down the hatches earlier. He had multiple rifles, handguns, and shotguns. All were out here on the balcony with her now, along with many boxes of ammunition. The rifle she was now using had an expensive scope. She knew it was expensive because she remembered when Dan bought it a decade ago, back when he was still an active hunter. He'd hemmed and hawed about spending the money, but in the end she talked him into it, telling him life was short and getting shorter all the time at their age. Besides that, they had no kids or grandkids to pass their savings onto when they were gone. Might as well spend what money you have on things you enjoy while you still can, that was her philosophy.

So Dan spent the money.

Now, all these years later, she was glad she'd talked him into it, because she could see the things with a startling HD-like clarity, as if they were right in front of her instead of many yards distant. She squeezed the trigger and took down another one as it came out of the trees. That one she eliminated just to again test accuracy and range. Still impressive. She was taking aim on a much closer creature when she began to perceive a strange pulsing sound coming from some indeterminate direction. There was an oddly resonant, warbling quality to it, a rising shrillness that set her teeth on edge and pebbled her arms with goosebumps as it grew steadily louder.

Grimacing, she lowered the rifle and looked up as a shadow began to move over the balcony. Her jaw dropped open when she saw the thing hovering directly above her home. Tojo came out on the balcony and started yipping frantically at the object, a sound vastly different from his usual full-throated barking. The fear that came over her then was more related to concern for the dog's safety than any worries she had for herself. She was old. She'd lived a long and full life. The dog was only a few years old. In the event something happened to her, someone else would need to take custody of Tojo and care for him for many years to come. She tried ordering him back inside, but the dog stayed where he was, standing now with his paws braced against the top of the railing and howling for all he was worth.

She considered raising the rifle again, this time to fire on the saucer-like craft, which was silver-colored and of some metallic construction. Lights along the circumference of the craft's underside blinked on and off in a repeating pattern of bright colors that made her wonder if it was trying to signal her. That didn't seem likely. This craft was not of this world. It was a UFO. How was she supposed to know what manner of message it was trying to communicate?

Something in the periphery of her vision made her look down again. Her mouth opened in amazement upon seeing that all the dead things had stopped in their tracks and were staring skyward. They seemed hypnotized either by the craft itself, the noise it was making, or the repeating pattern of lights.

Helen wondered if the beings at the helm of the alien craft might be responsible in some way for reanimating the dead. Why else would they be so affected by its presence when they were seemingly oblivious to everything else other than warm, living flesh?

The possibility angered her and she raised the rifle again, this time aiming it skyward. Before she could squeeze the trigger, a round black hole at the center of the craft's underside irised open and a brilliant shaft of light projected downward, enveloping the entirety of the balcony. The light soon grew so bright she couldn't see anything anymore. She heard Tojo yipping and howling. She heard the pulsing, warbling sound, now so loud it was making her ears hurt.

Next came a brief, gray moment of unconsciousness.

When she could see again, she and Tojo were sitting in the midst of a peaceful meadow with a picnic blanket and the contents of a lunch basket spread out around them. Tojo abruptly sat up and started barking excitedly. A tall, thin figure was approaching from the distance.

Helen stayed where she was, sitting cross-legged on the ground with a glass of wine dangling from her fingers. Dan would be here in just a few minutes. The three of them were going to be together again, now and forever. She smiled and sipped her wine, feeling better than she had in a long time. In years, in fact.

Tojo, however, could not contain his excitement.

He leapt to his feet and went running to meet his best friend.

Helen breathed a sigh of contentment.

Everything was perfect now. No more worries. No more fear. No more getting old. No more anything that made any of them unhappy.

Perfect.

EPILOGUE

THE FIRST THING OSCAR FELT upon opening his eyes was surprise at still being alive. He sensed the dead milling around him, but they were no longer mauling his shredded flesh. They were no longer even paying attention to him. In another moment, knowledge began to seep into his mind from somewhere else, like a download of information from the ether.

He was *not*, in fact, still alive.

Delight was more than a drug distributed by an advance invading force. It was a gateway. Though he hadn't ingested it voluntarily, the dead had transmitted its viral effects by biting him. His body was now undergoing a process of transformation. He was becoming a conduit. An alien consciousness was passing through the link between universes to take up residence in his brain.

He was now two beings existing in one reanimated body.

Oscar sat up and got to his feet. A loud fart popped out of his backside. The smell would've caused the living Oscar to recoil in disgust, but now he recognized it only as a side effect of the transference between worlds. The other intelligence residing inside him needed bio-fuel to operate at more than a basic level and continue the transformation.

Meaning human flesh and a lot of it.

Everywhere he looked, Oscar only saw other dead things. He

needed to find living people as soon as possible to assuage the burning hunger beginning to take hold of him. Groaning and grimacing at the pain the hunger caused him, Oscar started walking in a direction his new undead instincts told him was the right one. Then he felt an unnatural burst of intense energy and he began to run.

He couldn't wait to taste human flesh for the first time.

AUTHOR'S NOTE: The story that follows is a 10,000-plus word piece that was written inside of 24 hours. So if it reads as if it was written very quickly, well, you'll know why. This isn't a serious story. It's kind of a goof, actually. But I think most people who enjoy my books will at least find it fun. If it seems very random, there's a good reason for that as well. I had to come up with this story in a very short time frame. Because I wasn't sure what I wanted to write about, I posted the following message on my private Facebook page. This should help you figure out why the tale unfolds the way it does.

"That short story I have to come up with so quickly? Not sure what I want to write about. It can basically be anything within the horror genre. So I'm gonna do something a little different here and put it up for a vote. Refer to the numbers below to tell me what this thing should be about.

1. Zombies
2. Vampires
3. A serial killer or killers
4. Werewolves
5. Monsters lurking in the sewers
6. Lesbian cheerleaders with chainsaws
7. The cannibals next door
8. Nazi zombies risen from the grave
9. Some kind of combo of Nazi zombies, lesbian chainsaw-wielding cheerleaders, serial killers, and sewer mutants.
10. Fluffy bunnies."

So anyway, you may want to review this list again after you've read the story. By then you may be able to guess which answers were the most popular.

SOME CRAZY FUCKING SHIT THAT HAPPENED ONE DAY

DARBY HINSON'S GIRLFRIEND DIDN'T LIKE him smoking in their one-bedroom apartment. She didn't like the smell and she didn't like to watch him sucking poison down into his lungs. That was how she put it anyway. Of course, it was totally okay for her to fire up her bong and smoke weed all damn day. It wasn't the same thing, according to Lacy. Tobacco was stinky poison, but weed was organic, natural, and pure. It came from the earth, she said, and was one of God's most beautiful gifts to the world. Tobacco just made you sick, while weed made you mellow and happy and helped you see things in more enlightened ways and shit. Every now and then when she'd go off on one of her tobacco versus weed rants, he'd tell her that tobacco was a natural product that came from the fucking earth, too, and that, really, she was kind of a goddamn hypocrite. He tried not to lose his cool with her too often or even argue with her at all. She didn't like to be corrected or told she was wrong about anything. She'd get all wound up, start screaming and even throwing shit, which was no damn fun at all.

Kind of the total damn opposite of mellow, but, like, whatever, man.

So here he was again, strolling around the perimeter of the shabby two-story apartment building's little parking lot, puffing away on his fifth smoke of the day while again wondering what it was that kept him with Lacy Jones. As always, he recognized there was no easy answer to that question. He didn't like being alone for one thing. Who the hell did? She was good at sex. Like, really, really super phenomenally good. Probably because she was a former porn actress. So she was kind of a damn expert at fucking. Which was kind of awesome . . . except for when he started thinking about all the dicks that had been all up inside her over the years. That was kind of gross. These days she worked as a stripper down at the Sin Den on 10th Avenue, where, he suspected, she also turned the occasional trick. Lacy was a fine-looking babe, the hottest he'd ever hooked up with by a mile, but there were times, like now, when he wasn't sure staying with her was the right thing. Even leaving aside all the arguing and petty disagreements, the thought of his dick suddenly turning rotten with some funky venereal disease often kept him awake at night.

Such were his thoughts as his walk took him to the sidewalk and down to the street corner near the apartment building. He stood there and stared at the traffic passing through the busy intersection as he smoked his cigarette down to the filter. Then he tossed the butt to the ground and considered whether he ought to head back inside or stay out here a bit longer and have another smoke. While he was mulling it over, he heard the rumble of a big engine approaching from his left. He glanced in that direction and saw a yellow school bus rolling slowly through the intersection. Though the light was green, the bus slowed to a stop at the street corner.

Darby frowned.

What the fuck?

The door hissed open and a stunningly statuesque brunette in a black cheerleader outfit smiled down at him. "Hey, baby, want a ride?"

Darby had a fresh, unlit cigarette out already. He kept his eyes on the smiling stunner as he brought it to his mouth and drew on the filter. He kept his expression frozen as he realized he hadn't yet lit the cigarette. Then, smiling, he dropped his hand and exhaled imaginary smoke.

Man . . . I gotta look like the world's biggest fucking goof right now.

The cheerleader laughed. "You might want to actually light that, baby. Better that way."

Darby snorted. "Right, right. No shit." He fumbled his lighter out of a pocket and had a scary moment where it almost slipped from his fingers to the sidewalk. But he was able to close his fingers tight around the Zippo and hold it still as he snapped a flame to life. He lit his new smoke and smiled again. "Guess that didn't look too smooth, huh?"

The cheerleader giggled and wiggled her hips a little. It was pretty distracting. "It really didn't, but you're cute so it's okay. So . . . do you want a ride or not?"

"Well . . . I kinda wasn't actually going anywhere." He indicated the apartment building behind him with a tilt of his head. "I live over there. Was just out for a walk and a smoke."

The cheerleader pouted. "Aw. You sure you don't want a ride anyway?"

Darby gave that some thought. It wasn't like he had to work or had anything planned today. Sure, Lacy might be mad if he took off without saying anything, but she was in one of her fouler moods today and it might be nice to avoid her for a while. When he got back, he could just tell her he went on a really long walk. And hell, maybe she'd be too stoned to even notice he'd been gone at all. Wouldn't be the first time.

As he thought it over, he took note of the pom-poms the girl was holding. They were orange and black. Which made him think of Halloween decorations. They matched the black outfit she was wearing, which consisted of the typical short, frilly skirt and a tight, midriff-exposing top. Sewn across the front of the top was a bat insignia.

Not a baseball bat.

The kind with wings. A flying rodent.

Darby exhaled smoke. "What kind of school has a fucking bat for a mascot?"

The cheerleader giggled again and glanced over her shoulder. "He wants to know what school we cheer for."

Raucous feminine laughter exploded inside the bus. Darby's gaze swept the windows along the side of the bus. The vehicle was loaded with gorgeous cheerleaders. They hooted and hollered as they noted his scrutiny. Some waved. Others blew kisses. A few opened their mouths and did suggestive things with their tongues.

Darby blew out another cloud of smoke.

The cheerleader peering down at him through the open door said, "We cheer for the devil, Darby."

"The devil?"

"Satan."

"You're Satan's cheerleaders?"

"Yes."

Darby now figured this was a gag of some kind. They were having some fun messing with him. But he didn't mind. They were hot, so it was okay. And what the hell, he could play the same game. "All right, I'll take a ride with you gals."

The cheerleader he'd been talking to let out a whoop of delight. "Awesome!" She stepped aside and beckoned him inside. "Climb aboard, baby."

Darby frowned again. "Um . . ."

He'd figured they would laugh at him and close the door in his face the moment he called their bluff, maybe making mocking faces at him through the windows as they drove away. Suddenly unsure of himself, he experienced a momentary paralysis.

"What are you waiting for, baby?"

Darby swept his gaze up and down the block. Cars were backed up several deep behind the stalled bus. The intersection was effectively blocked as the backed-up vehicles haltingly jockeyed for position, hoping to slip into the other lane. Horns honked. Angry voices called out epithets. One man in a Volvo right behind the bus was getting out of his car. He was a big man and in his beefy right hand he clutched a big baseball bat.

Aw, shit.

Darby looked at the cheerleader. "Can I smoke in there?"

She beamed at him. "Of course, baby. You can do anything you want."

Darby nodded. "Cool."

Weird.

He climbed aboard the bus and the door hissed shut behind him just as the big man with the bat was closing in. He turned around and flipped the guy a middle finger as the bus pulled away from the curb. The guy screamed at him and smashed the bat against the side of the bus.

"That dude has anger issues."

The cheerleader he'd been talking to touched his arm and said, "Have a seat with me, baby."

She waved a hand at an empty seat at the front of the bus. He dropped into it and the cheerleader slid in next to him.

She smiled brightly at him and put a hand on his thigh. "My name is Lexie."

He glanced at the hand on his thigh. It was a slender hand. Pale as snow. It looked very soft. She wore a single silver ring engraved with the number 666. Though he was distracted by how very close to his crotch her hand was, he made himself look her in the eye. "My name's—"

"Darby," she said.

Darby's brow furrowed. He remembered now that she had done that once already, before he boarded the bus. "How do you know my name?"

"Satan."

Darby nodded. "Right. Satan. Of course." He glanced again at her 666 ring. Though he hadn't felt it move, her hand was closer to his crotch now. "You sure about that? I mean . . . and I don't mean to offend you or anything . . . but it sounds kind of crazy. You know? I mean . . . you know there's no such thing as Satan, right?"

Her hand came away from his thigh and snapped across his face. This was no love tap. It was a hard blow that rocked his head savagely to one side. He blinked rapidly and struggled to focus. "Jesus, girl."

She slapped him again.

He backed away from her. "What the fuck?"

She was still smiling. Strangely, it didn't look like the kind of mean smile Lacy sometimes flashed at him, the kind that invariably meant she was about to really unload on him. This was a genuine smile. A happy smile. It looked pretty out of place on the face of someone apparently bent on beating the shit out of him.

"I'm sorry, Darby. I don't want to hurt you."

"Well, don't then. Jesus."

She slapped him again.

He cringed away from her. "Oh, come on!"

The other cheerleaders appeared unconcerned with the strange altercation occurring at the front of the bus. Actually, they were completely oblivious to it, as far as Darby could tell. They were all too busy making out with each other. Everywhere he looked, curvy, busty, scantily clad hot girls were kissing other hot girls. Very passionately. As he stared with his mouth hanging open, one of the cheerleaders slid off her seat, dropped to her knees, and pushed her head beneath the frilly skirt of the girl who'd been sharing her seat. She was just the first. Others soon followed suit. Moans of ecstasy soon resonated inside the bus.

Christ, Darby thought. *It's a lesbian orgy on wheels. What the fuck?*

He looked at Lexie. "What the fuck?"

She smirked. "Do you really have a problem with any of that?"

"Well . . . no." His frown deepened. "I mean, it's hot as fuck. No shit. But it's strange as shit. This kind of shit doesn't happen every day." He gave that a moment's thought. "Okay, maybe in your world it does, but not for most people. And why do you keep hitting me?"

Lexie's hand was on his thigh again. "Because you keep misbehaving."

"I do? How?"

"Well, for one thing, you denied the existence of our dark lord, Lucifer. That's blasphemy. Don't do it again or I won't stop hitting you for hours and hours."

Darby gulped. "Um . . . okay. Was there something else? You said 'for one thing' . . ."

"You said the J-word."

"The what?"

"The J-word. Don't make me say the actual word."

Darby had no idea what she was talking about. Not at first. But he did a mental rewind and it came to him. What he'd said that offended her so. He'd said it twice and each time he'd received one of those thunderous slaps. It couldn't be a coincidence. "Okay. I won't say the J-word again."

She smiled. "Awesome." Her hand was on his crotch now. "Would you like to fuck in the name of Satan now?"

Darby couldn't help laughing.

Lady, I'll fuck in the name of whatever the hell you want.

"Well . . . sure."

She unzipped him and pulled out his erection. Her head dipped to his lap and she went down on him for several mind-bendingly pleasurable moments. He gasped as her mouth came away from him. She smiled again, raised her little skirt, and mounted him right there on the seat. By this point, he was unsurprised by her lack of underwear. Panties would just get in the way of fucking in the name of Satan, after all.

Lexie tossed her head back as she bounced up and down on him, her long, dark hair flailing and her mouth hanging open in a wide orgasmic O. She arched her back and thrust her pert breasts at him as she repeatedly screamed out . . . well, not his name. "Oh, Satan!" she screamed. "Oh, Satan! Oh, Satan! Oh, Satan! Oh, my beautiful dark fucking lord!"

It wasn't just her.

Other loud female voices called out the devil's name over and over.

Oh, man, this is some fucked up shit.

But it felt really fucking amazing, so Darby figured he'd just roll with it for now. At least until Lexie was done fucking him. Then, once the bus inevitably came to a stop again, he'd just hop off at the curb and leave this madness behind. Even in the midst of ecstasy, it was all so surreal. Seriously . . . cheerleaders for Satan? He had to be hallucinating. Maybe Lacy had slipped him something. It was the kind of sick fucking prank she would pull when she was really high. None of this really felt like a hallucination, but what other explanation made any kind of real sense?

When it was finally over, they reclined lazily in the seat, sharing a smoke as Lexie leaned against him with her head on his shoulder. "So . . . you never told me how you knew my name."

"Yes, I did, dummy. Satan."

"Oh. Right. So . . . Satan told you about me ahead of time?"

"That's right."

"Okay. And . . . he told you I'd be waiting on that street corner?"

"Yep."

"And that you should pick me up?"

"Yes."

"Okay. But . . . why?"

She groaned and snuggled closer against him. "Because Satan likes you and wants you to join the club."

"Oh."

"You should feel privileged. Not many motherfuckers get a direct invite."

"But . . . why me?"

She snorted and exhaled smoke before passing the cigarette back to him. "I don't know, Darby. The devil doesn't tell us everything. He'll tell you himself someday."

Darby tried to imagine having a conversation with the actual devil. Just a chill chat with the prince of darkness. It should have scared him. The dude was supposed to be the living embodiment of ultimate fucking evil, after all. But right now the prospect didn't unnerve him too much. Part of that undoubtedly was the very recent sexual release. Not much could bug him right after blowing a load. But a bigger part of it was this whole concept of hot Satanic cheerleaders. Evil or not, a guy with this kind of entourage couldn't be all bad, right? You could have a beer with a dude like that. Be buds, even.

The bus rolled to a stop at an intersection. Darby tensed, recalling the plan of action he'd conceived earlier.

Lexie sensed the change. "Something wrong, baby?"

Darby didn't say anything right away. He stared at the slice of curb visible through the closed bus door.

Stared at it until the bus driver changed gears and pulled away again.

He shrugged. "Nothing." He looked at Lexie and smiled. "Say . . . where are we going anyway?"

"The Nazi cemetery."

Darby opened his mouth to reply, but remained silent a long moment as what she'd said fully registered. "The . . . what cemetery?"

"The Nazi cemetery," she repeated.

Darby puffed on the cigarette and frowned. "Are you talking about, like, a cemetery for skinheads. Like neo-Nazis?"

Lexie giggled. "No. That would be lame. Real German Nazis from World War II. We're gonna perform some satanic rites and shit for them."

"A cemetery for actual WWII Nazis? Here in America? Are you sure?"

"Sure I'm sure. Would I lie?"

"I have no idea. Would you?"

"Not to you, baby." She sat up straight and stretched her arms above her, then dropped them and looked Darby in the eye. "It's a secret, you see. Hundreds of coffins were shipped here at the end of the war and buried at this special cemetery. They've been there all this time. Waiting."

"Waiting for what?"

She indicated the other cheerleaders with a head gesture. "Waiting for us."

"To do what?"

She smiled. "Isn't that obvious? To bring them back, silly."

"Oh."

Oh, shit.

"Right. Of course."

Darby looked out the window on his side, observing the passing cityscape with a new sense of longing. It still seemed remotely possible these girls were just a bunch of delusional crazies. It was what anyone observing from the outside would think, at least at first blush. But how likely was it anyone could convince a large group of devastatingly attractive young women to participate in this kind of lunacy if there wasn't some kind of real substance behind it? Which, though it seemed unlikely and absurd and insane, left just one viable explanation. Everything Lexie had told him was the absolute truth.

He looked at her. "Could you maybe have the driver stop somewhere? I need to take a leak."

"Thinking of running away, Darby?"

He tried not to look startled . . . but didn't entirely succeed. "Um . . . no, of course not."

"Good. Because that would be dumb. I'd have to be really mean to you and you wouldn't like that. Anyway, you can piss when we get to the cemetery. It's not far away now."

"Right. Sure. I'll hold it. No problem."

She patted his cheek. "I love you, Darby."

"What?"

"I love you."

"That's what I thought you said."

"Satan says you're mine. That means you are."

Darby nodded. "Right. Of course it does."

Lacy is gonna be so pissed when she finds out about this.

She patted his cheek again. A little harder this time. "So say it back, Darby."

"What?"

Another pat. Even harder, just a shade away from being a slap. "Say you love me."

The last thing Darby wanted was to have her really let him have it again. "Um . . . I love you, Lexie."

She squealed in delight and kissed him on the mouth. "I know you do, baby! I know you do!" She bounced up and down on the seat, apparently unable to contain her glee. "You'll make a great daddy."

"What?"

"I just conceived."

"What?"

"You're gonna be a daddy, Darby. We're gonna be parents!" She was doing that bouncing up and down thing again, this time hard enough that the dwindling cigarette was dislodged from his fingers. "Satan foresaw it. He sent me to seduce you and get knocked up with a little devil baby and that's just what happened. Aren't you happy?"

"Um . . ."

"We can start making wedding plans once we get back from res-urrecting the Nazis. Oh, Darby, I'm so excited!"

"Um . . ."

Darby snatched the fallen cigarette from his lap and drew heavily on it.

Oh shit, he thought. *Oh shit, oh shit, oh shit!*

Lexie kept babbling away about the wedding. "Naturally I'll want the ceremony to happen in a graveyard at midnight. It'll have to be a proper satanic wedding, of course, with human sacrifices and an orgy amongst the tombstones afterwards."

"Obviously," Darby muttered, lighting up yet another cigarette.

There was a squelch of brakes and a ratcheting sound as the bus driver changed gears again. Darby puffed smoke and looked out the window.

Lexie clutched his arm and squealed again. "We're here!"

Darby shuddered. "Great."

Darby departed the bus with the cheerleaders and accompanied them through the grounds of an immaculately maintained sprawling ceme-tery. The grass looked freshly mown, raked, and edged. Many of the graves sported fresh flowers. There wasn't a speck of trash anywhere. It all looked very nice and peaceful, like the kind of place where you'd want to be interred when it was your time. But it was maybe the big-gest cemetery Darby had even seen. Acres upon acres of lush, tomb-stone-spotted land. They walked and walked for what seemed like miles, baking beneath the heat of a summer sun shining brightly in an almost cloudless sky. Darby was in decent shape for a young man with so many unhealthy habits—chain-smoking and copious booze consumption being just two of them—but he soon grew uncomfort-able in his boots and tight jeans. Sweat dampened his Harley t-shirt and made it cling to his torso. But this physical discomfort was noth-ing compared to what he felt as he and the cheerleaders sauntered past a group of solemn-faced mourners at a graveside service. Many of the mourners glared at them as they went by. Darby couldn't read their minds, but he guessed they found the skimpy outfits disrespect-ful. He couldn't argue with that. It was disrespectful. The bubbly din of feminine laughter and conversation wasn't exactly appropriate ei-ther. But he wasn't about to suggest that the girls modify their behavior. It'd only earn him an ass-beating from Lexie and wouldn't do any good anyway.

He didn't relax at all until they'd put at least a hundred yards between themselves and the group of mourners. But even then he was left with the matter of his physical discomfort. He tugged at the collar of his Harley shirt. "Jesus, it's fucking hot."

Lexie had been walking arm-in-arm with him the whole time. She disengaged herself from him and placed a hand against his chest, stopping him cold.

Oh shit. Not again.

She slammed a fist hard into his gut, just beneath the sternum.

He gagged and doubled over.

When he was able to breathe again, he stood up straight again and looked at her glaring face. "I'm sorry."

"You know what you did."

"Yes. I do. I'm sorry. I just forgot."

"Next time I break something."

"There won't be a next time. I swear."

She took him by the arm again and this time she urged him to hurry along. The other girls had gotten ahead of them. By the time they caught up to the rest of the group, they had nearly reached a stand of tall trees that Darby assumed marked the edge of the property. But the girls kept on going, plunging into the dense knot of trees.

"I thought your Nazi friends were buried in that cemetery. Where the fuck are we going?"

"To the old cemetery."

Darby frowned. "A different one?"

"Same property, technically. Same owner. But an older part of the grounds, hidden away from prying eyes for obvious reasons."

"Right. Makes sense."

Actually, none of this made any kind of sense at all, but Darby knew he had passed the point of no return long ago. All the evidence of a lunatic brand of genuine Satanism aside, a small part of him kept thinking this might all still turn out to be some kind of elaborate gag. He was able to imagine a few possible alternate explanations. The one that seemed most likely was that these girls weren't Satanists at all, that instead they were actresses or performers en route to some sort of weird porn or B-movie shoot. That would account for the outfits and possibly even some of the offbeat behavior. But it didn't explain how Lexie knew his name.

The dense expanse of trees began to thin out and soon Darby was able to discern a clearing in the distance. He and the cheerleaders emerged through the last of the trees into the clearing a few moments later. And Darby saw at once that Lexie had not been lying about at least one thing. They really had come to an older section of the cemetery. The grass here was overgrown and patchy, but there were many tombstones protruding from the uneven ground. Some of them bore names, but others were just plain stones. Still others showed evidence of disrepair, lying shattered in pieces. And it was obvious kids had been using this neglected part of the cemetery as a place to party. Darby saw many empty beer cans and rubbers scattered about. Some of the tombstones had been desecrated with anarchy symbols and, appropriately, swastikas spray-painted on them. A few had even been dug up. Darby saw mounds of old earth and splintered pieces of very old coffins.

Darby lit up again and exhaled a cloud of smoke. "This is some spooky-ass shit."

Lexie giggled. "Just the way we like it."

"Be even spookier if you were doing it at night."

"I know, right?" Lexie rolled her eyes. "It would be fucking wicked as shit to do this at night, but this is the way the boss wants it."

"The boss being . . ."

She gave him a withering look. "Really, Darby?"

"Right. Satan. I know. I just keep thinking—"

"That this is all a hoax or something?"

He shrugged. "Well . . . not meaning to offend or anything, but . . ."

She nodded. "Sure. I get it. But your doubts are about to be erased, baby."

She gave him a wet smooch on the cheek and then bounced away from him, skipping across the patchy ground toward the largest tombstone in the clearing. Several other cheerleaders had already gathered there. Darby opted to remain where he was for the moment. He had no role that he knew of in whatever they were planning, nor did he know exactly what kind of crazy shit they had in mind, but for now he thought it'd be best if he just stayed out of the way.

A couple of long wooden crates were stacked against a side of the big tombstone. One of the cheerleaders—a platinum blonde with heavy, pendulous breasts—had produced a crowbar from somewhere and was using it to pry open one of the crates. She cranked the crowbar furiously up and down, making her big breasts flop around in that tight little top. As he watched her work, Darby prayed this would turn out to be exactly what he'd imagined—an epic porn shoot, some kind of horror T&A parody. That would rule. But so far no one had shown up with cameras or other moviemaking equipment. Maybe that was what was inside the crates.

The girl with the monster tits got the top crate's lid removed and a couple of the other girls helped her set it aside. Monster Tits reached both hands into the crate, got a grip on something, and slowly pulled it out. Lexie reached into the crate next and removed an identical instrument. Darby's mouth dropped open. The filter end of his cigarette clung to a wet corner of his mouth for a moment before tumbling to the ground.

Fucking chainsaws. What the hell?

One by one, the rest of the cheerleaders reached into the crate and removed more chainsaws. Once the crate had been depleted, it was tossed aside and the one below it was opened. It contained more chainsaws. The sight of all that potentially deadly steel made Darby feel queasy. So much so that he seriously considered a dash back through the trees to the pristine modern cemetery beyond. Each new thing that happened while he was in the company of these strange girls was just a deeper level of insanity. He shuddered to think what might happen next.

Lexie broke away from the other girls and came running at him with her chainsaw.

Darby screamed and staggered backward a few steps.

She laughed as she came to a lurching stop a few feet away from him. "You should see your face, Darby."

"Please don't kill me."

Lexie laughed some more. "I'm not gonna kill ya, silly. Daddy Satan has plans for you. But you look terrified. It's so fucking funny."

Darby sucked in a big breath and let it slowly out. He nodded as he listened to the frantic beating of his heart. "Yeah. Funny. Hilarious, even. Look . . . what are the fucking chainsaws for?"

"We're using them in the resurrection ritual."

Darby stared at her uncomprehendingly for long moments. She was smiling the whole time, looking at him in an expectant way, as if something truly wonderful and obvious was about to occur and she was just waiting for him to get it.

"I don't get it."

She sighed. "You'll see soon enough, baby." She held the chainsaw aside and leaned into him for a kiss. She lingered close to him for a moment as her voice dropped to a whisper. "I saw you staring at Candy."

"Who?"

"The chick with the monster tits."

"Oh. Yeah. Her."

Lexie's breath was warm against his face as she laughed softly. "If you want, we could have a threesome with her later. Would you like that?"

Darby couldn't keep his eyes from flicking in Candy's direction. She was swinging her own chainsaw around in some kind of crazy acrobatic dance, making her breasts do an enticing dance of their own inside the tight top. He licked his lips and looked at Lexie again. "You'd be okay with that?"

Lexie laughed. "Of course, baby. We're Satanists. You'll be my main man, but monogamy is against our beliefs."

"Huh."

Maybe there was something to this Satanism thing after all.

One of the other girls called out to Lexie. "Hey, Lex! It's time."

Lexie gave him another loud smooch on the cheek and bounded away from him, calling back to him over her shoulder as she went. "Enjoy the show, baby!"

He raised his own voice in answer: "I will!"

He fished another cigarette from the dwindling pack as he watched the girls gather into a loose crowd in the middle of the old cemetery. As they conferred, they spoke much more quietly than they had at any point since Darby had unsuspectingly hopped aboard Team Satan. The loose crowd became a tight huddle after a few moments, with the girls standing in a circle with their heads bowed, their chainsaws hanging loosely by their sides. Then a loud cheer erupted and the huddle broke apart. They spread out across the cemetery in a way that looked random at first, but soon they were forming precisely grouped rows of six girls apiece. Lexie, however, stood alone before them, with her chainsaw held ready at waist level. She looked kind of like the conductor of a demented symphony orchestra.

She raised her voice as she addressed them: "Ready, girls?"

General cheering appeared to indicate assent.

Lexie raised her chainsaw above her head. "Then in the name of our glorious dark father, let us commence with the resurrection of our honored Aryan brethren."

She yanked the starter cord on the chainsaw and it roared to life. The other girls followed her lead and in seconds the cemetery was alive with the sound of dozens of buzzing metal blades. The sound set Darby's teeth on edge and made his head hurt. He again was seized by the impulse to take off running while he still could. Now, while the girls were occupied with this weird fucking inexplicable goddamn thing they were doing. He'd never get a better chance. However, though he knew this was true, he couldn't take his eyes off the girls. Had he thought the events he'd witnessed and participated in on the bus were surreal? Well, they seemed almost ordinary by comparison with this.

Lexie marched backward a few steps while the other girls remained absolutely still. She then executed a stunningly graceful spin move. A pirouette. Darby was pretty sure that was what they were called in ballet. He was just as sure very few—if any—ballerinas had ever performed such a move while clutching an activated chainsaw. The other girls all performed similar moves, all while keeping their chainsaws perfectly poised above their heads. From this surprisingly elegant beginning, they transitioned to a perfectly choreographed but considerably more lewd series of dance moves. They shook their shapely asses as provocatively as any dance music diva's background dancers, twirling their chainsaws in the air like circus performers as they moved. At one point, they all squatted simultaneously and slid the whirring chainsaws between their spread legs, their contorted faces miming expressions of purest ecstasy. Then they were upright again, writhing and wiggling and spinning the chainsaws in the air. Several minutes into the performance, the girls stood rigid and flung the chainsaws high into the air above their heads. Darby's breath caught in his mouth as this happened and he cringed as the chainsaws began to descend again. He fully expected to witness at least one catastrophic accident. But each girl caught her chainsaw smoothly out of the air as it came back down. After that, they were spinning around and around again, their movements becoming more frenzied than ever. They were moving so fast after a while that Darby was no longer able to make out individual girls, just blurs of flesh and hungry, buzzing steel. Then, at last, each of the girls came to an abrupt, perfectly poised stop, with their chainsaws pointed toward the ground. At a signal from Lexie, the cheerleaders silenced their chainsaws.

Darby let out a breath. "Holy shit."

He raised his hands and began to clap them slowly together.

Lexie snapped her head in his direction and glared at him. "Quiet!"

Darby's hands froze in mid-clap. He opened his mouth to utter an apology, then realized that would be a mistake and shut it again. An eerie calm descended over the cemetery. No discernible sounds drifted over from the other areas of the cemetery. There were no animal sounds nor any buzz of insects, the latter a sound that was pretty much constant near any wooded area in Tennessee during the summer. The girls didn't talk and they stood as still as statues, all of them standing there with their eyes trained directly on Lexie.

Darby was unsurprised to discover Lexie was the leader of what he had to figure was the world's only squad of gorgeous, Satan-worshipping cheerleaders. After all, she was the one who had lured him onto the bus. In fact, she was the only one he'd interacted directly with at all. It made him feel special in a weird way. Prideful, almost. On the other hand, she was a servant of ultimate evil, which was a thing he should probably chalk up to the negative side of the ledger. Plus he wasn't much digging the whole fixation on dead Nazis. On one level, the idea of sexy cheerleaders who happened to be evil was kind of fun and hot. But the Nazi thing had the potential to leech the fun right out of the whole situation. Those fuckers were the true face of evil. It made sense that someone like Satan would want to align himself with them.

A faint, initially unidentifiable sound seemed to issue from nowhere. The girls still weren't moving. Their mouths were shut. No one else had entered the clearing. And yet here came the sound again, a rising whisper of murmuring voices. Voices coalescing into a chorus of groans. Something drew Darby's gaze to the ground by one of the nearest tombstones. A flicker of movement he perceived from the corner of his eye. He watched the tombstone for a while and began to suspect maybe he'd imagined it. But then it happened again. The ground moved. Shifted. A hole formed in the earth and loose dirt began to pour inside. Then the ground shifted upward again.

Darby took a tentative step backward.

Fuck this and fuck these hellbound bitches.

He took another step back. And another.

And then Lexie's head snapped toward him again. "Stay."

She didn't scream at him and she didn't blatantly threaten him.

But there was a deadly calm in her voice that instantaneously stopped him in his tracks. She held his gaze for a moment and when she was sure he wasn't going anywhere, her mouth curved in a smug way. A way that said, *You're my bitch now, Darby, and you and I both know it.*

Though Darby took no more steps backward, he remained in a deep state of panicky agitation. Every nerve-ending in his body screamed at him to get gone from this place, but his fear of Lexie was even stronger. He couldn't fathom why Lexie and the other girls were so unperturbed by what was happening around them. Because the earth disturbances were happening all over the clearing. And all of the disturbances were happening near tombstones. Darby's whole body was shaking by the time he finally connected the dots and figured out what was happening. The dead interred here were slowly clawing their way out of their graves.

Darby was unable to stifle a whimper.

Holy shit. Holy shit! Zombies. Nazi fucking motherfucking zombie fuckers!

Lexie had been telling him the total truth all along. They had come here to perform a resurrection ritual. The resurrection ritual being that kooky chainsaw dance. How a bunch of babes gyrating and throwing chainsaws around could bring a bunch of dead motherfucking Nazis back from the goddamn dead was well beyond his ability to comprehend. Or any normal person's ability, he was pretty sure. It was madness. And did it really even matter how they had accomplished it? The fact was, they had done it and now some kind of crazy zombie blitzkrieg was only moments away from getting underway.

Darby gasped as a withered, leathery hand punched through the earth by the tombstone nearest him. The hand flailed and clawed desperately at the empty air. Then another hand emerged through the ground a few feet from it. Darby groaned as an even larger shifting of dirt occurred and the head and torso of a long dead German soldier clawed its way to the surface. A thin layer of blackened, rotted skin clung to the zombie's skeletal face. The zombie hissed as its head jerked this way and that. Its empty eye sockets locked on Darby in the last instant before it pulled itself the rest of the way out of its grave. Though its eyes had rotted away a long time ago, Darby had the sense the hideous thing could see him plain as day. The dead soldier was dressed in a rotting black uniform, including a black helmet. Both the helmet and the uniform were adorned with SS insignia. The resurrected storm trooper got to its feet and took a staggering, lurching step in his direction. The clearing reverberated with the groans of other reanimated dead. There were many dozens of them. Maybe hundreds.

Lexie was shouting something about the glory of Satan and the everlasting Third Reich.

Right, Darby thought. *This right here is where I check out. I don't care how much that crazy bitch threatens me.*

He took a few quick backward steps and let out a startled grunt as he bumped into something. Someone was behind him. But that wasn't possible. There had been no one behind him . . .

Darby turned around and found himself staring up at a very tall dead Nazi.

Aw, shit.

He heard footsteps behind him. Rapid, strident, even on the patchy, rocky ground of the forgotten cemetery. "You're not going anywhere, Darby."

The towering Nazi opened its rotted mouth and hissed at him.

"Well, Lexie, that's where you're wrong."

He gave the zombie a hard shove and it went staggering backward, its claw-like hands flailing clumsily. These things had been underground a long, long time. They were dangerous, no doubt, but Darby's hunch that their debilitated physical condition could be used against them proved accurate. The creature's spindly legs buckled beneath it and it toppled to the ground.

Darby wasted no more time.

He vaulted over the zombie and took off into the woods. Lexie screamed at him and he had no doubt she was coming after him. Darby didn't bother looking back to confirm this. The only chance he had at getting free of this madness was to keep going all-out. So he focused on that, making his arms and legs pump just as hard as they could. He was running faster than he had at any point since leaving high school. But he was slower than he'd been back then. A decade of smoking had taken its toll. Despite being in decent physical condition, his lungs were straining. He sucked in great gasps of air as he ran, praying he could keep going long enough to get clear of Lexie and her lunatic cohorts.

He came out of the woods at a full gallop. The rolling grounds of the cemetery sprawled outward before him. He saw the roof of the school bus glinting in the sun in the distance. If he could get to it and overpower the driver before Lexie could catch up to him, he might have a chance. But his feet went out from under him and he took a tumble as he started down a steep slope. He heard Lexie laughing as he rolled and rolled on the ground, finally thumping to a stop as he slammed into a tombstone.

Then Lexie was standing over him with her hands on her hips, sneering at him. "Well, that was stupid, Darby. I'll have to punish you now."

"Fuck you."

She was close enough. He decided to take a chance.

He jerked his right leg back then kicked out at her. He heard a satisfying crunch as the heel of his boot connected with her knee. She cried out and toppled to the ground next to him. Darby drove an elbow into her face, snapping her nose and triggering an eruption of blood.

He got to his feet and looked up the slope to see an army of Nazi zombies and enraged lesbian cheerleaders swooping toward him. Some of the more rotted zombies tripped and went tumbling down the slope, much as he had. But there were so many of them. A lot of them would make it down the slope intact. At this point, though, he was more terrified of the goddamn cheerleaders. So he turned away from them and took off running again. He ran more easily now that he'd had a few moments to catch his breath. His side was hurting some where he'd collided with the tombstone, but it wasn't a crippling pain. He guessed maybe he had a cracked rib. It was something he could get taken care of if he managed to live another day and the odds of that didn't seem too good right now.

The original crowd of mourners they had offended had since dispersed, but now there was a new group of black-clad unhappy people gathered around another tombstone. This service was occurring in a direct path to the bus. He started screaming and waving his hands as he drew closer to them. The mourners turned toward the sound with an array of puzzled and angry expressions. But those expressions gave way to abject terror as they got a load of the horror rushing toward them.

"Get out of here!" he screamed at them. "Run! Run for your fucking lives!"

These apparently were not stupid people because they almost instantly abandoned the grave of the dearly departed family member and ran for their fucking lives. They scattered in several directions, evidently seeking the safety of their respective automobiles. Which was fine with Darby. It meant the path ahead was clear again. Darby hardly slowed down as he reached the bus, leaping through the open door and up the stairs to grab hold of the snoozing driver.

The driver was a heavy woman in a khaki uniform. She snorted and looked around in confusion as she came awake. "Wha . . .?"

"Sorry."

Darby hauled her out of her seat and heaved her through the open door. Her cry of surprise and fright was cut off as she hit the ground. Darby stared through the door and saw he had maybe thirty yards on the advancing horde of cheerleaders and zombies. No time to waste. Luckily, the key was in the ignition. Darby dropped into the driver's seat and worked a lever that closed the door. Then he turned the key and the engine sputtered to life. A glance through a window showed that the leading edge of the horde had cut the distance between it and the bus in half the time it took him to accomplish these things. Time was just about out. He was gonna have to run over some of these assholes.

He worked the gearshift and stomped on the gas pedal as he cranked the steering wheel, turning the long vehicle in an awkwardly sharp angle. The wheels of the bus bumped over a curb and rolled over a flat tombstone. He heard voices screaming at him and hands slapping against the sides of the bus. The bus bounced again as a body—cheerleader or zombie, he wasn't sure which—fell beneath one of the tires. There were meaty thumps as other bodies collided with the bus. Then he had the bus turned around and pointed back down the long drive leading toward the distant cemetery gates. He put the gas pedal to the floor and glanced at the rearview mirror. He winced at the sight of several bodies lying flat on the ground. Many were zombies, but some were cheerleaders. And the pursuit had not been abandoned. Many of the zombies were still staggering after the bus. He wasn't worried about them. They were too slow. But the cheerleaders were another matter. They were fast. Unnaturally fast. He grimaced when he saw Lexie at the head of the pack, moving faster than any of them. Of course. Why would it be any other way? Her bloodied face was a mask of fierce concentration.

Darby gulped.

That bitch is plain gonna kill me if she catches up to me.

A change of plans was in order. There was only one thing he could think to do. He could only hope Lexie was still far enough behind him that he could pull it off effectively. He kept the gas pedal all the way down, even when the bus occasionally clipped other cars parked along the side of the narrow road. His gaze kept nervously flicking back and forth from the rearview mirror and the speedometer. When the needle crested sixty mph, he looked at the mirror one more time and decided he was going fast enough to make it happen. Lexie was very far ahead of the pack now. They all had super satanic powers of strength and speed, but she was clearly more powerful than any of the others. Maybe more powerful than all the rest of them combined.

Darby's foot came away from the gas pedal.

And his other foot jammed down on the brake.

Something slammed into the back of the bus, hitting it with enough force to cause it to skid ahead faster. Darby looked at the rearview mirror again and saw Lexie facedown on the ground. It was as he'd hoped. She hadn't expected him to stop. And she hadn't quite been ready to pounce. So her unstoppable forward momentum had caused her to hit the rear of the bus at full speed. He kept his gaze on the mirror a few moments longer. She still wasn't moving. An impact like that would have killed any normal girl instantly, but Darby knew he couldn't count on her being dead. Lexie was no normal girl, after all. But she was definitely down for the count, at least for the moment. Knowing she might not remain that way long, Darby faced forward and hit the gas again. In a few more moments he was speeding out of the cemetery.

As he sped down the street that ran parallel to the cemetery, he glanced at the mirror a few more times. There was still no sign of further pursuit. So immense was his jubilation at his narrow escape that he didn't see the truck passing through the intersection ahead of him until it was nearly too late. The bus clipped the back end of the 18-wheeler and went skidding out of control. The wheel spun out of his hands as the big vehicle bounced over a curb and barreled through the parking lot of a convenience store. The side of the building loomed before him and he realized what was about to happen too late to do anything about it. The bus struck the building with great force, smashing a hole through concrete cinderblocks. Darby had the air blasted out of his lungs as he was thrown against the steering wheel. He fell awkwardly back into the seat, crying out in pain. He didn't feel like moving, but knew he couldn't just stay there. The police would have questions he couldn't answer. He might even have to go to jail. And that was assuming the law would get here before the cheerleaders.

He was much more afraid of the fucking cheerleaders.

He worked the lever to open the door and heaved himself out of the driver's seat, groaning in agony again as he did so. He had probably cracked another rib or two—at least—in the crash. Something else he could worry about later—if there was a later.

A crowd had gathered around the bus. He guessed some of them were owners of cars the bus had demolished en route to its rendezvous with the side of the building. One of them was a store employee. A middle eastern dude in a turban and a Kwik-Mart shirt. In his delirium, Darby knocked the man's turban off his head, further enraging him. He screamed at Darby and gesticulated wildly, jabbing a finger in his face repeatedly.

Darby winced. "I swear, man, that wasn't racist. I'm just not in my right head right now."

He scanned the rest of the crowd.

Pretty much everybody here hated his guts. He guessed he couldn't blame them, but they didn't understand the bigger picture—a bigger picture that was coming up fast behind them.

Darby lifted his chin. "Dude, behind you."

The store employee snorted. "I'm not falling for that, asshole."

"Seriously. Behind you. Fuck this shit, man."

They were maybe a hundred yards down the street.

But they were gaining ground.

Fast.

The cheerleaders and the zombies. He didn't see Lexie with them. So maybe she was dead after all. That could be a good/bad kind of deal. Good in the sense that she had been the biggest threat. Bad in pretty much every other sense. If she was dead, the rest of these psycho Satan worshippers would want some payback.

Which basically meant his ass.

A commotion arose in the street and the store employee reluctantly turned away from Darby to check things out. His posture changed at the sight of the onrushing horde. No longer aggressive—and apparently no longer at all concerned with Darby and the damage he'd caused to his store—he took off running.

Darby figured this was a wise move so he did the same.

The first thing he did was to put the bus between himself and the approaching horde. There was a tree-dotted hill behind the convenience store. Darby climbed the hill and pushed through the stand of trees, emerging into a residential area. He staggered into the parking lot of an apartment complex much larger than the one where he lived with Lacy. He could hide here, if he could convince someone to let him into their apartment. That didn't seem likely, but maybe he could steal a car. The complex was comprised of several buildings. He'd wended his way into the heart of it by the time he finally spied someone getting out of their vehicle. A middle-aged woman stood at the back of her black SUV. The rear door stood open and she was reaching inside for something. He approached her as stealthily as he could. Which wasn't very stealthily at all, given his beaten-up condition. She sensed him coming and whirled toward him before he could reach her. In her hands was a big wire cage.

The cage was swinging in an arc toward his head.

Inside the cage were . . . two fluffy bunnies.

Aw, shit.

The cage struck his head and knocked him to the ground. The woman started kicking him as the cage hit the parking lot pavement and the door to the cage sprang open. The bunnies emerged from their wire prison and chittered excitedly as they hovered curiously near his head.

Fucking bunnies. Go away, assholes.

Meanwhile, the woman was still kicking him repeatedly. "Teach you to mug somebody, you fucking filth! You scum." The toe of her shoe drove into his already very tender abdomen yet again. "You're nothing but human garbage. You're—"

Enough of this shit.

Darby rolled away from the woman before her next kick could connect. He felt something soft squeal beneath him and realized he'd rolled over one of the bunnies.

Oops.

The woman was screaming louder than ever now and was yelling for someone to call the police.

Darby started running again. By now, he'd gotten turned around and had no idea where he was going. Every building in the complex looked exactly the same. For all he knew, he was heading right back toward the convenience store. Which meant he might well be delivering himself into the arms of the avenging cheerleaders. The prospect should have terrified him, but he was suddenly finding it hard to care. He was tired and he was in pain. A lot of fucking pain. It might be easier all around to just let them have him. They were clearly relentless. They would have him sooner or later anyway.

But then he staggered around the corner of yet another building and saw a street. It was not the same street where he'd crashed a bus into a convenience store. He saw other businesses. More convenience stores and fast food restaurants. An auto garage. He limped out to the sidewalk and watched the cars going by in opposite directions.

A 70's era Firebird pulled to a stop at the curb. An attractive blonde woman in sunglasses peered out at him. "Need a ride?"

Darby just stared at her for a long moment.

All the day's madness and carnage had started with a very similar question asked by another very attractive woman. What was it with random gorgeous babes suddenly wanting to give him rides all the time? Somehow that shit had never happened much at all before.

The woman slid the sunglasses down her nose a little and squinted at him. Her eyes were a breathtaking shade of sky-blue. "What's wrong with you? Are you mute?"

"Am I what?"

"Mute. And never mind. Do you need a ride or what?"

Darby considered the question a moment longer. Then he said, "You don't worship Satan, do you?"

She laughed. "What kind of crazy-ass question is that?"

Darby didn't say anything.

Either she worshipped Satan or she didn't. Either way, he was about out of other options. He circled the car, opened the door on the passenger side, and got in.

She smiled again and pushed the sunglasses back up the bridge of her nose. "Where to, handsome?"

Darby told her where he lived.

"That's close. We'll be there in no time."

"Appreciate it."

"No problem."

Darby expected her to chatter at him non-stop, but she stayed silent for most of the ride. For which he was immensely grateful. He didn't feel like talking. And he sure as shit couldn't explain what he'd been through today in a way that wouldn't make him sound like an escaped mental patient.

Then there was a loud thump from the back of her car.

Darby frowned.

The thump came again. Actually, a series of thumps.

Thump-thump-thump.

This was followed by a muffled cry for help.

Darby's head swiveled slowly to the left. "What, um . . . is that?"

The blonde kept her gaze on the road. "My husband. He's in the trunk."

"Why?"

"He's been bad. He hit me."

"Oh. Well. Are you gonna kill him?"

"Yeah."

Darby sighed.

Awesome.

"Will you help me do it?"

Darby looked at her again. "Could you just take me to my apartment? I've kind of been through a lot of shit today. I ain't up to participating in a murder."

The blonde shrugged. "Guess I can understand that."

"Yeah. Thanks for . . . understanding."

Her handbag was wedged into the space between the seats. She dipped a hand inside it and pulled out a pistol. She clutched the pistol in her lap as she continued to navigate her way through the city streets. She glanced at Darby as they stopped at a red light. "Maybe I should put you in the trunk, too."

Darby looked at the gun. Then he looked at the woman's smiling face. Should a woman bent on killing her husband smile so much? It didn't seem right. "Look, I don't care what you do with your husband. Kill him. Fuck it. I've just, you know, like I said, been through a lot of shit and I just wanna get home and get really fucked up and then sleep for about eighteen hours."

The thumping from the trunk resumed.

The blonde laughed. "I can see you've been through some shit. You're all bruised and bloodied. It's part of why I stopped. You wanna know something?"

"Not really."

She ignored him. "That's not really my husband in the trunk."

Darby sighed again. "I don't care if you have the fucking pope in your trunk."

"I'm a serial killer."

Darby laughed. "Of course you are."

"What's funny?"

Darby shook his head. "Oh . . . pretty much everything."

She stared at him for a long moment as the light turned green. Angry motorists stalled behind the Firebird laid on their horns. The blonde's expression was thoughtful. "You're a weird guy."

"You're a weird chick."

She put the gun back in her handbag and drove on through the intersection. "I guess maybe I won't put you in my trunk."

"Thanks."

"I'll have to find someone else, of course."

He snorted. "Obviously."

They drove the rest of the way in silence. The blonde guided her Firebird to a stop at the same street corner where the bus full of satanic cheerleaders had picked him up earlier in the day. She leaned over in her seat and studied the building where he lived for a second or two before looking at him again. "This where you live?"

"Nope."

She laughed. "Liar."

"Well . . . I'm getting out now. Thanks for the ride."

"You're welcome."

He got out of her car and stepped up to the curb. Before he could go, she called out to him. "Hey, handsome?"

He knelt at the waist to peer in at her. "Yeah?"

"Be seeing you."

She hit the gas and the Firebird peeled away from the curb. Darby watched her go, staying right there on the corner until her car disappeared in the thicker traffic further down the road. There was one cigarette left in his pack. He smoked it to the filter, scanned the street for signs of impending satanic doom, and saw only the usual urban chaos. He flicked the filter aside and returned to his apartment.

Lacy was sitting cross-legged in front of the sofa in the living room. Her bong was on the floor beside her and she had a video game controller clutched loosely in her hands. Her eyes were glassy. The air inside the apartment was thick with the pungent odor of chronic. The good stuff. She was high as fuck.

She acknowledged him with a woozy grunt as he sat down beside her.

He picked up the bong and her lighter and helped himself to a hit. "Lacy?"

Her head turned slowly in his direction. "Yeah?"

Another burble of bong water before he replied. "We have to move."

She nodded slowly. "Cool. Whatever."

"Like, I'm thinking maybe today would be a good time to do it. I'll just pile some shit in the car and we'll take off. What do you say?"

"I can dig it."

He frowned. He was surprised. "Really?"

She smiled and snuggled up against him. "Yeah, really. I've always said you needed to more spontaneous. Take chances. That's what life's all about, baby. About time you figured that out."

Darby laughed.

And laughed some more.

A little later that day they were on their way to another town.

THE RESTLESS CORPSE

AUTHOR'S NOTE: An EC-comics/*Creepshow* kind of tale.

LINCOLN "LINK" BOOTH WAS DEEP into a 12-pack of Bud when he started hearing the racket from down in the basement. The first thing he heard was a loud crash. This was followed by a clatter of things being thrown around. His heart almost stopped upon first hearing these things. These were impossible sounds. There was no one in the basement. He knew that for a stone-cold fact. No one capable of raising that kind of ruckus, anyway.

He nonetheless hit the mute button on the TV and perked up his ears, turning his head in the direction of the kitchen as he waited to hear any additional noise. Close to a full minute elapsed before he let out the breath he'd been holding. What he'd heard was probably only his imagination. It'd been a stressful day, after all. You couldn't blame a guy for being jumpy or prone to hearing phantom sounds after the things he'd been through today. And on the off-chance the noise wasn't a product of jittery nerves, it didn't necessarily signal anything sinister or troubling. It was possible he'd bumped into one of the many crowded shelves down there the last time he was in the basement, which had been earlier this afternoon. He might have jarred something which had only just now gone crashing to the floor.

He'd nearly convinced himself of the likelihood of these rational explanations when more noise emanated from the basement. This time it was different. What he was hearing now sounded like somebody rattling the doorknob from the other side of the door. Again, this was impossible. There was no one down there capable of doing such a thing. His wife's corpse was wrapped up in a sheet and stashed away inside an old wooden storage trunk. He'd put her there a couple hours ago after accidentally killing her. But there was no chance he'd been mistaken about her being dead, not with the side of her skull being staved in so gruesomely. Yep, she was dead as a damn doornail, absolutely no doubt about it.

Putting her down there in the trunk was nothing more than an act of pure panic. After it happened, his brain sort of short-circuited. He didn't know what to do. The fact she was dead had been immediately obvious. There'd been no chance to save her. Calling 911 was the obvious thing to do. The expected legal thing. But visions of being slammed in a jail cell and left there to rot forever filled him with an icy terror. Or even worse, being sent to death row. Link didn't want to die. That was the main thing he knew in those first moments. He hadn't even meant to do it, goddammit.

Carrie had been needling him mercilessly again about a wide range of things, as per usual. Household chores that needed doing. Home repairs he'd been neglecting to finish for far too long. She went on and on about all the overdue bills and how he needed to be working more overtime at the warehouse to get them caught up. On top of all that, she was pissed off because he was late refilling the prescription for his boner pills. She was horny and hadn't gotten laid in too long, which was making her extra agitated. Agitation was Carrie's default state, so being around her when she was extra agitated was like being in the eye of a fucking hurricane. At the end of what turned out to be her final rant, she was right up in his face, her face turning red as she screamed at him. It was too much. He couldn't help reacting. All he did was shove her away from him. A simple act that shouldn't have resulted in such a total goddamn disaster.

But it had.

She tripped over her feet as she went stumbling backward and wound up falling at just the right angle to bounce her head off a corner of the kitchen island. She dropped to the floor and didn't move. There was a lot of blood. So much goddamned blood. A spreading pool of bright-red horror. At first Link could only gape at her unmoving form in astonished, paralyzed disbelief. When he finally did get moving, he knelt over her to check her pulse, but this was only a formality. The smashed-in shape of her head told him all he needed to know. The woman he'd been married to for fifteen years was gone. Just gone. In the blink of a fucking eye. It didn't seem real. It didn't feel like it could be real. Just a few moments earlier she'd been alive, a perfectly healthy human being. And now she was gone, abruptly erased from this mortal coil. Like she was nothing more significant than a bug squashed beneath someone's shoe.

After confirming her demise, Link spun away from the corpse and vomited profusely into the kitchen sink. When he was done heaving, he went into the hallway and grabbed some spare sheets from the linen closet. He wrapped Carrie's body up in those sheets and carried her down to the basement, dumping her in the old crate that had once belonged to his father. There'd been nothing in it but a bunch of moldy old newspapers and nudie magazines. He pulled these things out, dumped his dead wife in the trunk, and closed the lid.

Next he went back upstairs, locked the basement door, and set about scrubbing the floor clean in the kitchen. This involved the use of an ungodly amount of Lysol and three whole rolls of paper towels. The bloody paper towels went into a black plastic garbage bag, which he then stowed in the back of his pickup truck for later disposal.

With these things out of the way, he set about numbing himself with booze and football on TV. The Dolphins were playing the Raiders. It was late in the third quarter and the Raiders were leading by a touchdown. Link didn't particularly care about either of these teams, but he liked football in general and having the game on gave him something to occupy his mind, which might otherwise slide in more troubling directions.

At the point when he started hearing the noise from the kitchen, he was deep into a state of intense denial. He would not let himself believe the tragic thing that had happened had actually happened. It was a dream. A nightmare. Had to be. Link was no saint, but he wasn't a bad person either. Most people would call him generous and kind. Horrendous, awful things weren't supposed to happen to good people, hence he could not really have killed his wife. He could not have made the terrible mistake a now-distant part of his mind was saying he had. Shutting that part of his brain down was easy. All he had to do was keep guzzling down the beers. Increasing inebriation made it easier to buy into the denial rationalizations. Carrie's not dead, he told himself. She's gone out shopping, that's all. Probably be gone a few hours. Maybe longer. Maybe a lot longer.

The rattling of the doorknob commenced again, louder this time.

Link turned up the volume on the TV and popped the top on another beer, his eighth of the afternoon. Or maybe it was number nine. He was starting to lose count. This struck him as a good thing. He wanted things to get fuzzy, craved the oblivion of drunkenness. He instinctively understood this would make it even easier to buy into his denial fantasies.

The Dolphins were driving down the field now and had entered the red zone. Looked like they might be on the verge of making this a tied-up ballgame. Link hoped so. A good, competitive game could only help with keeping his mind away from certain inconvenient and upsetting realities.

Link guzzled beer and pumped a fist as the Dolphins' QB lofted a pass into the corner of the endzone, where it was caught by a leaping TE. He'd drained the can of nearly half its contents when he heard a sound of splintering wood. A sharp, slapping sound followed this one. In the next instant, he realized it was the sound of the basement door flying open and slamming into the side of the refrigerator. Then came a sound of leaden, lurching footsteps slapping against kitchen tiles. From the sound of it, those footsteps were headed in this direction, toward the living room.

Link went as still as a statue and listened intently to the approaching footsteps. He kept telling himself what he was hearing couldn't be real. His wife's corpse had not reanimated and busted out of the basement. Ridiculous things like that only happened in movies or in stories by crazy horror writers. They never happened in the real world because the supernatural didn't exist. The real world was ruled by science and reason. By the laws of physics and shit like that.

The footsteps nevertheless kept coming.

Link let out a breath and remained where he was as he began to mutter reassurances to himself. "This isn't happening. This shit isn't real. I'm imagining it. Go away, you dead fucking bitch."

His breath stuck in his throat again when he sensed a presence looming over him. Still, he didn't move. Getting up and running away in terror wouldn't accomplish anything other than making him feel like a fool. He refused to acknowledge the reality of what his senses seemed to be telling him.

Then he felt the presence behind him reach around him and place the edge of a sharp blade against his throat.

Link sighed. "Well, shit."

Carrie's reanimated corpse tore the blade of the razor-sharp butcher knife across his throat.

Link's last conscious thought was, *Damn, I guess those crazy horror writers actually get it right sometimes.*

Dead Carrie seized a handful of the scraggly, greasy hair at the top of his head and forced him to watch the arterial spray of his blood with the last of his fading vision. When she was sure he was dead, she dragged him down to the basement and heaved him into the trunk.

Then she climbed in after him and closed the lid.

CHAINSAW SEX MANIACS FROM MARS

AUTHOR'S NOTE: Fun story, I think. Title pretty much explains all.

THE NEED TO PEE CAME over Tanya Logan so quickly and with such overwhelming force it caused her to bolt outside through the trailer's open back door without saying a word to anyone. Her objective was the outhouse in the isolated rural lot where Yancy Malone kept his decrepit old trailer. The strains of an old Lynyrd Skynyrd shitkicker song remained audible as she awkwardly scampered across the patchy ground with a hand pressed between her legs and her thighs pressed together.

Tanya and some of the other regulars at Duke's Tavern had adjourned here after Duke had shut the place down at two in the morning. The local college football team won a big game earlier in the night and the whole town was in celebration mode. Nobody wanted the party to end, so when Yancy said anyone who wanted to could head on down to his trailer and keep things going there, more than a dozen drunk redneck guys and gals took him up on the offer. Now most of them were crowded in together in the cramped little trailer, but a few others were hanging around out front, swigging rancid moonshine from clear glass jugs and occasionally shooting off their guns. Now and then they howled at the moon like wolves, a sound that sent an icy tingle of dread up Tanya's spine. A couple of those boys had been giving her creepy looks ever since Duke kicked them all out. They were guys she'd never liked. Bo Gatlin and Jim Loomis. She was thankful the rest were all people she knew well and trusted to keep her safe.

Her bladder felt like it was about to bust by the time she reached the outhouse and yanked open the rickety wooden door. She pulled the door closed as she entered the outhouse and latched it from inside. The outhouse was distressingly dark inside, with the only faint illumination coming courtesy of moonlight streaming in through a hole in the tin roof. She knew Yancy always took an electric lantern with him when he came out here to do his business in the middle of the night, but she'd taken off without thinking to ask for it. Oh, well. She'd have to make the best of it.

The moonlight was enough to ascertain the location of the toilet. It was at the back of the outhouse. A small window was a few feet above it. She wasn't worried about anyone peeking in, though. They wouldn't be able to see shit, it was so dark in here. There were a few rolls of TP in a basket next to the toilet. No wash basin, though. She'd have to wash her hands back in the trailer.

Whimpering with the need to relieve herself, she hurried over to the toilet, grabbed one of the rolls of TP, lowered her flimsy denim cutoffs, and sat herself down on the toilet's somewhat less than ideally sanitary seat. She grimaced as she felt moisture on the backs of her thighs. One of the nasty fellas she was partying with tonight had drunkenly and carelessly sprayed his piss all over the thing. More than one of them, most likely.

Whatever, though. The damage was already done. A little icky moisture wouldn't kill her. She'd clean it off with TP as soon as she was done doing what needed doing in here. Her bladder began the process of emptying itself, which this time took far longer than usual. The sense of relief that gripped her as that pressing need faded caused her to moan in an almost sexual way.

She was almost finished when a light much brighter than the moon shined down from somewhere high above the outhouse, filling the little structure's interior through the hole in the roof. Tanya turned her head up, squinting against the glare. She couldn't fathom what could possibly be the source of anything so bright in Yancy's little dump of a lot. There were no streetlamps out here. She wondered if maybe a helicopter was hovering around somewhere up there, shining down a spotlight. It was common knowledge that Yancy grew pot out there in the woods beyond the edge of his property. Maybe this was the DEA doing a late-night raid. Never mind that people out here never got raided for pot these days. People had stopped caring much about that sort of thing. Besides, no one would ever rat out Yancy to the law. Everybody loved the big galoot.

Funny thing, though. She wasn't hearing any motor or rotor noise. She'd been around helicopters a time or two. They were noisy as hell. Yet the only things she could hear were the distant sounds of music and some hooting and hollering from the party. Overall, though, the night was still enough for her to hear the buzzing of the crickets from the woods.

Curious, she hurriedly wiped herself, pulled up her cutoffs, unlatched the door, and went outside. She took the one creaky step down to the ground, moved a few feet away from the outhouse, and turned around, putting a hand to her brow as she tilted her face toward the sky. The bright light was indeed coming from somewhere directly above her. She was still squinting, straining to make out the source, which she figured must be some sort of airborne craft. Because it was so high up there, though, the shape of it remained hard to discern. If it wasn't a helicopter, what could it possibly be?

There were others around her now. She sensed them without seeing them. One person was almost directly behind her. Though she couldn't see whoever it was, she felt a fresh tingle of revulsion, she shuddered and hunched her shoulders as a creepy-crawly sensation twisted her up inside, a feeling akin to having thick, wriggly worms slithering through her guts.

Turning her head around, she saw Bo Gatlin staring at her ass. His mouth was hanging open and he had that familiar dumb, dull-eyed look on his face. Sensing her sneering scrutiny, he looked up and smirked, but didn't say anything. As they eyeballed each other with increasing hostility, Jim Loomis sidled up next to his creepazoid pal and smirked at her in a similarly sleazy way. She would have been nervous if not for the presence of the others. Most everybody was out back of the trailer now, staring up at the mysterious bright light in the sky.

Catching sight of Yancy and Daryl Monroe, his best friend going back to middle school days, Tanya headed over there, away from the creeps. She felt their loathsome gazes on her every step of the way.

Yancy had his head tilted up to the sky, but glanced Tanya's way as she approached. He grinned and waggled an index finger upward. "Hey, girl. What do you reckon that is?"

She smiled and shrugged. "Don't know, Yance. Was thinking

DEA maybe, but don't hear no rotors."

Yancy snorted laughter. "Ain't drug enforcement. I'm too low-level to warrant their attention. Air Force base ain't that far away. Could be some kind of experimental aircraft."

Daryl Monroe gulped Miller High Life from a can. "Or maybe a weather balloon."

Candy Hopkins had joined them by then. She was another of the regular girls from Duke's Tavern. Candy and Tanya could almost be twins, going on looks alone. Both were bottle-blondes and tonight they were each wearing denim shorts cut down nearly to the size of bikini bottoms along with bright-colored skimpy halter tops. Candy was a little younger, though, and maybe a teeny smidge cuter. Tanya hated her. The fucking slut. Bitch was always trying to get with any man she showed any interest in.

Candy pressed herself up against Yancy and put an arm around his back. She looked up at the sky and said, "Guys, that's not a weather balloon. That's a UFO."

Yancy glanced down at her, eyeing her with genuine perplexity etched in his features. "You mean like a flying saucer? Really?"

She nodded. "Gotta be. Them are aliens up there. You can tell by how there ain't any sound."

Tanya rolled her eyes, but she had to admit Candy had a point. That lack of engine noise had puzzled her from the start. Debate continued along the same lines among the crowd gathered behind Yancy's trailer for several minutes, with the light hovering in that same fixed point high above the clearing the whole time.

Just as some among them began to lose interest and head back to the trailer for more beer, the object in the sky began to descend at a rapid rate, triggering a collective gasp from the gathering. Those who had started back toward the trailer stopped in their tracks and turned around.

Daryl's Miller High Life slipped from his fingers and thumped on the ground. "Goddamn. It *IS* a flying saucer."

Now that it had descended so drastically, Tanya could see that the craft was indeed saucer-shaped. As it neared the ground, landing gear appeared in the form of four metallic legs. Tanya was overcome with a profound sense of astonishment as the craft touched down in a spot out there beyond the outhouse. The look of the thing was like something out of a black-and-white sci-fi movie from the 1950s. Her head began to feel swimmy as she contemplated this, the result of a combination of all the cheap beer she'd consumed and the surreal nature of what she was seeing.

Minutes passed and nothing happened. As time ticked by, people began to edge closer to the eerily quiet craft, drawn forward by equal measures of sheer awe and curiosity. Everyone had heard stories about flying saucers. The tales had been handed down through the decades ever since that incident out there in Roswell. There were believers and non-believers. The non-believers scoffed and poked fun at the UFO nuts. Any concrete evidence either didn't exist or was locked up so tight no normal person would ever lay eyes on it. And now here they all were, confronted with indisputable proof that flying saucers were real. Tanya knew she should be afraid. The beings inside this craft might have hostile intent. They might be capable of anything. The sensible thing for all of them would be to take off running and get as far away as possible.

Only one person gave in to the flight instinct. A big guy named Nick Bolton let out a yelp and took off running. Moments later, they all heard the sound of his pickup truck's engine roaring to life and then speeding away. The rest of them stayed right where they were. Tanya didn't know about anybody else, but she felt an almost spiritual sense of privilege at being able to witness this amazing thing. They were all present for something momentous, possibly something that could alter the course of human history itself.

A hiss sounded as an opening appeared at the bottom of the craft and a ramp with stairs began to lower until it touched the ground. A light tinged with green emanated from inside the craft. More minutes passed with nothing else happening. Tanya and the rest of them continued to inch closer in giddy anticipation of actually seeing alien life forms.

And then one form appeared at the top of the steps. After a moment, it began to descend step by careful step. Other similar forms appeared and began to follow the first one down. From the first moment, the fact that these were indeed creatures from another world was not in doubt. The resemblance to the so-called "grays" known to all from various popular culture depictions of aliens was amazing. Physically, they looked exactly like that. Other things about them, however, came as a great surprise.

Daryl's face twisted in a way that conveyed deep confusion. "What the fuck? Are those chainsaws them boys are carrying? And . . . are they wearing coveralls?"

Yancy nodded slowly. "Yeah. You know, I'm thinking maybe we should all consider getting the fuck on out of here. This don't look right at all. I got a bad feeling."

Tanya was in full agreement on that point. This was nothing at all like what she had been expecting. "Surreal" didn't even come close to describing it. She felt like she'd slipped into some bizarro alternate cartoon dimension.

The first alien to reach the ground plucked a toothpick from a corner of its mouth and spoke a robotic brand of English that seemed to emanate from some kind of translation device. It was nonetheless perfectly intelligible. "Yep. Reckon y'all dumb meat-sacks 'bout to get fornicated and buzzed up right nice."

Candy disengaged herself from Yancy and began to back away. "What did that thing say?"

The alien made a chittery sound that might have been laughter. "Gonna blow a load of Martian spunk up yonder blondie's poophole. Best believe."

Then the creature started the chainsaw, raised it above its head, and came charging at them in a lightning-fast waddling motion. The other aliens followed suit. And just like that, the spell that had held Tanya and the rest of them in place was broken as everyone dispersed and ran screaming for their lives. Tanya turned and ran straight for the trailer as the night filled with the sound of chainsaws tearing through human flesh. She didn't know where else to go. Her car was back at Duke's tavern. She'd ridden here in the back of Yancy's pickup. Maybe she could find his keys and take the truck.

Before she could reach the trailer, however, she stumbled over a rock and went crashing to the ground, banging her knees with debilitating force. She twisted her head around and saw one of the alien rednecks heading right toward her. Tears appeared in her eyes. She had no hope of getting away, not with her knees hurting like this. Then there was a blur of motion in her peripheral vision. Yancy came hurtling out of nowhere to tackle the alien and drive it to the ground. Tanya was grateful for the intercession, but she was in no condition to help her rescuer fight the creature.

The trailer was close. She started grabbing at the ground and pulled herself under it, crawling deep into the shadows. The sounds of carnage continued. She heard screams and loud grunts that sounded like a product of carnal exertion. Telling herself not to look, she did so anyway.

It was a panorama of horror and inter-species perversion.

There were chain-sawed body pieces everywhere. Lots of blood on the ground. Most of the aliens had shucked off their overalls and were thrusting their surprisingly large penises into every imaginable orifice. They fucked the living and the dead. They fucked flesh holes made by the chainsaws. She saw Candy get bisected by one of the buzzing blades. Prior to cutting her into two halves, the lead alien had indeed done her up the poophole. It went on seemingly forever, until virtually all the humans out there were dead. At least one person was still alive, though. She could hear someone blubbering. At first she was unsure who might have survived, but then the aliens began heading back toward the craft at the edge of the clearing. One of them had hold of a whimpering and naked Bo Gatlin by an ankle and was dragging him toward the flying saucer. He cried out, pleading for help that would not be coming. His head thumped roughly against each of the steps on the ramp as the alien pulled him up into the craft with no concern whatsoever for his well-being.

Once they were all back inside, the ramp retracted and the craft rose into the air again. It hovered a couple dozen feet above the ground for a moment before abruptly shooting upward and out of sight.

Tanya stayed under the trailer until the first hints of sunlight began to tinge the sky. She did this just to be safe, in case the alien hicks came back. When she finally crawled out and got to her feet again, she spent a moment gaping at the bloody horrors arrayed around her. They were all dead. Every single one of them. Even sweet Yancy, her savior. She then went into the trailer and vomited into his kitchen sink. When she had finished voiding her stomach, she hunted around until she found his keys, then she went outside and found his truck, which she wound up ditching about a half mile away from Duke's Tavern. She didn't want to be seen showing up in it.

She retrieved her car and drove home, where she took several of the strongest pills she had and passed out.

She never told anyone about the redneck aliens.

Who the hell would believe her?

THE THING IN THE WOODS

AUTHOR'S NOTE: Slice-of-life from days gone by interspliced with creature feature horror.

I'M GOING TO TELL YOU about something I've never told anyone else. Something that happened a long time ago. Every word of this is true.

It was a warm summer night in middle Tennessee. The sky was clear and a luminescent silver moon was shining down on us through the slanted roof beams of a house under construction. As was so often the case when we were out roaming through the neighborhood at night, we were up to no good. The house was still in the early stages of construction. The foundation had been put down and the wood frame was up. The rest of it—the drywall, the insulation, the wiring, etc.—had yet to be done. It was the perfect place for a gang of young hooligans with nothing else to do to hang out and blow off a little steam.

The little ball inside the can of spray paint clutched in my right hand rattled as I gave the can a good shake. I aimed the nozzle at the plywood board in front of me and pressed down the valve button. Black paint began to hiss from the nozzle as I started adding the finishing touches to my latest piece of graffito.

This particular graffito was the Van Halen logo. I had already perfectly (in my estimation, at least) rendered the stylized VH part of it, with the slanted H nestled up against the V. I just needed to add the little wing-like lines. There were three of them extending from each side of the logo. Each descending line was just a little shorter than the one above it. Once I had accomplished this, I stepped back to admire my handiwork and found it worthy. Eddie Van Halen would have been pleased, I was sure.

Tom Keller stepped up next to me and squinted at it. He took a swig from a can of Budweiser and wiped his mouth with the back of a hand. "It's crooked."

"I did it like that on purpose. An artistic touch. It's more rock and roll that way."

Tom belched. "That's a ten on the belch-o-meter. And bullshit it's an artistic touch. It's crooked because you're drunk."

"It's artistic because it's slightly off-kilter. It symbolizes what rock and roll is all about. Rebellion, rejection of conformity, that kind of thing. And fuck you, by the way. Your Ozzy logo looks like a retarded monkey did it."

It was true. Tom had spray-painted an Ozzy logo on a section of the plywood floor. Ozzy's logo featured crisply-defined letters with a little horizontal line through the middle of each of them. There was nothing at all precise in Tom's rendering of it. The letters were wavy. The "O" looked more like a long oval shape. And the supposed-to-be-horizontal lines through each letter were fucking crooked. Talk about hypocritical.

Tom shrugged. "Whatever, man. I was being artistic and rebellious and shit, just like you. I gotta fuckin' piss."

He wandered off to another part of the house. In moments I heard a strong stream of beer-fueled urine hitting another plywood wall panel.

There were four of us there that night. The other guys were Shane Cunningham and Mike Harper. My name, by the way, is Trent Bates. I had turned eighteen the previous month. Mike was nineteen and had graduated high school a year earlier. He had subsequently attended Memphis State University (now called the University of Memphis for some reason) for one disastrous semester the previous fall. The other guys were still in high school.

Shane and Mike were guzzling beers and hanging out in a part of the house that would one day be its kitchen. As I came into the room through an archway, they were arguing about Van Halen. In particular, about whether their new album sucked or ruled. The album was *Diver Down* and it had come out just a few months earlier. My personal opinion was that it neither sucked nor ruled. It didn't quite kick gargantuan amounts of ass the way all their previous albums had, but it was still Van Halen, which automatically made it better than just about anything else.

Shane crushed an empty Bud can and tossed it on the floor where it joined several of its drained aluminum companions. "The album's got four fucking good songs on it. The rest of it's a bunch of covers and shit. It's too poppy and wimpy-sounding. Where'd the originality go? And what happened to the fucking heaviness?"

Mike belched. "That was a ten."

Shane scowled. "That was not a ten. It was a five at best." He glanced my way as I fished a can of Bud from the dwindling supply in the cardboard carton on the floor. It was the big kind that held twenty-four cans. There were maybe four or five brews left in it. Another, already empty suitcase had been ripped to shreds and scattered across the floor. It's fair to say we were all somewhere in the vicinity of completely fucked up. "What do you say, Trent? That a ten or a five?"

I peeled the ring-tab off the lukewarm can and tossed it aside. I had a thoughtful look on my face as I took a long swig from the can and pretended to mull over the issue. "It was more like a four. Maybe even a three."

I wasn't busting Mike's balls. It'd been a weak-ass little bitch belch.

Mike gave me the finger. "Fuck you guys. Get your ears checked. And why does every Van Halen album have to sound the same? So what if *Diver Down* isn't super heavy? Did every Beatles album sound the same? I think it's good they're trying something different, like the little synthesizer touches."

Shane grabbed a can of Bud from the suitcase. As he did this, I took another huge swig from my own recently opened can. I recall wanting to drain it fast and get one more can for myself before the other guys could finish off the rest. I didn't know it then, but this was a harbinger of things to come later in life, this need to always be sure I had more than enough booze on hand to quench my prodigious thirst and then some.

Shane opened his can and guzzled. We never sipped beer back then. Beer wasn't for savoring. It was for getting wasted. Totally obliterated, man. "Synthesizers are for wussy bands."

Mike's first response to this was another raised middle finger. "Van Halen are not a wussy band, you fucking traitor. You should be more open-minded."

Shane laughed. "I'm no traitor. I still love Van Halen and expect Dave and the boys to rip it up when we see them next week, but synths are for wussy new wavers. There can be no disputing this."

Tom staggered into the kitchen, cursing as he banged a shoulder against an archway beam. "You fucking alcoholics haven't drank all the beer yet, have you?"

Mike snickered. "Who you calling an alcoholic, you goddamn lush?"

I was about to chime in with something undoubtedly witty in the extreme when we detected the sound of a slow-moving car in the street outside the house. The house we were in that night was one of several under construction in Weakley Hills at the time. Weakley Hills was the name of our neighborhood, just to spell things out for you again. It was at a corner of a loop encircling the top of a very steep hill. There were other, already occupied houses not too distant. I assume one of the upstanding adult homeowners somehow became aware of our nefarious activities and called the police.

We all fell silent as we heard the car pull to a stop outside and, as quietly as we could manage, shuffled deeper into the shadows at the back of the house, in hopes that the darkness would shield us from sight. At that point, we were not yet aware that this was the police. There was no streetlight and we could only dimly perceive the outline of the car from our vantage point. That changed when the spotlight mounted on the side of the cruiser popped up and lit up the interior of the house like a movie set. An amplified voice squawked at us from the cruiser. The words themselves didn't matter. In the midst of our fright, they were unintelligible. The tone was what mattered. It was authoritarian and angry. We heard the cruiser's doors pop open. Someone was getting out, maybe multiple someones.

They were coming to get us.

Someone among us—it could have been me or any of my friends, I honestly don't remember—shouted, "Run!"

We dropped our beers and abandoned our cans of spray paint as we vaulted out of the house at the rear. I stumbled and fell when I hit the rocky, debris-strewn ground behind the house. It would not be the last time I lost my footing over the next several minutes. There were shouts behind us, stentorian voices drawing closer by the second, flashlight beams waving in the night. The area that would one day be the property's backyard bordered a line of trees, the beginning of that big expanse of woods that stood between the top of the hill and the part of the neighborhood where my parents' house was located. My booze-fogged brain was reeling at the prospect of arrest. Arrest would be bad enough, but facing my parents later would be worse. It may well have been that thought that got me off the ground so quickly and got me moving again.

My friends were already gone, swallowed by the dark woods. I started running and plunged through the tree line after them, heedless of the shouts behind me. The cops were screaming at me to stop. By now I could tell there were at least two of them. Looking back, I think much of the increasing agitation in their voices came from an almost instant recognition that they would not be able to catch up to me. Though I was no athlete, I was young and fit and could really move when I was motivated to do so, which I certainly was on this occasion. The steep downward slope also helped me build speed.

I knew I was putting some distance between myself and the cops, but escape was by no means a given. My pursuers seemed determined to get me, at least initially, pursuing me deeper into the woods. Their curses and pounding footsteps propelled me onward, made me strive to go even faster. My greatest adversary at that point was the deep darkness of the woods. I couldn't see for shit. I kept banging into—and bouncing off of—trees. Low-hanging branches snapped against my face. On at least two more occasions I stumbled and fell. Each time I bounced right back up and kept moving. There was pain each time I fell, but one time it was especially pronounced. I'd hit something on the ground, something hard—a rock, I guess—and when I got up again I felt wetness and cool air against bare skin. That rock, or whatever it was, had ripped open my jeans and opened a big gash in my flesh. That wetness was blood sliding down my leg, but I wouldn't be fully cognizant of that until the next day, largely thanks to what was about to happen.

I got up and got moving yet again. By then the sounds of pursuit had ceased. There were no more shouts, no pounding footsteps, and no more flashlight beams dancing in the darkness. I was aware of this on some dim level, but I didn't allow that recognition to slow me down. The cops would be returning to their car and soon they would be circling the neighborhood, searching for wayward delinquents with their goddamn spotlight. I needed to get out of the woods and back inside my house before they could reach my part of the neighborhood.

Soon I began to perceive the glow of a streetlight through the fast-approaching line of trees. I slowed down a little at that point, knowing it would be dangerous to come bursting out of the woods at full speed. There was a vacant lot just beyond that line of trees. It stood between the edge of the woods and my parents' house. In the center of the lot was a deep, foliage-obscured depression. You could almost call it a pit. In fact, we had called it that back when we were little kids and used to play war games in the lot. Years earlier, back when the very first houses in the neighborhood were being built, a number of large slabs of rock were excavated from the ground there, thus forming the pit. These rock slabs were then moved via heavy machinery to the property owned by my parents, where they were arranged in a kind of border along the side of the property. When we were kids, we thought of the rock border as a kind of castle wall, though it wasn't very tall. It was a perfect place to pretend you were lying in wait for enemy soldiers. For a long time, it was one of the neighborhood's most distinctive landmarks.

It's gone now.

Anyway, I stumbled and fell yet again when I slowed to a jog. My foot had snagged on a vine and there was no way to prevent another painful rendezvous with the ground. I braced my hands on the brambly ground to push myself up again, but I stopped cold when I sensed someone or something behind me. I didn't know who or what it was, just that I was pretty sure it wasn't a cop. At first I hoped I was imagining things. I told myself there was nothing behind me. But then I heard that deep and rumbling exhalation of breath. I didn't yet know what was behind me, but I began to have a strong sense that it was not human. In fact, it sounded more like some kind of . . . beast.

A thing.

Instead of getting to my feet, I turned over and gaped up in disbelief at a creature that looked as if it had emerged from the depths of my most lurid, movie-inspired fevered imaginings. The beast had the general shape of a man. It was a biped, with very long arms and legs. But it was abnormally tall. It towered above me, seeming at first as tall as the trees surrounding us. This was a false impression exacerbated by the darkness and my prone position on the ground. Even so, the thing was extraordinarily tall, reaching a height of perhaps nine feet. You might be thinking the high level of alcohol in my bloodstream was distorting my powers of perception. But that absolutely wasn't the case, I swear.

The creature's mass was also abnormal. Two NFL offensive line-men squashed together would be almost as huge, though not nearly as tall. The creature's bare, glistening flesh was bursting with muscle. Its claw-like hands looked like they could tear me apart as easily as I'd tear apart a sheet of notebook paper. But the most fearsome thing about it—the thing that made my insides quiver like jelly and nearly made me pee my pants—was its head, which was, of course, enor-mous. It was also grotesquely misshapen, a bulbous and swollen rot-ting pumpkin of a head. The scalp was pink and hairless. Its eyes were huge black orbs. It had large and sharply-pointed pink ears, a detail that would later cause me to describe it as looking like Mr. Spock from *Star Trek* after having turned into a gigantic and hairless were-wolf. Its chin was also pointed and extended outward in a way that made me think of goblins from some of the darker fairy tales. Worst of all, though, were the teeth. Rows of them were visible as the thing hissed at me. They were long and sharp and dripping saliva. Its lipless mouth seemed designed to display them prominently, making them even more mind-bogglingly terrifying.

Clutched in its claw-like right hand was a human arm. A twinkle of moonlight helped me spy a wedding ring affixed to a stubby finger. The ragged, bloody stump end of the arm indicated it had been torn from the body to which it had formerly been attached. The strength necessary to accomplish such a thing was, of course, astounding. As the creature stared at me, it raised a fleshy part of the arm to its mouth and tore off a bite.

I felt like puking. I also knew I should get up and start running again. And yet I felt paralyzed, completely incapable of movement or action of any kind. And even if I could move, what good would it do? It would give chase and catch up to me with just a few strides of its long and powerful legs.

But I had to try. What choice did I have?

After scooting backward several feet, I got shakily to my feet and started backing away from the thing. I was afraid to turn my back on the thing out of fear that it would pounce as soon as I did. This caused me to lose my footing yet again when I stepped on a large rock. But this time I was able to maintain some semblance of balance and only dropped to one knee rather than falling flat on my back again. I bounced right back up and resumed my backward retreat.

The creature opened its strange, lipless mouth wider and hissed at me. I was sure it was about to come at me, but before that could happen the sound of a branch snapping somewhere out in the woods distracted it. Its head jerked to the right and that was when I finally mustered the courage to turn tail and start running for my life. Within moments, I emerged through the tree line, moving at full-speed through the overgrown vacant lot. My terror was such that it overwhelmed whatever level of critical thinking might have been available to me in my drunken state. In another moment, I was no longer running. Instead I was falling, having plunged into the foliage-choked pit at the center of the lot. I experienced another jolt of pain when I hit the bottom, but the foliage at least cushioned my fall, so it could have been worse. That small bit of silver lining was canceled out by yet another jab of pain when I blindly grabbed a thorny vine in a desperate effort to pull myself upright again. I cried out and let go of the vine, but my palm was already leaking blood in several places.

But by then I was in so much pain—and in such a state of overall distress—that a little more agony didn't matter much. I got to my knees and began to crawl up a sloping side of the pit. Fear of being caught by that hideous thing out in the woods was a big part of what drove me onward and made me push through the pain, but I was also motivated by how close I was to home and perceived safety. I'd glimpsed my house upon emerging through the tree line. Had I been watching where I was going, I could've been back in my own room by now. Just then that was what I wanted more than anything else in the world. I wanted it more than I wanted a million dollars. More than I wanted to party with Van Halen. More than I wanted to have sex with Christie Brinkley.

It was an absolutely staggering amount of want, is the point I'm trying to get across.

But just as I reached the top of the pit, I heard a car moving slowly down the street in front of my house. And it was coming in this direction. I groaned and ducked down when I saw the spotlight sweeping across the front yard of the house. Within a few moments, that spotlight would illuminate the vacant lot, but I was pretty sure the cops wouldn't see me if I just kept my head down. In the interest of further obscuring my presence, I allowed myself to slide a few feet deeper back into the pit. The vegetation choking the lot would also help. Unless the cops got out of their cruiser and came out to the lot to poke around, there was a good chance I would remain undiscovered. I nonetheless flinched when the spotlight's bright beam swept over the lot. The sweep of the beam happened with excruciating slowness. That cruiser was just inching along. I had no doubt these were some seriously pissed off cops. And they were aching to give someone a beating, I was sure.

After a seeming eternity, the spotlight completed its sluggish sweep of the vacant lot and the cruiser finally moved on. I crawled up again and poked my head out of the pit. A check of my surroundings revealed no signs of the monster. Part of me was already beginning to wonder if I'd really seen it, after all. A more sober examination of my memories would soon stifle my brain's instinctive attempt to protect me against the horror of what I'd seen by throwing up a wall of denial. In that moment, though, nothing at all was clear, except that I had to get home.

So I hauled myself out of the pit and took off running again. Soon I'd vaulted over the rock barrier and was sprinting across my yard. There were no lights on in the house. No one was waiting up for me. This wasn't a big surprise. It was past midnight and my dad was a very early riser. He and my mother went to bed at ten sharp every night. Though the dark windows were what I'd expected, my relief was immense. It was the one lucky break I'd caught all night that didn't involve not being devoured by a monster.

I headed for the far end of the house, where I flew right by the closed garage door at the top of the driveway. I continued around the garage and came to the six-foot-high privacy fence that encircled our backyard. After scaling the fence with the ease that comes from years of late-night practice, I dropped into the backyard. There was no lawn back here. Instead there was an inground swimming pool with a concrete deck. To my right was a large pool house. There were no lights on back here and I could only faintly discern the shapes of lounge chairs and wrought-iron deck furniture. Conscious of a need to make as little noise as possible, I made my way around the pool house by treading as lightly as I could across the pebbled landscaping and the deck. Finally, I reached a door that opened into the garage. I dug my keys out of a hip pocket, clutching them tight to keep them from jingling. I got the door open, slipped inside the garage, and let myself into the house.

Fortunately, my room—or living area, really—was immediately adjacent to the garage. There was a short hallway through the door into the house. If you continued to the end of it and through the open archway to the left, you would enter the kitchen. To the right, however, was a door I normally kept closed. I opened it and slipped into a room that had been a rec room when my sister and I were kids. But now it was part of what my parents had been calling my "apartment" for the last couple years. The ping pong table and other games that had once occupied the space were gone. It was now outfitted with a refrigerator, a bathroom with a shower, an old sofa, some chairs for guests, and a big Zenith floor model television my parents had passed down to me.

I left the lights off as I closed the door to my apartment and continued through the outer room to the door that led to my bedroom. Once I was in there, I closed and locked that door and again left the lights off as I fell facedown onto my bed. I crawled to the headboard, wrapped my arms around the double-stack of pillows, and immediately began to drift down toward unconsciousness.

I didn't think of my friends again until those last few moments before the darkness swallowed me. A twinge of guilt made my eyes snap wide open for a brief moment as a wild panic gripped me. I had no idea what had become of them. Had they all made it home safely or had they been apprehended by the police? Worse still, had any of them encountered the thing in the woods?

As much as these questions troubled me, I knew there would be no answers to them tonight and allowed my eyes to flutter shut again.

Seconds later, I was asleep.

That return to consciousness was not a gentle one. It came courtesy of a banging on my door. This was my mom waking me up to tell me breakfast would soon be ready. The way the door rattled in the frame told me she'd been trying hard to wake me for a while. She was a little cross with me when I finally came to and acknowledged her entreaties, but she didn't further berate me. Instead, she wandered back off to the kitchen after I groggily reassured her I would be out there in a bit. By then both my parents were well-accustomed to me sleeping late after returning home from a night out with the guys.

The first thing I was aware of after mom retreated to the kitchen was my overall miserable physical state. My head felt like someone had dropped a truck on it. The ache was huge and seemingly all-encompassing, but I soon realized I had other problems. My mouth was so dry I could barely swallow or move my tongue. When I did attempt to swallow, it was like trying to force a razor blade down my gullet. This dryness, however, was a typical consequence of failing to hydrate prior to crashing after a night of heavy drinking. It was something I could remedy easily enough.

Less ordinary was the pain I was feeling in so many other places. I felt beaten up, as if I'd tumbled down the side of a mountain. There were several raw places on my legs. Some of the lingering grogginess began to dissipate as I tried to remember the reason for that. That was when the first memories from the night before came to me. I didn't know the term "panic attack" back then, but I had one then. Flashing images from my delirious dash through the woods danced through my head. If I had been capable of it in those moments, I would have sat bolt upright in bed, my eyes bulging in their sockets as I gasped for breath, but something in me recognized that this would be a bad idea in my current state and blocked the impulse. As it was, my heart galloped and my eyes were wide as I remembered the grotesque face of the beast.

A bad dream, I tried telling myself. That's all it was. Just a really bad fucking dream.

I grimaced as I turned onto my side to stare down the length of my body. The physical effort made all my various pains even worse, but I had to know what I was dealing with here. My jeans were shredded, ripped and torn open in several places. I remembered tripping and falling in the woods, and I remembered a tearing sound and that feeling of wetness, but the actual damage was beyond anything I had expected. The reason my skin felt raw was now obvious—my legs had endured numerous abrasions and cuts. I felt dried blood on my skin.

There were blood stains on the sheets.

And something else that rolled out of my long, tangled hair as I tried to sit up—a badly-mangled human finger. I could only surmise the beast in the woods had spat at me as I turned and ran, and the blood had caused it to stick in my hair, where it had remained all through the night.

It had been real. All of it.

That terrible, hideous thing.

I never went into the woods again. Any woods, anywhere.

Would you?

A SLASHER'S DILEMMA

AUTHOR'S NOTE: Sometimes even serial killers have to balance home life and career aspirations.

THE MAN AREA MEDIA HAD long ago branded "The Lone Star Slasher" started getting impatient after an hour of waiting for his intended victims. He was standing hunched-over in a cramped bedroom closet. A low shelf kept him from standing fully erect. It was an uncomfortable place to hide, in purely physical terms, but being in the closet put him in perfect position to do the work he'd come here to do. He was therefore reluctant to vacate the closet in search of a hiding place that would place less strain on his aching back.

Having been at the hack 'n' slash game for more than twenty years, he still had much of the zeal for killing that had characterized his long career in serial murder. Thanks to advancing age and a changed set of priorities, however, opportunities to engage in his life's greatest passion had become increasingly rare in recent years.

When he first started out, he had a lot more freedom to go wherever he wanted any time he wanted. He was young and single with no serious attachments and little in the way of outside obligations. Other than the six hours he used to put in at his part-time job at the video rental store five days a week, his time was his own. In his lone wolf days, he'd been free to prowl the streets of various Texas cities in search of victims for hours on end. Back then there'd been no social

127

media and the internet had been in its infancy. The world was less connected and it was easier to get up to nefarious nocturnal activities. There were no smartphones and less constant surveillance of citizens in general. He hadn't known it at the time, but it'd been a golden age for mad slashers.

Not that he was actually "mad" or otherwise mentally inhibited. He was a bit above average in intelligence and, as far as he'd ever been able to tell, was perfectly sane. He knew the difference between right and wrong and had no problems separating fantasy from reality. There were no voices in his head telling him to do what he did. Aside from that one time when he'd tried peyote in his college days, he'd never hallucinated. Nor were his urges driven by abuses or traumas he'd experienced in his youth. He understood this was a common scenario in cases of serial murder, but it wasn't the case for him.

To the contrary, he'd grown up in an ordinary and happy middle-class home. His parents loved him and he received all the support a kid could ever ask for. He didn't get bullied at school, and while he hadn't been part of the popular crowd, he hadn't been a social outcast either. To all outward appearances, he was the most normal guy ever. None of his friends or acquaintances would ever guess he'd committed more than forty vicious murders over the course of almost a quarter-century.

With one exception.

His wife knew all about his hobby. In fact, they only met because she'd been one of his intended victims. It happened on a chilly winter's night almost a decade ago. Lydia was returning home after a night of bar-hopping in Austin, walking alone to her apartment in the wee hours after parting ways with a trio of gal pals. Having trailed them from bar to bar much of the night, he'd been thrilled by this development. The gals were all pretty sexy, but Lydia was the hottest of them all by a mile. Following along behind her as she drunkenly stumbled her way down a series of dark sidewalks, he had plenty of time to admire her leggy form, emphasized to great effect by her short skirt and heels. At some point during that long walk, his interest in her shifted from murderous to amorous. He caught up to her and initiated a conversation. At first she was wary. After all, he was a stranger and she was an attractive young woman walking alone at night. But he turned on the charm and she wound up inviting him to her apartment. If she'd been sober, it almost certainly wouldn't have happened that way.

Even after being invited into her apartment, he still thought he'd wind up killing her after having sex with her. It wasn't his usual way of doing things at all. The murders he committed were never sexually motivated. He never copulated with corpses or did other super-weird stuff like that. Guys like Ted Bundy and Jeffrey Dahmer weren't his role models. He didn't have some deep-seated hatred of women. As far as he was concerned, women were superior to men in virtually every way that mattered. He had great respect for them. All of which made it so weird that he enjoyed killing them so much. And he did enjoy that a great deal. The screams. The struggling. All that blood. The sound a knife made punching through vulnerable flesh. All of it was so thrilling and gave him a rush no drug could ever equal. And yet none of that impacted how he interacted with or felt about women in the context of normal, everyday life. His was a highly compartmentalized existence. The way he saw it, these polar opposite sides of himself need not negate each other. With just a little effort, they could coexist. It wasn't even that difficult.

He didn't wind up killing Lydia, though.

They got to talking and he found himself genuinely intrigued by her on an intellectual and emotional level in addition to the lust he felt for her. She was a smart lady. They liked a lot of the same things. Maybe it was the booze talking, but she kept turning the conversation in daring directions. She kept hinting at a deeply kinky streak and confessed to a morbid interest in murder and death. Her bookshelves were lined with true crime books. By the time she broke out her collection of autopsy photos, he was falling in love with her. After they fucked, he compulsively confessed to her that he was the Lone Star Slasher, who'd already been notorious for years even back then. She didn't believe him at first, but then he showed her the knife he carried with him every time he went out on a killing expedition. After admitting he'd initially followed her with the intent of stabbing her to death, she did a strange thing. She smiled. When they had sex again a short time later, she had him hold the knife to her throat the entire time.

Obviously they were meant for each other.

They dated for less than a year before getting married. She got pregnant with their first child. He got a better-paying job and soon they moved into a nice suburban house a lot like the one in which he'd grown up. Less than a year after their first child was born, Lydia was pregnant again. Now they had three kids under the age of ten. His free time was down to almost nothing. Providing for his family displaced murder as the dominant factor in his life. Almost a year and a half had passed since his last kill. He knew the clock was ticking on his career. All serial killers aged out of the game eventually, growing too weak and infirm to overpower younger victims. He wasn't naïve enough to believe it wouldn't happen to him, too. The truth was, after being at it for so long, the day when he'd have to call it quits for good was almost upon him. All he wanted now was to indulge in one more round of kills and go out in style.

Lydia was supportive of this idea. She told him to go for it, which was all the encouragement he needed. He began keeping an eye out for prime opportunities to again indulge in his craft. That was how he thought of it, as a craft. He was a skilled artist, albeit one who worked with blood and body parts rather than paints and canvas. His kill sites were his canvases and he liked to decorate them as gaudily as possible. If crime scene investigators and forensics teams didn't feel as if they had walked onto the set of a horror film, what it meant to him was he hadn't done his job correctly. These would be his final kills. He wanted them to be spectacular.

To better facilitate this goal, he'd brought along an extra set of tools tonight. His trusty hunting knife, the one he'd been using since his first kill all those years ago, would see a fair amount of action tonight. It wouldn't, however, suffice for everything he had in mind, which would include the severing of multiple body parts. He needed more heavy-duty tools for that. In the bag at his feet as he waited (and waited) in the closet were a hatchet, a bone-saw, a meat cleaver, a hammer, a box of long nails, more knives of varying types, a serrated surgical scooping tool, and a scalpel. The scalpel he would use for some of the finer bits of work, such as slicing off eyelids and lips. He hoped he'd be able to do that part of it while his victims were still alive, but that wasn't always possible. They sometimes bled out from the initial wounds he inflicted before he could get around to torturing them, but even if that happened, he would still have fun aplenty. Taking apart the bodies and leaving them in creative places and poses would more than make up for any such unfortunate occurrence.

His targets tonight were a young couple. High school students. It was a classic slasher scenario, like something right out of an 80s stalk 'n' slash movie. The girl who was his primary target was a babysitter. Tonight she was looking after a pair of young kids whose parents had gone out for a night on the town. Her boyfriend was planning to come over after the kids were put to bed for the night. They would do their fooling around in this bedroom. He knew all this because he'd eavesdropped on their conversation while dining alone at a nearby restaurant.

Containing his excitement as he listened to them talk was close to impossible. The entirety of his attention was so focused on what the high school seniors were saying that he stopped eating with his meal half-finished. His right hand remained poised with a knife over the plate in front of him for a stretch of several minutes, a fact he was unaware of until a waiter abruptly snapped him out of it by asking if everything was all right with his meal. After flinching in surprise, he said he wasn't feeling well and asked the waiter to bring his check.

After paying his bill, he went out to his car and lurked in the parking lot, waiting for the couple to emerge. When they did, he followed them at a discreet distance until the boy dropped the girl off at her house and drove away. He circled the block and called Lydia to tell her what was going on. She agreed it sounded like an ideal scenario. There was just one problem. His parents were coming to town for a rare visit. Their flight was scheduled to arrive shortly after ten. He'd promised to pick them up personally so they wouldn't have to get a cab or rent a car. In order to get there on time, he would have to be done with his work here no later than 9:30.

He grimaced when he checked his watch again. It was now five minutes after nine. The kids the girl was babysitting should have been put to bed over an hour ago, but he could still hear the faint sounds of them squealing and playing somewhere downstairs. The sound was driving him nuts. The girl had been so specific in telling her boyfriend how the evening would unfold, including when the kids would be in bed and when they would be free to fool around in the guest bedroom. Thus far, though, none of it was working out the way she'd said. The lengthy delay already meant he wouldn't get to do the more elaborate things he'd planned. If another ten or fifteen minutes (at the absolute outside) elapsed with no sign of the girl and her boyfriend, he wouldn't get to kill them at all. He'd have to abort the whole thing and wait for another opportunity to arise. One would come up eventually, but odds were it wouldn't feel as perfect as this one had at the outset.

The next check of his watch showed another nine minutes had elapsed. Those play sounds from downstairs had died down, but he could still hear faint sounds of chatter. The kids weren't in bed yet. A deep disappointment welled up inside him. It was time to face facts.

This wasn't happening tonight.

He took out his phone and sent a text to his wife explaining the situation, also telling her he'd be slipping out of the house in just a few minutes to head to the airport. Her initial response was a sad-face emoji. Before he could respond to that, flashing dots that meant she was composing another response appeared on the screen. He waited to see what she would say next, fully expecting an additional gesture of sorrow on his behalf.

What she said instead was this: No fucking way. You do you, baby. You need this. I'll pick up your folks.

He quickly sent back a response: Are you sure?

She sent back smiley-face and heart emojis. Then she told him, Hell yes. I only ask that you bring me back a souvenir. You know the kind I like.

Grinning almost ear-to-ear, he typed in his next response: You got it. I love you so fucking much. You're the best.

Shortly thereafter, he put his phone away and resumed the wait. Just over twenty minutes later, the girl and her boyfriend came into the room and crawled onto the bed together. Sounds of incipient passion soon ensued. The Lone Star Slasher observed them through the slats of the closet's accordion-style door, waiting until they were fully disrobed before he donned his famous mask, pushed the door open, and emerged into the bedroom.

He spent the next hour doing so many of his favorite things, things he'd been unable to do for such a long time. There was a tremendous amount of hacking and slashing. Blood was sprayed all over the room. He used all the tools he'd brought with him to great, satisfying effect, disemboweling the corpses and severing every limb. Before he left the house, he took the babysitter's severed head out to the hallway and set it at the top of the staircase, nailing it to the carpeted floor. The boyfriend's head he placed in the room shared by the sleeping kids, who hadn't stirred the whole time. Lydia's souvenir (the boyfriend's surgically-removed cock) went into a Ziploc bag.

On the way home, he stopped off at a grocery store and bought her a dozen red roses and the most expense bottle of merlot they had. Lydia was such a wonderfully supportive wife. She deserved more than just another piece of severed flesh. He'd given her many such tokens over the years. The flowers and wine would be a nice extra surprise.

He couldn't wait to see her face light up when he saw her again.

PILGRIMAGE

A TOUR BUS PULLED INTO an almost empty parking lot early in the afternoon on the sixth day of August in the year 2019. Adjacent to the lot was a single one-story building. The only other vehicle in the lot was an unoccupied 1970s-era Chevelle. The old muscle car was in pristine condition, with new paint, new tires, and a set of fancy new rims that gleamed in the brilliant glare of the San Francisco sunshine. Of the eye-catching ride's owner, there was no sign, but Jason Dobbs knew one thing for sure—whoever the owner was, he or she was rolling in cash. That or in hock up to their eyeballs, because a top-notch restoration job on a car of that vintage couldn't be done cheaply.

He nudged the person in the seat next to him, then pointed out the window. "Hey, George. Check out the sweet wheels."

George Sanderson took a break from making out with Karla Donahue, his girlfriend, and craned his head around to look in the indicated direction. "Oh, wow. Nice old school transpo."

Jason nodded. "Hell, yeah. Can't you just see yourself rolling down the strip back home in that thing in, like, 1976 or whatever?"

George grinned, warming to the idea. "Sure can. Bunch of hot girls in the back. Bell-bottom jeans and tube tops. Awesome tunes cranking on the 8-track player while a fat blunt gets passed around."

Karla leaned over the guys for a look at the subject of conversation. She did so at an angle that allowed Jason to see straight down the front of her top. The view was pretty breathtaking. She had incredible breasts. His face flushed hot as he stared down the valley between them. He was pretty sure she'd done this on purpose. It was not the first time she'd blatantly taunted him with her sexuality. As always, he felt a mixture of titillation and shame. This was his best friend's girl. He felt he should do something to discourage the behavior, but how he might go about doing that without making things awkward or even hostile between the three of them, he did not know.

She had choppy dyed-black hair that wasn't quite shoulder length and was dressed in the manner of rock and rollers from a bygone era. The outfit included a studded black leather biker jacket, a studded dog collar around her throat, a tight, low-cut red top that left very little to the imagination, black-and-white striped pants, and Doc Martens. Rings adorned nearly every finger. Some were plain bands of various colors, but the selection included multiple skull rings. Dramatic black eye makeup rounded out a look Jason figured was best summarized as "rock and roll wet dream."

She pulled back from the window, returning to her seat on the other side of George. "I don't think they had that term back in the 70s. Blunts. That came out of hip hop. I think."

Jason turned his face toward the window, hoping the others wouldn't see the bright red tinge to his cheeks.

George, at least, seemed oblivious to his embarrassment, regarding his girlfriend with a frown as he said, "Okay, enlighten me. What was the preferred vernacular of the time?"

She grunted. "Doobies, I think."

George snorted. "Doobies? Like the fucking Doobie Brothers or some shit?"

"Yeah. Where do you think those guys got their name? They were a bunch of pot-smoking hippies."

George laughed. "You sound pretty knowledgeable on the subject. Name one song by the fucking Doobie Brothers."

"Shut up. That's not the point."

George laughed again and nudged Jason. "You listening to this shit, man?"

"Yeah, Jason," Karla said, her tone playful but with a subtle undercurrent of mockery. "We need your opinion on this all-important matter. You're the authority on all things retro."

Enough of the heat had faded from Jason's cheeks that he felt comfortable turning away from the window. "Actually, I don't—"

An abrasive burst of loud static from the overhead speakers made him grimace and fall silent. The abrupt sound elicited startled gasps of displeasure from several other people on the bus. All heads turned to the front, where a tall, abundantly bearded fat man stood with a radio handset gripped in one of his massive paws. He coughed and thumbed a button on the side of the handset. "Sorry, folks. Was having some technical issues. Anyway, I'm sure at least a few of you recognize the very famous building off to our right. It's been featured in several documentaries and a great number of the most iconic photos in the history of rock and roll were taken inside this storied edifice."

Some drunken-sounding individual from the back of the bus let out an obnoxiously loud whoop. "David Bowie! Woo!"

The fat tour guide smiled in an indulgent way. "You are correct, sir. Woo, indeed. David Bowie was indeed one of the many legends to play a show on these hallowed grounds. Others you might have heard of include Led Zeppelin in their infancy, the Doors, Humble Pie, Jefferson Airplane, the Grateful Dead, Van Halen when they were starting out, and many more. Lot of the biggest and most influential punk bands of the 70s played here, too."

The same drunk from the back let out another whoop. "Sid Vicious! Sex Pistols! Woo!"

Karla snorted laughter and raised her voice in a whoop of her own. "Woo! Rock and roll! Woo!"

The drunk in the back laughed so hard Jason worried the force of it might result in a self-induced seizure. On the bright side, at least it would shut him up.

The tour guide's smile looked strained now. He cleared his throat and again thumbed the button on the side of the handset. "The Shantyman has always been more than just a legendary place to see live music performed. It is a destination. It is living history. The venue has played host to a dizzyingly diverse range of artists, including some who later became figures of myth in their own right. And it is a place where the ghosts of the past never seem far away, where guitar chords struck at the end of legendary performances decades earlier seem to linger in the air still, at least for those attuned to the right mental frequencies. For those with a deep love for music, there is something almost sacred about the Shantyman. Little wonder, then, that so many are willing to travel from so far away to experience the special vibe of the place firsthand."

Like us, Jason thought.

The guide sounded like he was reading from a memorized script and probably was.

Karla raised a hand. "I have a question."

George smirked. "Oh, look at the proper schoolgirl. Being all courteous and shit. Not bad for a high school dropout."

Karla glared at him. "Shut up."

The tour guide sighed heavily into the live handset, a sound replicated in distorted fashion through the overhead speakers. "What would you like to know, miss?"

The angry look on Karla's face was immediately displaced by a mischievous smile. "Is it true Johnny Kilgore of the Sick Motherfuckers blew his brains out right over there?" She twisted in her seat to point in the general direction of the venue's entrance. "Right about where that penis on wheels is parked?"

A few of the other passengers giggled at this remark. Predictably, the drunk in the back honked more obnoxious laughter. Jason wished he had a hatchet to bury in the guy's head. In a way, it was more than a bit hypocritical. He had, after all, indulged in his fair share of public drunken buffoonery in the past. It occurred to him that what was really bugging him here was the way the guy seemed so locked in on Karla with his over-the-top reactions to her every remark. He was jealous of the spontaneous camaraderie that had developed between her and this stranger. Which was ridiculous. She wasn't his girlfriend. The only one entitled to any feelings of jealousy here was George, who either was oblivious to their rapport or simply didn't care. In his friend's place, Jason would have a hard time being blasé about it.

The tour guide again cleared his throat and spoke into the handset. "That is the unfortunate truth, yes. The year was 1979. The band to which you referred had just played their first headlining gig at the Shantyman, which was a big deal for them. Back then, it wasn't easy for a band with a name like that to market themselves effectively. The sign on the marquee billed them as the Sick M.F.'s, which caused some drama between the band and venue management. This apparently offended the late Mr. Kilgore's sense of punk rock purity, and near the end of his band's set that night, he announced he would be killing himself as soon as the show was over. Unfortunately, it seems no one took this threat seriously. Not until it was too late."

Some on the bus made clucking sounds of disapproval while

others with grim expressions shook their heads at this tale of rock and roll tragedy. Jason wasn't one of them, having been familiar with the details for years. The same was true for Karla, of course, who was being a tad disingenuous by inquiring as to the veracity of something she already knew all about.

The tour guide paused for a moment while some of the passengers aimed their phones at the venue to snap pictures. When he sensed the majority of his customers had finished recording this moment for something resembling posterity, he again thumbed the button on the side of the handset. "Okay, then. If there are no other questions, it's time to move along to the next stop on the tour. We've got a ways to go before we're done and a schedule to adhere to."

Karla abruptly stood up and moved into the center aisle between the rows of seats. "We'll be getting off here."

George did a double-take at this unanticipated declaration before glancing at Jason with raised eyebrows. "Uh, you heard her. Guess we're debarking. Any objections?"

Jason sighed. "Would it matter if I had any?"

George chuckled. "Not really, man. It's cool. We'll just get an Uber back to the hotel later."

"Fuck it, then. Let's go."

They both began to rise from their seats.

As the three of them began to move down the aisle toward the front, the tour guide moved aside to allow them room to pass. When they were within range, he addressed them without speaking into the handset. "It's early in the tour, guys. Sure you want to get off now?"

By that point, Karla had already descended the short set of steps at the front of the bus and was standing in the parking lot, where she was lighting up a cigarette. George glanced back at the tour guide, grinning in a sheepish way as he shrugged. "Already a done deal, looks like."

The tour guide nodded. "No skin off my back. Just remember there aren't any refunds. Doesn't matter where you get off."

George cackled and said, "That's what she said, bro."

He descended the steps to the parking lot without another word.

Jason directed a cringing look of silent apology at the tour guide, shrugged, and followed his friends out the door. He held a hand to his brow to shield his eyes against the glare of the sun as he approached them. His friends had donned sunglasses as soon as they'd stepped out into the sunlight, but he'd left his own pair behind at the hotel. George had one of Karla's cigarettes wedged into a corner of his mouth, and she was holding the flame of her Zippo to its tip to light it for him. Jason had known George for a long time, going back to middle school. He'd never smoked at all until hooking up with Karla about a year ago, but now he indulged on a regular basis. She had a habit of taking two cigarettes from her pack and passing one to him without asking if he wanted one. Jason had a feeling George just went along with it because he thought his girlfriend would disapprove if he didn't. And Jason kind of idolized Karla. In private conversation with Jason, he often called her "the coolest chick I've ever fucking met."

Jason didn't much care for the smoking, but he could understand. He kind of idolized Karla, too.

And now he felt a bit awestruck at the sight of her. Dressed like she was while standing outside one of the most storied music venues in the world, she looked like a rock star who had arrived early for a gig. With his shaggy dark hair, black clothes, and lanky good looks, George could pass as one of her bandmates. Unlike his girlfriend, however, the guy couldn't play a lick of music. His singing voice wasn't such hot shit, either. He did have that same effortlessly cool 70s rocker look, though. This sometimes made Jason feel a little lacking by comparison. He was just an ordinary, kind of nerdy-looking guy. The kind of guy a wild child like Karla would never go for, or so one would think. A tiny hint of a smirk dimpled one side of her mouth when she glanced his way and caught him staring at her.

He glanced away from her just as the door to the tour bus hissed open again, allowing one more passenger to disembark. A skinny young guy in a tie-dyed shirt and raggedy jeans grinned and waved when he saw them. He had fair skin and what Jason thought of as lazy, heavy-lidded eyes. They were the eyes of a dedicated weed-smoker. He also had long blond dreads.

The tour bus pulled away from them, turned about in a wide circle, and drove out of the Shantyman's parking lot, leaving the four of them alone there. Aside from the unoccupied car parked by the entrance, there was no indication of any other human presence in the other area. Though he would have had difficulty articulating why in that moment, this made Jason feel uneasy.

"Hey, yo," the hippie kid said, calling out to them with a big, goofy grin on his face. "There room for one more at this party?"

Jason winced at the sound of the guy's voice. He always found that lethargic stoner drawl irritating. So many of those guys sounded just like that. But that wasn't the real reason for his instinctive dislike of the interloper. He'd heard this particular obnoxious stoner voice several times already. This was the annoying guy who'd spoken up several times from the back of the bus.

He looked at his friends and mouthed the word "no" as emphatically as he could manage. They were both looking right at him as he did this. There was no doubt they understood what he was trying to silently communicate. George gave a slight nod of understanding, and Jason knew his old buddy was on board with his desire to send the guy on his way.

Karla, however, had other ideas.

"Sure, pal. So long as we can have some of whatever you've been smoking."

The stoner's grin got bigger and goofier. He hooked his thumbs under the green straps of a backpack and tugged at them. "Absolutely. Got plenty to go around. Got some magic mushrooms, too, if you're interested. Really potent shit, yo."

Karla laughed. "We'll keep that in mind for later, maybe. Meanwhile, break out the fucking weed."

The guy removed the backpack, unzipped a side pocket, and took out a baggie filled with an ample supply of the green stuff. Also stuffed inside the baggie was a glass pipe. He took out the pipe, tamped some weed into the bowl, and fired it up, after which he took a big hit and held the smoke in as he held the pipe out for whoever wanted to hit it next.

Karla flipped her half-smoked cigarette away and snagged it from him, held the flame of her Zippo to the bowl, and took a big hit of her own. She then passed the pipe to George, who took a more modest hit before offering it to Jason.

Jason declined with a wave of his hand. "Not interested."

George shrugged. "Suit yourself."

He and Karla took turns taking additional hits before passing the pipe back to the hippie kid at his request. The kid pinched another nug out of the baggie and refilled the bowl. He sparked it up again with the plastic gas station lighter he'd used before, put the pipe to his lips, and inhaled deeply.

Karla coughed a couple times and made a face. "I feel a little weird. Not high exactly. Just weird. Like my head's inside a glass box or something, disconnected from my body and the rest of the world.

There's something not right about your weed, man. I've got this chemical taste in my mouth." Her features shifted, conveying anger as she grabbed hold of Jason to keep from toppling over. "Jesus. It's laced with something fucked-up, isn't it? Industrial solvents or some shit. Pesticide, maybe."

The hippie kid laughed as he took the pipe away from his mouth. "Nothing so mundane as that. This is my own special blend, though. Designed to induce a certain pliable state of mind. Open to suggestion. Some of the ingredients are what you might consider . . . exotic."

Karla took a lurching step sideways, dragging George along with her. They took another awkward step together before simultaneously dropping to their knees. Karla looked at Jason. Her mouth moved, but no words emerged. There was a look of pleading in her eyes. She wanted help with something, but he had no clue what manner of assistance she needed. In another moment, she and George fell over and lay motionless on the ground.

Jason gasped in shock. "Fuck!"

The hippie kid laughed again and took another long drag from the pipe, his puffed-out cheeks turning red as held the smoke in for an extended period. In the grip of a mounting panic, Jason grabbed hold of the guy by an arm and roughly spun him about so they were facing each other.

"What have you done to them, asshole!?" He snatched the pipe from the kid's hands and squinted at the bowl. At a glance, the partially charred substance inside it looked no different from regular weed, but that didn't necessarily mean anything. He held the bowl to his face and sniffed. The odor did seem off in a way that was hard to pinpoint. "You better not have poisoned them, motherfucker."

The kid opened his mouth and expelled a pungent cloud of smoke directly into Jason's face. Some of the smoke went up his nostrils while more of it went straight into his open mouth. He relinquished his grip on the kid's arm as he gagged and took a staggering step backward. At once he detected that chemical taste Karla had described. It made the inside of his mouth feel like it was coated in a fine layer of liquid metal. The sensation was horrifying and he felt an instinctive, all-consuming need to rid his body of it as soon as possible. He gagged again and bent over at the waist as he repeatedly spat phlegm at the parking lot asphalt. No amount of this relieved the strange sensations plaguing him.

He dropped to his knees and in another moment toppled over

and rolled onto his back with a groan. The hippie kid came closer and knelt next to him with the same blissed-out smile as before, but there was something in the set of his features that hadn't been there originally. Something sinister. There was also something not quite right in the texture of his skin. The longer he stared at the kid, the more that skin didn't look real at all. It looked kind of fake, like stretchable plastic. He had the feeling that if he could lift his hand and reach out to the guy, he would be able to peel back that phony outer layer of pseudo-flesh and reveal the true horror beneath.

But he didn't have the strength for that.

He was still conscious, though. Unlike his friends, he was still able to groan and squirm around minutely on the ground. He supposed he'd gotten a weaker dose of whatever had crippled them because he hadn't drawn the smoke directly into his lungs via the pipe. The hippie kid with the fake-looking skin blew another cloud of smoke into his face, causing him to cough and gag yet again.

The kid shook blond dreadlocks out of his face and grinned. "You're right, you know. About the diluted effect of the second-hand smoke. No worries, though. You'll get the necessary dose soon enough."

That this creature could read minds didn't even rank among the top five most scary things about it, as far as Jason was concerned. This thing masquerading as a hippie kid wasn't even human. It was some kind of monster or demon. And it had targeted him and his friends for reasons he couldn't even begin to fathom.

He coughed so hard it made his lungs hurt. "Wh-what . . . are you?"

The creature smiled. "I am The Traveler. Time is an illusion. Did you know that? I could explain it to you, but there's no time. Hah-hah. Anyway, she wanted you, you know. That girl. It's true. I looked into her mind and saw it. She wanted you to fuck her, but you didn't have the guts to go for it." He glanced at the girl's unconscious form. "Such a shame, really. To let down a girl that pretty." He grinned as his gaze returned to Jason. "Your problem, Jason, is that you're too much of a good guy. You'd never betray a friend's trust. What you don't know is George killed that kitten of yours that went missing a few years back. Such a cruel and petty act. There was no real reason for it. Other than pure malice, that is. Dear, sweet George has a hidden inner darkness. Guess he was never really worthy of your blind loyalty, huh?"

Tears misted Jason's eyes. "Why . . . are you doing this?"

The creature chuckled, a sound that made Jason think of the tour guide's distorted voice crackling through the speakers in the bus. "Because I can. Because it amuses me. Your friends are not dead, by the way. Quite the contrary. I'm sending each of you on separate journeys through the timestream, all in some way connected to that building over there. The girl asked about the night Johnny Kilgore killed himself. Well, she's about to witness the event firsthand."

Jason sniffled as his vision began to blur. "This is . . . crazy. Can't be real."

"Oh, but it is." The creature inhaled deeply from the glass pipe, held the smoke in for a moment, and then expelled it into Jason's face. "Did you know that the Stooges played a show here fifty years ago tonight? It's true. It was the day after their first album was released. Little known historical fact, several members of the Manson family were in attendance that night. This was three days before the infamous Tate-LaBianca murders. The raw violence and energy in the protopunk music they heard that night had a galvanizing effect on some of them. It's too bad ol' Charlie wasn't there. The experience might have elevated his game, made him an even more effective sower of chaos and dread."

Jason coughed. "I have no idea what you're talking about. And none of that sounds true."

The creature laughed. "The timestream consists of an inestimable number of interweaving strands. Along some of those strands, what I've told you is demonstrably false. Along others, it is the absolute truth. As you're about to find out."

The plastic baggie full of that toxic weed was in the thing's hands again. Now he scooped out a handful of it and forced it into Jason's mouth. Jason gagged and spat some of it back out, but the creature clamped a strong hand tightly around his jaw, closing his mouth and forcing him to swallow the weed. A short time later, he experienced something similar to the sensation Karla had described. His head felt separate from his body, somehow heavy and weightless at the same time.

The brilliant blue hue drained out of the sky above within seconds. Darkness engulfed him.

An indeterminate period of incognizance ensued, during which he drifted in a formless black void. It was as if he barely even existed anymore.

As if nothing existed.

Then, abruptly, awareness returned in the form of the driving backbeat of a distantly familiar tune. That rhythm was one he knew well, but an overwhelming sense of disorientation prevented him from identifying it right away. He heard other sounds, as well. Raised voices struggling to be heard over the amplified music. The hoots and hollers of a cheering audience.

He opened his eyes and saw that he was right up front inside the Shantyman, watching a primal rock band barrel its way through a song he now recognized as "1969", a track from the self-titled debut album by the Stooges. Leading the band was the young Iggy Pop, a frenetic whirlwind of manic energy.

I'm not really seeing this, Jason thought. I'm not really here. This is power of suggestion bullshit. A drug-induced hallucination. That's all.

He stood there swaying mindlessly to the beat a moment longer, feeling the heavy thrum of the rhythm section in his body. The floor seemed to vibrate beneath his feet. The bodies of others in the audience jostled against him. He detected the acrid scent of pot permeating the smoke-filled air.

Sure feels real, though.

The apparent reality of it all was suddenly too much. He spun away from the stage and began to push his way through the tight press of bodies. The closeness of those bodies and thickness of the smoke was oppressive, made him feel like he was suffocating. He needed to get out of the club, out into the clean night air. The press of bodies became less oppressive, less dense, as he neared the bar at the back of the club. This allowed him to take a longer look at the people around him. They looked strange, not right for the audience at a punk show. There was a lot of long, greasy hair. A lot of hippie garb and regalia. Headbands, peace symbol buttons, and so forth. Then it hit him. The audience didn't look right to him because this was the time before punk, when the Stooges were just the newest stage in the ongoing evolution of rock.

There were a lot of people at the bar. And a lot of drinks on its crowded surface. At one end sat an unguarded beer that looked like it had just been opened, its contents untouched. He snagged it while no one was watching and hurried out of the club, heaving a breath as he emerged into the warm California evening. The parking lot that had been empty before was full now. Surveying the sea of vehicles, he felt like he'd stumbled upon a vintage car show. He saw Mustangs and VW vans, as well as numerous sedans and sports cars of various makes. There was nary a sign of a Prius or any other modern vehicles.

All real, he thought. *I'm really stuck in 1969.*

Laughing with tears in his eyes, he took a swig of beer and sat his ass down on the curb. He didn't know what to do with himself. Accepting the reality of the situation presented a whole new host of problems. He had no connection to anyone in this time. His parents were out there somewhere on the other side of the country, but they were kids. There would be no point in seeking them out. He drank more of the beer as he sat there and thought about it. It all seemed so hopeless. He had no idea how to go about starting a new life in what essentially amounted to a foreign land, a place where he did not officially exist. Not on paper, anyway.

Then he thought about what the thing that called itself The Traveler had said. He was sending Karla back to 1979, to the night Johnny Kilgore of the Sick Motherfuckers killed himself not far from where he now sat. A tiny spark of hope flared to life inside Jason.

All he had to do was somehow survive the next ten years and return to this spot on that infamous date. He knew the details well. He could be right here at the appointed time when Karla arrived. He'd be a decade older than her at that point, but that wasn't such an insurmountable age difference, was it? He didn't think so, especially now that he knew about her private feelings for him. She would be thrilled to see him, he was sure of it.

And who knew what might happen then?

A voice spoke from somewhere right behind him: "Hey, cutie."

He shifted about on the curb and craned his head around, frowning at the familiar face staring down at him. It was a girl. A not unattractive one. She was no Karla, but she wasn't half bad, either. But he knew that face, was sure he'd seen it somewhere before.

He frowned. "Do I know you?"

She smiled. "I don't think so. We're just now meeting. My name's Suzie."

Then it came to him. Where he'd seen her before. Mostly from black and white photos in the pages of a dogeared old paperback book that had belonged to his father. This was Susan Atkins.

One of the Manson girls.

Before he could say anything else to her, he felt another presence rushing at him from somewhere off to the side. He turned his head around just in time to see another familiar face. This time the name came to him faster. Charles "Tex" Watson, another member of Charlie's family. He had something in his hands. A burlap sack.

Jason dropped the beer and tried getting to his feet, but a kick from behind sent him tumbling back to the ground. Then Tex and Leslie were on him. The bag was pulled over his head and cinched tight. Others crowded around him then, and he felt multiple sets of hands lifting him off the ground. He tried thrashing his way out of their grip as they carried him across the parking lot, but to no avail. An attempt to cry out for help earned him a hard thump over the head. A short time later, his abductors came to a stop and dumped him inside the spacious trunk of a car.

"Sit tight, cutie," he heard the one called Suzie say. "We're just going on a little adventure and wanted some company."

Jason squirmed around inside the trunk. "Where are you taking me?"

"To the desert. We've got this big thing we're doing soon. Some real Helter Skelter shit. We're sending out a message to the piggies of the world. One they won't be able to ignore."

A man chuckled. Tex, probably. "That's right, darlin'. But before the main event, we're gonna practice on this poor son of a bitch."

The trunk lid slammed shut.

Jason screamed with every bit of lung power he had as the Manson family members piled into the car. He screamed some more as the car's engine started and kept screaming as the car was steered out of the parking lot and into the city streets.

No one heard his screams or pleas for mercy.

No one except Charlie's chosen few, that is.

And no one else ever would.

Because all that remained of Jason Dobbs' future—aside from his pending agonizing death—was a rendezvous with a lonely hole in the dusty desert soil. A forgotten unmarked grave that would forever go undiscovered.

WE ARE 138 GOLDEN ELM

"MAYBE WE SHOULD TRY CALLING them again."

Jim Matthews shifted in his seat and adjusted his grip on the Audi's steering wheel. He scanned the surrounding area as he took the car slowly down yet another in a seemingly endless series of non-descript suburban streets. They all looked pretty much the same. Well-kept lawns. Modest-sized houses in varying styles, but nothing too ostentatious. Most of the cars parked in the driveways and at the curbs looked relatively newish, but none of them were luxury rides. Working class people lived here. Well-paid unionized factory workers and middle-management types. There were no one-percenters with Bentleys and Ferraris. Everything looked so damned normal, but appearances, as Jim well knew, could be deceiving.

"Did you hear me?"

Jim sighed. "I heard you."

Tanya Carlson heaved a sigh of her own, one invested with a high degree of exaggerated petulance. "Well? Should we call them again? We've been driving around in circles forever. You must've gotten the directions wrong."

Jim shrugged. "Okay."

They drove on in silence until reaching the end of Edward Avenue, which intersected with Bronson. Jim glanced at the rearview mirror as he brought the Audi to a full stop. No other cars were approaching from behind. He took his phone from the slot beneath the radio, pulled up the number from the recent calls list, and put the phone to his ear.

The call was answered on the first ring. "Hello?"

Jim cleared his throat. "Hey, Mr. Quist, this is Jim Matthews again. We must've gotten our wires crossed or something because we're having a hard time finding your street. Pretty sure I've taken at least one wrong turn."

Tanya snorted. Jim ignored the disdainful noise, keeping his gaze on the rearview mirror. Patience was not one of Tanya's virtues, to understate. Mostly he was okay with it, because she seemed to genuinely love him. Also, she was easily the best lay of his life and was open-minded when it came to some of his more non-traditional interests.

The man who'd given his name as Michael Quist chuckled from the other end. "Easy to do out here if you're not using GPS. We're at 138 Golden Elm Lane. Where are you right now?"

"End of Edward Avenue, facing Bronson."

A barely audible voice issued from the other end. The words it uttered were indistinct. Someone—the man's wife, maybe, though gender was impossible to determine with any certainty—was speaking to Michael Quist in hushed tones. "Yes, yes, I know," Quist said, obviously addressing the mystery party. "They'll be here soon, I promise." He cleared his throat. "Sorry, Jim. We're pretty anxious to see you and get down to business." Another chuckle. "The good news is you're really close now. Take a right and drive on down to Parker Street. You'll pass a couple stop signs before you get there. Take a left at Parker and drive down a couple blocks. That'll take you to Golden Elm. Take a right there and you'll practically be here. We're three houses down on the left. Got that?"

Jim nodded. "Three houses down on the left. Got it."

"See you soon, Jim."

"See—"

Jim took the phone away from his ear and stared at the dark screen a moment. The call had already gone dead. It'd been slightly rude of the man to click off so abruptly, but it didn't really matter, did it? They didn't know each other. They weren't friends. This was an arrangement ostensibly devoid of emotion, a convergence of like-minded adults interested in doing things together polite society might frown upon. Ostensibly.

Tanya snatched the phone from his hand. "What's the address?"

Jim glanced again at the rearview mirror. He saw headlights behind him, approaching from about a block away. He took a right turn out onto Bronson, keeping in mind what Quist had said about having to pass through two stop signs.

Tanya's fist slammed against his shoulder.

Jim grimaced. "Ow. Damn, Tanya. That hurt."

"I told you to give me the address. That's what you get for ignoring me."

"Jesus. It's 138 Golden Elm Lane. But we're almost there. I've got it straight in my head now."

Tanya grunted. "Yeah. Okay. I'm putting it in Google Maps anyway, just in case."

She swiped at his phone's screen and started tapping in the address. After staring at the screen a moment longer, she took a look around and nodded as they reached the first stop sign. "We're getting close. You'll take a left at Parker. It's just up ahead."

Jim already knew that, but he didn't say anything. Even though it was true, it would come out sounding as petulant as she'd sounded a moment ago. She'd accuse him of being a snotty jerk and they'd get in a pointless argument. It wasn't worth it. Better all around to let her think she'd set him straight.

"Turn here," she said as they reached Parker.

Jim took the turn, said nothing. He did the same when she told him to take the right turn at Golden Elm Lane. Their destination was right where Michael Quist had said it would be, the third house down on their left. The driveway was empty and no cars were parked at the curb on that side of the street. The house looked dark and foreboding in the deepening dusk. Not much light remained in the sky and there were no lights on in the house that Jim could see.

Tanya made a sound of exasperation. "Are you sure this is the right place? It looks empty."

Jim couldn't argue with her there, but there was no doubt this was the house to which Quist had directed him. The large gold numbers reading 138 on the side of the mailbox were visible even in the fading light.

Jim nodded, gesturing at the mailbox. "Yeah. I mean, this is definitely 138. And we're on Golden Elm, just like the ad said. And just like the man told me several times."

Tanya twisted in her seat and leaned over him, peering intently at the dark house. Her pretty face was tinged with a deep confusion. "It really doesn't look like anybody's home. No lights on. No fucking cars." She glanced at Jim, arching an eyebrow. "Are you sure it's supposed to be 138, not 148 or something else that sounds similar?"

Jim sighed. "I'm sure. The man said so. And you saw the ad. This is definitely the place."

Tanya made another of those fretful, annoyed sounds before pulling away from him. "Park in their driveway."

"But—"

"Just do it."

Jim shrugged. "Okay."

He pulled the Audi into the driveway and moved the gearshift over to park. A closed garage door was directly in front of him. It had no windows. There was no way to tell, but it was possible—likely, even—that the Quists' cars were parked behind that door. Knowing this dispelled that feeling of foreboding to some degree, but not entirely. The absence of any exterior lighting or visible indoor lighting still struck him as a bit strange.

They sat there in silence a long moment, staring at the dark house. At last, Jim let out a big breath and glanced at his girlfriend. "Well, what do you think? Do we go up and ring the doorbell?"

Tanya had her arms crossed tightly beneath her breasts. A deep line was creasing her forehead. "I don't know. This is starting to feel a little sketchy."

Jim nodded. "Yeah. I guess. The guy sounded friendly enough on the phone, though."

Tanya shrugged. "If you say so. You're the one who talked to him, not me."

"Look, if you want to write this off and just leave, I'm okay with it. We'll find another couple."

"It's up to you," Tanya told him, that deep line on her forehead still in place as she continued to eye the split-level house with obvious wariness. "This is your deal, really. You know that."

Jim frowned. "But I thought you were into it. That's what you've always told me."

Tanya grunted. "I don't mind it once we're into it, but it's not something I need. You're the real enthusiast here."

"I guess so."

Tanya looked at him. A little smile shaded the corners of her mouth as she reached out and touched his leg. "Don't sound so bummed. I like it. I do. And I want to make you happy. So we'll knock on the door. If they answer and everything seems chill, we'll go on in. If something seems off . . ."

Jim nodded, smiling now, too. "We'll leave. Maybe go see that Von Trier movie you wanted to check out."

"Good plan. Let's go."

She opened the door on her side and got out before he could say anything else. Jim was still in place behind the wheel as she threw the door shut. Still eyeing the house, he patted his leather jacket's inner pocket and felt the reassuring weight of the 9mm pistol. It was loaded with a full magazine. A switchblade was nestled in there along with it. He glanced at Tanya and saw the big purse dangling from her shoulder by a thin strap. She was packing a snub-nosed .357 Taurus and a blade of her own, a big serrated hunting knife. He smiled again as images from the last time she'd used it flitted through his mind.

The thought of his gorgeous girlfriend pushing that big blade into soft human flesh and making it gush crimson made his cock twitch. This in turn triggered a fresh surge of the dark hunger that had always driven him. It was powerful enough to dispel the last of his wariness.

He got out of the Audi and joined Tanya on the sidewalk. Together they traversed the sidewalk and climbed the steps to the front porch. Jim was reaching for the doorbell button when Tanya said, "Look at that."

Jim glanced at her, confused. "At what?"

She indicated the door with a tilt of her chin. "It's open."

Jim followed her gaze, frowning again as he noted that she was right. The door was open just the tiniest crack, maybe a quarter inch of vertical blackness standing between the edge of the door and the doorframe. "That's a little strange."

Tanya adjusted the strap of her purse and moved back a step to peer up at dark second level windows. "It's more than a little strange. Oh, wait." She moved back another step, teetering for a moment on the edge of the porch before righting herself. "I saw something."

Jim joined her at the edge of the porch. In the dark, the smaller second level looked a bit like a huge, squat gargoyle perched atop the sloping roof. It had two windows facing the front yard. Both were dark. Jim stared at them a moment and saw nothing.

"I don't see anything."

Tanya made an exasperated sound. "I saw it, Jim. I fucking know I did."

"What was it?"

She shook her head. "It looked like a face."

"One of the Quists, probably."

"Do they have a kid?"

Jim frowned. "Not according to the ad. You saw a kid?"

Tanya let out a shuddery breath as she again shook her head. "I don't know, but it sort of looked like one. It was just a little, pale face at the bottom of the window. I saw it for, like, a split fucking second before it was gone again."

Jim turned his head about, glancing at the tall streetlight on the opposite side of Golden Elm. He thought maybe she'd caught a glint of that light reflecting on the window.

Tanya scowled. "I know what you're thinking. It was no optical illusion. I saw a face. A kid's face, I'm pretty sure."

"That just doesn't make any sense."

"I know what I fucking saw."

Jim nodded. "Okay. Maybe they lied about not having a kid. Does it make a difference?"

Tanya's features became pinched with thought a moment before she shrugged and said, "Not really. There was a kid that first time, too."

"And it really doesn't bother you?"

"No."

"You're sure?"

Tanya stamped a foot on the porch. "I'm fucking sure. Now let's get on with this before I lose my nerve."

Jim reached out and tapped the doorbell button. He tapped it twice, a long-standing habit dating back to early childhood. It'd been one of the first symptoms of his OCD. He always had to do lots of things twice or in multiples of two. It was a pain in the ass sometimes, but he'd learned to live with it.

The doorbell produced no sound.

Jim made a sound of aggravation and stabbed at the button with his index finger two more times, thinking he merely hadn't hit it hard enough the first time. Again, there was no sound. With the door open, the chime should have been audible from inside if it was functioning properly.

Jim grunted. "Broken."

"No shit. Try knocking."

Jim raised a hand and rapped his knuckles against the door eight times in four rapid multiples of two. He moved back a step after that, anticipating an approach of footsteps from somewhere inside at any moment. They stood there in silence for almost a full minute. Again, no sound of any kind issued from inside the house.

"This is ridiculous," Tanya said, sounding more aggravated than ever. "The door's open. We should just go on in."

Jim thought about it. They could do that, sure, but his sense that something was wrong here was growing by the moment. In the half-decade that had passed since beginning his career as a serial killer, he'd learned to trust his instincts. They were almost always right and right now they were telling him to turn around and leave this place.

And yet he hesitated.

Four months had passed since they'd killed that couple in Tallahassee. Since the start of his life as a killer, there'd only been one gap between kills longer than that, a six month stretch three years back. That break had been necessary in the wake of his most high-profile crime, the brutal slaughter of a family of four in Orlando. That had been before Tanya's entry into his life. As a team, this was by far the longest break there'd been between kills.

Jim was feeling antsy. He needed to feel that one-of-a-kind rush again. Tanya wanted it just as badly as he did. She was just playing it cool, like always, trying to make out like she didn't enjoy it the way he did. But he'd seen that look of wild glee on her face while slashing apart human bodies too many times to buy that.

"Fuck it. Let's do this."

He glanced at Tanya. She was smiling. She had a hand deep inside her purse.

The door creaked as Jim pushed it open. It was a loud creak, as if the hinges hadn't been oiled since at least the Eisenhower administration. It was a sound he'd expect from the door to some crumbling ancient estate. This struck him as strange. The house didn't seem that old, but maybe it was older than it looked.

Whatever, it didn't matter.

They were going in, anyway.

Jim pushed on the door until it was all the way open and stepped into a dark and empty foyer. He felt along the wall to his right, groping for a light switch. He found a panel with three switches and flipped up the first one. The foyer remained dark.

He tried the next two.

Again, no light.

Stranger and stranger. Those finely-honed instincts were screaming at him now. Something was definitely not right at the Quist residence. Given the interest in an extreme level of kink expressed in the Quists' online ad, a certain degree of strangeness was not a huge shock. But Michael Quist had sounded so normal on the phone. Then again, Jim was capable of coming across as very normal to regular people when he put his mind to it, so you just never knew.

The heels of Tanya's boots clicked on the foyer's hardwood floor as she followed him into the house. "What's going on?"

Jim flipped all three switches up and down eight more times to the same result. "No power," he said, giving it up at last. "Or the bulbs are all burned out."

Tanya hugged herself and shivered. "It's cold in here."

Jim frowned.

He hadn't noticed it before, but she was right. The air in the house was significantly colder than the air outside. The difference had to be a minimum of ten degrees. Maybe more like twenty degrees. He could think of no good explanation for that. If anything, the house should be warmer inside. It was just another bit of oddness in an overall pattern of oddness.

Deciding at last to listen to what his instincts were telling him, Jim glanced at Tanya and said, "Let's get the fuck out of here. Something really isn't right."

She nodded. "Sorry, baby. I know how bad you wanted this. We'll find some trashy crack whore and spend all night fucking her up. Will that make you feel a little better?"

Jim smiled. "You know, I think it will. Come on, let's go."

He took her by an elbow and they started back toward the open door. Before they could get there, the door swung shut right in front of them with astonishing force, slamming into the doorframe hard enough to make both of them flinch.

Tanya shrieked in fright. "What the fuck!?"

Jim rushed to the door and grabbed the doorknob. He tried turning it to no avail. He tried again, this time gripping it with both hands and twisting with all his might, but it was no use. It would not budge. In frustration, he pounded on the door with the base of a fist. Predictably, this also accomplished nothing.

"Wh-what's going on?" Tanya's voice sounded thin and brittle, more like the voice of an overwhelmed little girl than a grown woman. "What's happening?"

Jim kicked at the door. "I don't know. It's stuck or something."

"I'm scared."

She sounded a bit more than just scared. Frightened out of her goddamned mind was more like it. Jim turned away from the door and saw her standing in the center of the dark foyer. She had her phone out and had turned on the flashlight function. The beam projecting from the back of the phone was aimed right at his face, making him squint.

He held up a hand to block the glare. "Aim that thing somewhere else, please."

She shifted the direction of the beam and now it cast faint illumination over the base of a spiral staircase to Jim's right. "I'm so fucking scared. This place is haunted or something."

Jim's heart was pounding hard in his chest and his breath was coming in quick gasps. He was scared, too. For good reason. Something was very not right here. That was undeniable. But he couldn't help laughing at Tanya's wild assertion, which he found hysterical. "Bullshit. There's no such thing as ghosts. Somebody's fucking with us."

A sound came from somewhere else in the house. A low moan. Tanya squealed in fright again upon hearing it. The sound came again a moment later. This time Jim was sure it was tinged with a note of sensual pleasure. His gaze went to the staircase. He was pretty sure the sound had come from somewhere up there.

"Somebody's playing games, baby." Jim's elevated heart rate began to ease back into the normal zone. He was pretty sure he had a sense of what was happening now. "These people are even freakier than they let on in their ad."

Tanya made a petulant, frightened sound. "What the hell are you talking about? That door closed itself, Jim. You saw that with your own damn eyes."

Jim smirked. "I saw a trick. This is some kind of spook show game. These people are horror nerds or something. They get off on this shit. Just listen to them." He paused as he waved a hand at the staircase. Yet another of those low, sexual moans issued from upstairs. "They've already started. You wait. When we get up there, they'll be dressed as Victorian vampires or some other shit like that."

"Are you serious?"

Tanya sounded more frustrated than ever, which Jim would not have thought possible.

He chuckled. "Yeah, I'm serious. Isn't it obvious? We're supposed to go find them and join in the action. We'll probably run into more of these spook house gags on the way."

Tanya turned her phone's light beam again, illuminating her face, which was now set in a look of deep disdain. "That's the dumbest load of shit I've ever heard."

Jim shrugged. "Never said it wasn't dumb. It's just what they're into, that's all."

Tanya shook her head, the look on her face indicating that she wasn't buying it. "I don't think so. I'd almost believe you if not for this weird fucking cold. It's like on the ghost hunter shows on TV. Haunted houses have cold spots."

Jim sighed, growing weary of the inane debate over ghosts. "More tricks. They probably dialed the thermostat down as far as . . ."

A scowl twisted Tanya's features as he trailed off. "I don't think so. I don't think there's any A/C running in here. The air doesn't just feel cold. It's stale. It's . . . hey . . . what's wrong?"

She'd at last taken note of the look of alarm that had dawned on his face.

Jim shook his head, temporarily incapable of speech as his mind struggled to make sense of the thing looming up behind his girlfriend. The light from her phone made its hideous face visible in the darkness as it came closer. It was a visage of pure horror, the kind of impossible abomination that could only exist in nightmares—or so Jim would have thought if he hadn't been staring right at it.

The thing's head was huge and deformed and tinged a sickly shade of green. Large, pustulant sores further marred the sickly-looking flesh. As it came closer to Tanya, its jaw opened wide to display a mouth bristling with fangs. The stretching of the flesh caused many of the oozing sores to pop open and spray Tanya's back with pus.

Tanya had continued yelling at him, but it was just so much noise in the face of this looming monstrosity. Now she scrunched her face up in disgust as she felt the unnatural vileness spattering her back. She turned around to see what was behind her.

Too late, Jim called out a warning. "Don't!"

Tanya screamed and staggered backward a step. The creature let out a roar and opened its mouth wider, impossibly wide, its fangs becoming longer and curved. Tanya's body language suggested flight was imminent, but she didn't act quickly enough. The creature's abominable head snapped toward her, its mouth opening so wide it was able to take the entirety of her head inside its mouth. There was a crunch of bone as those knife-like fangs clacked together and severed her spine.

Jim screamed.

He opened his jacket and fumbled for the 9mm concealed in the inner pocket. The creature gave its head a savage twist. Tanya's head came away from her body. A geyser of blood shot up into the air from the neck stump. For one horrific, frozen moment, Tanya's corpse remained upright in the middle of the foyer as that spray of blood arced up toward the ceiling. Then it staggered backward a step and toppled to the floor.

Jim finally had a solid grip on the 9mm. He yanked it free of the inner pocket, tearing the pocket's lining in the process. The creature eyed him with what might have been amused contempt as it chewed on its morsel of flesh and bone. The crunching, grinding sound Jim heard as the thing ate his girlfriend's head turned Jim's stomach.

It was crazy. He was a killer. Any normal person who, upon hearing details of the things he'd done, would describe him as a madman, possibly as inhuman. A monster. But he felt real grief in the wake of Tanya's death. He'd loved her. He experienced a moment of profound regret. This was obviously some kind of cosmic punishment for the many horrible things he'd done. In that moment, at least, it was the only explanation that made any sense. Right then, he wished he could take it all back. He'd give anything to have a normal life with Tanya.

But that wasn't going to happen.

Not now.

The thing finished gulping down the last of Tanya's now thoroughly masticated head. Then it opened its mouth again and belched. A blast of putrid, hot air issued from its mouth, making Jim's eyes water from more than a dozen feet away. The creature made a sound that might have been laughter.

Then it took a step toward him.

Jim got the gun up and aimed in time to squeeze off four quick shots. Each bullet found its target, ripping bloody holes through the diseased-looking flesh. None of the wounds affected the thing in the slightest. It kept lurching forward, that hideous mouth opening wide again.

Backing away from it, Jim felt for the doorknob with his left hand and found it. He tried to turn it, but it didn't budge. In the face of such horror, he'd forgotten about the knob being frozen in place. His head snapped to the right and he again glimpsed the base of the spiral staircase. Tanya's phone was buried somewhere under her body. The only reason he could see at all was ambient light from various outdoor sources—moonlight and the glow from that streetlamp on the other side of Golden Elm—shining through the windows.

Window, he thought.

Even in the midst of grief and horror, he realized that breaking one might be his only way out of this insane predicament. First, though, he'd have to live long enough to do that. And that meant getting upstairs and away from this fucking monster.

The creature let out another roar as he made a break for the staircase. Jim fired two more shots in its direction as he hit the stairs running. Again, both bullets found flesh, one of them passing right through one of the creature's bulbous yellow eyes. Judging from the fresh roar that ensued, this was the first of the wounds to actually hurt it.

Suck on that, you ugly fuck, Jim thought.

Jim was breathing heavily as he reached the second-floor landing after vaulting up the stairs two at a time. He took a quick look around. There wasn't much to see. Significantly less of that ambient lighting was filtering through to this smaller second level. He felt his way around and arrived at a door to the room he was pretty sure had those windows facing the yard. He meant to get in there, break out one of those windows—shoot it out, if necessary—and shimmy down to the yard.

A thunderous sound from below made Jim yelp in fright. The creature was clumsily tromping its way up the winding staircase.

Jim sighed in relief as the door to the room opened easily. He closed it behind him as he entered the room. The door was equipped with a basic lock. He turned it, despite knowing that the flimsy lock and plywood door would be no more effective at keeping the monster out than a sheet of rice paper.

Turning away from the door, he spied the window he'd noted from outside earlier. That had only been a few moments ago, which struck him as surreal. Those few moments felt like a lifetime. He started toward the window, but froze in his tracks when the little girl materialized directly in front of him. One moment she hadn't been there, then she was. Jim flashed back to Tanya's assertion that she'd seen a child peering out at them. He'd been sure she was seeing things, but apparently not.

"Get out of my way, kid. I don't want to have to hurt you."

Another thunderous, earthshaking sound came from right outside the door as the creature arrived on the second-floor landing.

"We are 138 Golden Elm Lane."

Jim frowned. "What?"

And now he was aware of other presences in the room. He glanced around and saw wispy forms emerging from the shadows. Some looked more solid than others. A few of the apparitions were dressed in old-timey outfits, while others wore more modern clothes. Some looked barely there at all, like faded remnants of things lost long ago. They were saying things. No. That wasn't right.

It was all the same thing.

We are 138 Golden Elm Lane.

"We are 138 Golden Elm Lane," the little girl told him again, giggling. "And now so are you."

And that was when she plunged the knife deep into his belly.

Jim thought, *No, no. I can't die. I can't die.*

But then he did.

The next morning two men stood on the sidewalk outside 138 Golden Elm and stared at the house where the serial-killing couple had gone to their demise. These men knew two human beings had died in the house the previous night, but they knew nothing of the couple's background. As far as they knew, the two had been complete innocents, just like most victims of 138 Golden Elm.

These men were Tom Clifton and Michael Everett. Both men were long-time residents of Golden Elm. They had raised their families here. They had lived prosperous, happy lives here. But that happiness came with a price.

Tom scratched his chin and let out a breath. "The key will be in the mailbox like usual, I guess."

Michael nodded. "Should be. Whose turn is it to get rid of the car?"

His was the voice Jim Matthews would have identified as belonging to the fictional "Michael Quist".

Tom grimaced. "Mine, I think."

Michael glanced at him. "I can do it if you'd rather."

Tom shook his head. "No, it's my turn. We do this right. We do our part. I'll ditch the car. You go online and pull that ad."

Michael shrugged. "Yeah, okay. Until next time, anyway."

Tom grunted. "Right. Until it's hungry again."

Both men stared at the long-unoccupied—by living humans, any-way—house of death another moment. They didn't like doing any of this, but it was part of the sealed-in-blood deal they'd made so long ago. For better or worse, they were bound to it for life. Until they were dead and others were lured into taking their place.

Tom went to the mailbox and opened it.

The keys to the Audi were waiting.

THE BARREL

AUTHOR'S NOTE: A little bit of *Black Mirror* and a little bit of the EC Comics inspiration. Plus Satan.

THE BARREL WAS IN HIS backyard when Martin Sanchez got up to let his dogs out that morning. He'd had a few drinks the night before—okay, maybe more than a few—and had stumbled bleary-eyed and still half asleep through the kitchen on the way to the back door. He glimpsed the barrel as he got the door open and let the dancing, antsy dogs outside. In the grip of that deep grogginess, however, its presence initially did not register at the forefront of his consciousness. He'd seen it, but not seen it. Not really. Not yet.

He closed the screen door and left the inner door open as he turned away from the view of the yard and the scampering dogs. One of them—it sounded like Hank—was already barking at something. Probably a squirrel up in one of the trees that lined the other side of the tall privacy fence surrounding his property. Ignoring this, he sleepily fumbled with his refrigerator's door handle a moment before getting a grip on it and hauling it open. That accomplished, he rubbed at his eyes and stared in at the fridge's severely depleted contents.

Martin sighed heavily.

The fridge was a kind of metaphor for the current state of his life—nearly empty and devoid of anything truly nourishing. It'd been different before the divorce. The fridge had always been fully-stocked with all the staples when Carol was still around. Condiments, lunch

160

meats, various cheeses, vegetables, and the full array of hearty break-fast foods. She'd seen to all of that every week without fail. He'd barely even thought of it back then. Things were so much simpler—open fridge, find whatever you needed, go on with your life. The way things were supposed to be.

Now, though, all he saw were some stray bottles of beer—lefto-vers from various six-packs purchased over the last few weeks—a bottle of ketchup, and a clear plastic container of cheap cheese dip. What Martin really wanted was a heaping plate of eggs, bacon, and pancakes. Unfortunately, if he wanted to eat, he'd probably have to settle for cheese dip and some stale leftover tortilla chips. There was a week-old bag of Tostitos in one of the cupboards. He could have that. He was hungry.

But not quite that hungry.

Making a mental note to go to the store later that afternoon, Mar-tin grabbed one of the beers from the fridge and flipped the refriger-ator door shut. After twisting the cap off the longneck bottle, it slipped from his grasp and clattered to the dirty floor. He stared at it a moment in groggy irritation before kicking it under the fridge.

Hank was still barking outside. He was being really loud. Louder than usual. Martin groaned and took a deep slug of beer. The last thing he wanted was for old Mr. Sloan to come over and start bitching about the noise. He shuffled over to the screen door and peered through the window.

He was a little more awake now thanks to the rejuvenating dose of hair of the dog and this time the presence of the barrel truly regis-tered. The dogs weren't barking at squirrels. Instead they had their teeth bared and their hackles up as they stood on opposite sides of the barrel and growled and barked. Martin had the lip of the bottle poised at his mouth for another swig, but now he lowered it as a look of confusion began to twist his features.

"Huh. That's weird."

Weird was perhaps an understatement. The barrel looked like one of those big metal oil drums. It was all black and it was sitting on the ground about fifteen feet away from the back stoop. Martin had no idea where it had come from or who might have left it there. The one thing he did know was it had not been there the last time he'd let the dogs outside, which had been around two in the morning.

Its inexplicable presence was just one component of the overall weirdness of the situation. Another was the behavior of the dogs. The

German Shepherds were acting as if they'd cornered a malevolent intruder. He couldn't fathom why they were freaking out over an inanimate object. He was troubled by the thing's unexpected arrival in his backyard, but that was because he knew it shouldn't be there. Someone—some stranger, possibly—had come onto his property while he was sleeping and put this thing there. It was scary. But Hank and Lucille were dogs. They couldn't know it didn't belong there.

Or could they?

He knew better than to underestimate the perceptive ability of dogs. He'd owned dogs all his life. They picked up on more than people realized. Maybe there was something in the barrel they didn't like. The longer he observed them, the more likely this seemed. Martin tried to imagine any non-troublesome explanation for that and couldn't come up with anything.

The barrel was just sitting there, but the dogs were becoming steadily more agitated. They crouched and dug their claws into the ground. Hank started barking again, louder than before. He looked almost frenzied, like a rabid junkyard dog.

Martin opened the screen door and held it open as he stepped out onto the back stoop. He put his fingers to his mouth and let out a loud whistle. "Hank! Lucy! Come the fuck inside!"

The dogs glanced his way, but they remained where they were and resumed growling. Martin raised his voice and shifted to his "I mean business" tone as he yelled at them again. This time they came away from the barrel, but they did it slowly, with obvious reluctance. Hank in particular glanced back at it several times on his way to the stoop.

Martin hurried them inside and closed the screen door. He heard them whimper as he stood on the stoop and eyed the mystery barrel a while longer. He took another big gulp of cheap lager and tried to figure out what to do about the thing.

The barrel and its contents—if any—might well be harmless, but there was no guarantee of that. He could think of no reason why anyone he knew would put the barrel in his backyard. For all he knew, it might contain a body. Or an explosive device. Those things seemed wildly implausible, but how could he know for sure without peeking inside?

Ah, but therein existed the conundrum. In the unlikely event the barrel did contain a body, he risked contaminating any evidence if he touched it. Doing so might even cast suspicion on him. Leaving the thing the hell alone and calling the police was the obvious answer to this dilemma. Let them open it up and see what was inside it. That way, there'd be no risk to him and he wouldn't wind up smearing his DNA all over the goddamn thing.

This made perfect sense, yet for some reason he continued to linger here on the stoop rather than going back inside to fetch his phone and place a call to 911. His curiosity was growing the longer he stood out here and stared at the barrel. There was something compelling about it that went beyond the obvious, beyond what he could see, an indefinable something that tickled something in his subconscious mind.

Martin glanced down and saw that he'd moved to the edge of the stoop without being aware of it. He frowned as that tingly something in his subconscious became more pronounced. This was accompanied by a nervous sensation in his gut, a feeling similar to the butterflies he'd experienced when asking girls out as a teenager. There was a strange sense of yearning in it. Martin had no idea why that might be.

At first.

On further reflection, he thought maybe the feeling was rooted entirely in the unexpectedness of the object. For many years, everything about his life had played out in ways that rarely contained any element of genuine surprise. Even the disintegration of his marriage was something he'd seen coming from years back. The actual serving of divorce papers had been almost anticlimactic. He was an ordinary guy living the most ordinary, unremarkable life possible. But now here was this thing, this fucking barrel, and it was calling to him.

Martin glanced down again.

He'd moved down a step, again without being aware of having done so. Just one more step remained between his feet and the ground. The alluring element of the mystery aside, this was odd and disturbing. It was almost as if the thing was actively drawing him toward it, as if it had projected a kind of psychical tractor beam, one that had hooked into his body and soul and was drawing him inexorably forward. Sounded absurd on the surface, but that was how it felt.

To prove to himself he remained in control of his body and will, he took a deliberate step back up onto the stoop. Once he was there, he stared at the barrel a moment longer and downed the rest of the beer. That tingly sensation was still there, but it was slightly diminished. It was hard not to take this as confirmation that the power of the barrel's pull increased with physical proximity. This in no way eased his fears about the thing, but that strange sense of nebulous yearning remained.

Martin went inside and closed the screen door. He again left the inner door open so he could continue his observation of the barrel. The pull of the thing remained palpable, but it wasn't as strong from inside the house. He tried to convince himself what he'd felt was imaginary, the result of a combination of lingering grogginess and a general feeling of unsettledness caused by the thing's mysterious arrival. This sounded every bit as sensible as the inclination to call the police, but somehow he couldn't quite fully buy it.

Something else was happening here, he was sure of it. Something . . . strange.

After tossing the empty in the trash, Martin grabbed another beer from the fridge, screwed off the cap, and took a big swig. He'd done this without thinking, which seemed to be the emerging trend of the day. It wasn't uncommon for him to have a little hair of the dog the morning after knocking back a bunch of brews, but it almost always stopped there. He wasn't some raving alcoholic who required a steady influx of booze to keep functioning throughout the day. Yet something in him was telling him today was different. Today he would need the comfort of at least a mild buzz to get through what was ahead.

Hank was growling again.

The dog was standing at the screen door and staring out at the barrel. His hackles were still up and he was quivering with either excitement or fear, maybe both. Lucille was whimpering from somewhere behind him.

Martin took another slug of beer. "You guys calm down. This is nothing to get excited about. It's just a fucking barrel."

The dogs seemed unmoved by this sentiment. Hank kept on with the growling while Lucille paced and panted. Thinking to soothe the animal closest to him with a reassuring touch, Martin reached down to stroke Hank's back. The dog flinched at the touch and the volume of his growling increased.

"Okay, okay," Martin said, sighing. "I'll do something about the fucking thing. Just give me a minute."

Taking the beer with him, he went to his bedroom and retrieved his phone from the nightstand. The screen lit up when he hit the home button, displaying a message that informed him of a missed call and a voicemail. His heart raced as he recognized the number.

It was Carol's number. He hadn't heard from his ex-wife in months. She was off having a high old time with her new boyfriend, a much younger guy named Nathan. A fucking pretty boy. The last thing she'd said to him was she never wanted to talk to him or see him again.

Now this.

Maybe she'd had a change of heart. Maybe the whole thing with Nathan had soured after the initial whirlwind and now she was ready to give him a second chance. He was surprised at how badly he wished for this. Even though he'd seen it coming, her exit from his life had hurt him deeply. Also, being alone was just a drag in general. Given the chance, he'd take her back in a heartbeat, he knew it.

Heart hammering, he pushed the voicemail button and put the phone to his ear. "Hello, asshole," came Carol's familiar voice. He flinched at her harsh tone and felt a new churning in his gut. "You'll be served papers by the end of the day. I'm going for bigger alimony payments, you piece of shit. Much bigger. I recommend you agree to the terms without a fight." She laughed. "Unless you want me to flood your family's inboxes with those pictures from your, ahem, 'experimental' phase. You know the ones I mean."

She laughed again and the recording ended.

A wave of disappointment assailed Martin as he took the phone away from his ear and stared at it a moment. He couldn't believe what he'd just heard. During their marriage, Carol had never spoken to him so nastily. Not once. He couldn't understand it.

He also couldn't afford significantly higher alimony payments. Slightly higher, maybe, but not anything like what she seemed to be suggesting in the message. And yet the threat was real. Those pictures existed. For a moment, Martin felt on the verge of a panic attack.

In the next moment, he heaved a breath and told himself to calm down. He chugged down the rest of that second beer and went back out to the kitchen, where he took a third beer from the fridge and joined Hank at the screen door.

The dog glanced up at him. Martin read a sense of fear in the animal's eyes. He was still agitated, but he was afraid of the barrel and was hoping his master could make the perceived threat go away.

Martin scratched the dog's neck. "Don't worry, buddy. I'm gonna take care of this. Move aside."

He nudged Hank out of the way and went back out onto the

stoop, closing the screen door again. The barrel was still there. A part of him had half-expected it to be gone, revealed after all as a figment of diminished, drowsy perception. For better or worse, that was not the case.

After taking another big gulp from the third beer, Martin let out a breath and stepped down from the stoop. That prickling in his brain returned, as did the tingle in his gut. His brow creased as a new perception came, an impression that the barrel was bigger than he'd first thought. In the next instant, however, he realized this wasn't true. It just seemed larger. In a repeat of his previous experience, he'd moved closer to the barrel without being conscious of it.

This was undeniably disturbing.

And yet this time he felt no inclination to resist whatever was happening. That sense of deep yearning was back, stronger than before. He felt a prickling along his arms as gooseflesh rose and hairs stood up. There was a thrumming undercurrent of strange electricity in the air, like before a big storm.

Only there were no dark clouds in the sky.

Martin chugged down the last of the third beer and tossed the empty to the ground. A dim, disconnected part of him made a note to pick it up later.

The barrel was calling to him.

It was here for him. Specifically for him.

Only for him.

After reaching the barrel, he moved around it in a slow circle, squinting as he examined it closely. There wasn't much to see, really, nothing additional he couldn't have ascertained from the stoop. The barrel was entirely black. There were no markings at all, no brand symbol, nothing like that.

The pull of the barrel was stronger now. Much stronger. The sensation enveloped him, consumed him, obliterating any remaining tiny shred of resistance. He crept closer still, leaning over it to examine the lid. As he did this, he saw that it was not entirely devoid of markings after all.

Something in a tiny white font was printed along the edge of the lid. The sense of excitement gripping him intensified. He was sure this was significant, the first real hint of why the barrel was here. Logic said this was probably just a company name printed on the lid, but that prickling in his brain was telling him something else.

He put his face closer to the lid and squinted. This is what he read:

#blackbarrel

After staring at the tiny letters without moving a muscle or making a sound for at least one full minute as his face registered an ever-deepening confusion, Martin stood up straight and looked at his phone. He swiped at the screen and pulled up the rarely used Twitter app. Unlike his ex-wife, Martin had never been a big social media user. A quick glance at his profile showed that nearly two years had gone by since he'd last tweeted anything. He had twelve followers—all of them either relatives or co-workers—and he was following twenty-eight people, most of them celebrities.

Though he was never going to be anyone's idea of a social influencer—not even close—he did recognize a hashtag when he saw one and he knew what to do with it. A few seconds after opening the app, Martin Sanchez sent out the following tweet:

BadAzzSanchez: #blackbarrel WTF!?

A response to the tweet arrived almost instantaneously in the form of a direct message:

BB999: Black Barrel is a gift.

Martin stared at the screen and frowned. The response came so fast it couldn't have come from an actual person. It had to be an auto-response. He highly doubted the mystery of the barrel could be solved by interacting with a fucking bot, but the fact that the interaction had happened at all elevated his excitement level. At the very least, he now had a strong indication that the barrel's appearance here wasn't as random as he'd first surmised.

It was a gift, according to this thing, but who had sent it to him and what did it contain? These were the essential questions he'd had from the start, but now they were invested with a deeper level of mystery. Despite his lingering confusion, the existence of an apparently official Twitter account did a lot to make the thing seem less sinister. This was some kind of internet thing, some new creative form of gift-giving. He'd heard of such things.

Martin figured its forbidding outward appearance was intentionally misleading. The barrel was most likely filled with a hodgepodge of novelty and joke items. Maybe there would be some kind of supposedly hilarious theme to it all. The more he thought about it, the more sense this made. He could almost see some of his co-workers getting together and pooling their resources to have something like this sent to his house.

Some of the guys had attempted to cheer him up in the wake of the split with Carol, inviting him out for drinks and such. He didn't consider those guys especially close friends—they didn't come over to the house for Sunday football or anything like that—but, sure, it was possible, maybe even likely.

He had some of their numbers in his contacts. A call or two might have this situation sorted out in just a few minutes. He figured he'd wind up doing just that, but first he wanted to see what additional information, if any, he could extract from the bot.

Tapping rapidly at the screen, he replied directly to the DM.

BadAzzSanchez: What the fuck is this thing and the fuck am I supposed to do with it?

Again, the response was instantaneous.

BB999: Black Barrel is a gift. Open the barrel.

More tapping on the screen, followed by the ensuing exchange.

BadAzzSanchez: What's in the goddamn thing?
BB999: Black Barrel is a gift.
BadAzzSanchez: You already said that. Will it blow up in my fucking face?
BB999: Black Barrel will not harm you. Black Barrel is a gift.
BadAzzSanchez: Who sent it?
BB999: Black Barrel is a gift.

By that point, Martin felt like screaming. He was going round and round with the bot and not getting much of anywhere, except for the information that the barrel would not harm him. This should have been reassuring, as it fit with his latest line of thinking. What didn't fit with any of that, however, was that sense of having been physically pulled toward the barrel by some invisible force. Your standard internet gag didn't have that kind of capability.

Martin sighed and tapped at the screen again.

BadAzzSanchez: Okay, Black Barrel is a gift. Who sent the gift?
BB999: A friend.
BadAzzSanchez: Which fucking friend?
BB999: Black Barrel is a gift.

This time Martin did scream. The sound was so loud and shrill it alarmed old Mr. Sloan's Golden Retriever, which barked from the other side of the privacy fence. His own dogs barked and whimpered in response. This was followed by an extended round of back and forth barking, which became increasingly agitated.

Ignoring the growing canine cacophony, Martin tapped at the phone's screen yet again.

BadAzzSanchez: Fine. Don't tell me. Fuck you.
BB999: Black Barrel is a gift. Open Black Barrel.

Sighing in resignation, Martin dropped the phone in the pocket of his bathrobe. It was clear he'd learned all he could from the bot. He gnawed on his bottom lip as he stared at the barrel and continued to ponder what to do. The strange undercurrent of power emanating from the thing was just as palpable as ever. That was still somewhat disturbing. In the wake of his interaction with the bot, however, his fear level remained at a low ebb.

Holding his breath, he reached out to the barrel with a tentative, slightly shaking hand and touched the lid. The pull of the thing again intensified with the physical contact, but this didn't frighten him. He felt suffused with a warmth and deep peacefulness, the likes of which he hadn't experienced in years, maybe decades.

Martin dug his fingernails underneath the edge of the lid and pulled at it with all his strength, but he was unable to budge it. After stepping back and staring at it in consternation for a long moment, he went back into the house, grabbing his keys as he went out to his car, which was parked in the driveway. There was a beep as he hit a button on the key fob. The trunk lid popped up as he arrived at the rear of the car. It took a bit of rooting around in the junk-crowded trunk, but he soon found what he wanted.

After closing the trunk, he marched back through the house and back out into the backyard. Hank tried to squeeze through the screen door with him, but Martin held him back and closed the door. Both of his dogs whimpered from the kitchen. He could feel their anxious canine stares on his back as he descended from the stoop to the ground. Martin wished they could feel what he'd felt upon touching the barrel. Their fears would go away. Maybe later, after he'd opened the barrel and learned its secrets, he'd bring them out here and gently coerce them into touching it. He smiled as he pictured Hank sloppily lapping at the barrel with his big tongue, a wide doggy grin on his face.

Martin wedged the claw end of the crowbar beneath the edge of the lid, pushing it in as far as he could. Once he'd done this, he gripped the other end firmly with both hands and pushed down as hard as he could. The lid did not yield easily to the pressure—the seal was tighter than the most stubborn pickle jar lid by a factor of about a thousand—but it did finally begin to come away from the top of the barrel.

His face shining with sweat, Martin cranked the crowbar up and down a few more times and finally the lid came free with a loud pop. Heaving a big breath, he tossed the crowbar aside and wiped sweat from his forehead.

Well, this is it, he thought. *Time to see what's inside this bugger.*

Before he could lean over it and peek inside, he felt a vibration in the pocket of his bathrobe. Frowning, he took the phone out and stared at the screen. A Twitter alert told him he had a new DM from BB999.

Martin grunted. "Huh. That's weird."

The bot couldn't possibly know he'd removed the lid. Could it? It was just a piece of computer code, not a person. But maybe there was some kind of hidden sensor embedded in the barrel. Maybe the sensor had sent out a signal as soon as the lid was removed.

Martin nodded.

Made sense. Sort of.

He opened the Twitter app and looked at the DM.

BB999: Black Barrel is everything you ever wanted.
BadAzzSanchez: We'll see about that.

Martin dropped the phone back in his pocket and leaned over the barrel. His brow knitted in confusion as he lowered his head and peered inside. He stood there with his hands on his knees, studying the barrel's interior for several minutes.

It was empty.

He saw no gag gifts. No bottles of whiskey or tins of artisan cheeses. There was nothing. The barrel's metal interior was spotless. It looked fresh off the production line, as if it had never contained anything at all. A thought occurred to him. Maybe the barrel's emptiness was the gag, a lame 21st century equivalent to pet rocks or some shit like that. He hoped that wasn't the case. What a rip-off that would be. And yet the barrel's emptiness was impossible to deny. There just wasn't anything in the damn thing.

Nothing he could see, anyway.

The strange, thrumming power that continued to emanate from the barrel was the only reason he didn't immediately give up on it. In fact, he felt it more strongly than ever now. Something he couldn't see, something inside the barrel, was still pulling at him.

The phone buzzed in his pocket again. He took it out and was unsurprised to see a new DM.

BB999: Black Barrel is everything you ever wanted.

BadAzzSanchez: I never wanted an empty barrel so I'm pretty sure that's a load of shit.

BB999: Black Barrel is everything you ever wanted. What do you want most, Martin Sanchez?

Martin's eyes widened and his grip tightened on the phone as he read these words.

They know my fucking name! What the fuck!?

He took a few deep breaths and started to calm down. This wasn't anything ominous. Of course they knew his name. The asshole (or assholes) who'd paid for this thing would have provided that information. He let out another big breath and reread the question posed by the Black Barrel bot. That wave of soothing warmth continued to flow from the barrel, further easing his anxiety.

What do I want most, huh?

He thought about that for a while. For quite a few minutes, in fact. He wanted a lot of things. They were the things everybody wanted. Love. Money. Happiness. An array of cool material things. Boats. Fast cars. A bigger house. Season tickets to his favorite teams. Hell, scratch that. His own private luxury box at the football stadium and the hockey arena. Hey, why not dream big? It was all fantasy bullshit, anyway.

The power flowing from the barrel seemed to rev up for a

moment. It again raised gooseflesh on his forearms and stirred the air around him. Martin heard Hank's paws scrabbling against the screen door's window. He was barking again. It was a shrill bark, filled with terror.

Then the power cut off abruptly.

Martin shivered as he felt the air around him go still. A single dead leaf from one of the nearby trees fluttered lazily to the ground. The dogs were still whimpering a bit, but they were no longer barking in that shrill, panicked way. After eyeing it warily for some moments, Martin again touched the barrel.

Nothing happened.

Not even the faintest flicker of its former power. It was just a barrel. A simple metal construct. Probably that's all it'd ever been. Yet he knew what he'd felt. That had been real enough, but perhaps it'd been some kind of trickery, a current of electricity—or whatever—generated by some cheap device embedded in the metal itself. This seemed unlikely, but what other rational explanation could there be?

Martin kicked the barrel.

A dull clang resonated inside it.

Shaking his head, Martin went back into his house and spent some time consoling his dogs, who were very happy to have him inside again and away from the barrel.

The calls started coming in about an hour later.

First he heard from his boss. The guy had always been kind of indifferent to him. Cordial, but nothing more. Now, suddenly, he was Martin's number one fan. He wanted to offer him a new position at the company, a top management spot. Never mind that he didn't have the proper experience. He could learn on the job. Martin didn't know what to make of any aspect of this. He didn't know which was stranger, the offer itself or the boss man's effusive praise of his job performance, which Martin himself knew rated only a hair or two above the merely adequate.

Martin told the man he'd have to think about it and hung up on him.

Next came the call from Carol. She was a tearful mess. First she told him to tear up the court papers when they came. She wouldn't be going forward with the case. Then she told him about Nathan. He'd just gotten a call from his doctor. The results of some routine tests had come back with some not so routine results. He only had weeks to live. After hearing the devastating news, Nathan tearfully confessed he was only with her for the money and had secretly been fucking a bunch of guys behind her back. At that point in her accounting of events, Carol broke down in hysterics and begged Martin to take her back.

Smiling as he spoke in a semi-consoling tone, Martin said, "Aw, that's too bad, baby. We'll get together for coffee or something and talk about it. Or whatever. Next week maybe."

He hung up on her.

And so it continued throughout the afternoon. Call after call from colleagues, friends, and acquaintances, all of whom inexplicably wanted to offer him things. Money. Tickets to major events. A night out on the town, all expenses paid. A smoking hot female coworker called and confessed to having a major crush on him. She offered to come over and allow him the use of her body. He could do whatever he wanted to her. Or she could do any freaky thing he wanted her to do to him. "Anything goes," she told him.

He gave her his address and told her to come over later that night. Then he hung up on her.

He looked at Hank and Lucille, who were curled up on the floor in front of him in the living room. Hank lifted his head and eyed Martin in a way that could be interpreted as vaguely reproachful.

Martin grunted. "You know what's weird, buddy? I don't remember ever giving that gal my number. Oh, well. Whatever."

Later that afternoon, Martin went down to the corner store and bought a Powerball ticket. The jackpot was over $300 million and rising. He was feeling lucky and considered buying more than one ticket. In the end, he bought just the one. Whatever was happening here, luck had nothing to do with it. This was the right ticket, the only one he would need.

The knockout coworker came over that night and did every freaky thing he asked her to do, including a few that might have been borderline illegal. At the end of the long, exhausting romp, he told her he intended to take her to Vegas in a few days and marry her. She did not object to this idea.

The next day came the news that a single winning Powerball ticket had been sold. The entire jackpot would go to the ticketholder. Martin was unsurprised to learn that the ticket had been sold at a store down the street from where he lived. That the winning numbers matched the numbers on his ticket also did not come as a surprise.

Martin called the state lottery office and made arrangements to come in the following day.

Immediately after hanging up with the lottery office, his phone buzzed. He stared at the screen and felt his pulse rate quicken. A new DM had come in from BB999. He swiped at the screen, tapped on the app, and saw the following message:

BB999: Monetary cost for services rendered is $666.66.

Martin laughed. "Of course."
He tapped at the screen.

BadAzzSanchez: No problem. How do I submit payment?
BB999: PayPal amount to bb999@gmail.com.
BadAzzSanchez: I'll do it tonight.
BB999: Spiritual cost for services rendered is 100 souls.

Martin frowned. "Huh. That's weird."
More screen tapping, then . . .

BadAzzSanchez: 100 souls?
BB999: Correct.
BadAzzSanchez: I mean, I'll sign over my own soul, no problem. It'd be worth it. But 100? How do I do that?
BB999: You must harvest 100 souls within a 6 year period or all will be taken away.
BadAzzSanchez: How in fuck do I 'harvest' 100 souls?
BB999: Simple. Kill 100 people.

A deep chill went through Martin as he read these words. Not because of moral qualms. He was past that. No, his hesitation stemmed from other, more practical matters. Killing that many people in that short a time frame would be a lot of work. Messy work. Moreover, he didn't see how he could pull it off without getting caught.

He resumed tapping on the screen.

BadAzzSanchez: I'll get caught. I don't want to go to jail.
BB999: You will be protected. You will face no serious consequences in the mortal realm.

By now Martin was pretty sure he was no longer talking to a bot. There was an intelligence behind this interaction and not an artificial one.

BadAzzSanchez: You sent the barrel, didn't you? Not a friend.
BB999: Yes. But we are friends. Black Barrel is a gift. The greatest gift of all.

Martin hesitated before tapping the screen again, swallowing a lump in his throat before sending the next message.

BadAzzSanchez: Are you Satan?
BB999: I am legion. Click the following link to digitally sign form and accept spiritual price.

Martin tried eliciting more information from the other user, but each time the only response was a repetition of the last message with the link. After thinking about it for a solid ten minutes, he shrugged and thought, fuck it. He clicked the link and signed where indicated.

A final DM came from BB999.

He read it and sighed.

Should've seen that coming, I guess.

On a whim, he went out to his backyard.

The barrel was still there. He needed to put the thing in his basement, at least until he was able to move into the secluded mansion he meant to purchase with his lottery winnings. When he moved, the barrel would have its own room. A special place, sort of a shrine kind of thing.

The last DM from BB999 had read: Black Barrel is a receptacle. Fill it with 100 human hearts.

He figured he'd have to keep an assload of incense burning in that special room at all times.

Hank and Lucille had come outside with him. Lucille was off loping around the yard, looking for a place to squat and take a shit. Hank sat on his haunches next to Martin on the stoop. The dog's eyes turned a dark shade of crimson as his owner scratched his neck.

Once Lucille was done taking care of business, Martin and the dogs went back inside.

Tina, his wife-to-be, was where he'd left her earlier, lying naked on the bed and awaiting his renewed interest. She sat up with a big smile on her gorgeous face as he came into the room.

"Darling!" she exclaimed with a squeal. "Are you ready to fuck me again?"

"In a little while," Martin replied, as he started pulling on going out clothes. "Meanwhile, I've got a question for you."

"Anything for you, baby."

We'll see about that.

"How would you like to go cruising the bad part of town with me?"

"Slumming it can be fun."

Martin smiled. "How about if he we pick up a hooker and ritually sacrifice her soul to Satan? I'm not joking, by the way."

Tina was still smiling as she slid off the bed and came to him, mashing her beautiful naked body against him. "Sounds like a good time to me."

Martin kissed her. "You're perfect. Do you know that?"

Tina giggled and kissed him back.

A few minutes later, they were on the road, headed for a part of the city inhabited largely by its less fortunate citizens. Martin knew of a likely place for picking up prostitutes. Not because he had any experience in that area, but because he'd seen a story on the news. And offing a hooker seemed like a good way to get his feet wet in this whole harvesting souls for Satan business.

He sighed at the thought.

He had a lot of work ahead of him. A *hell* of a lot of work.

AUTHOR'S NOTE: Lots of EC Comics-style horror in most of these stories, even more so than usual. With the exception of "South County Madman", they were short and to-the-point by design.

TAKE A WALK

UNTIL THAT NIGHT, PAUL MALDONADO had never gone for walks around his neighborhood. Not during the daytime and certainly not in the midst of the lonely wee hours of the early morning. But he was bored at what felt like an almost terminal level. Bored with everything on the TV. Bored with the vast selection of streaming music available on Spotify. He was even bored shitless with the internet, sick unto death of surfing through the same fucking websites dozens of times a day every damn day.

But Paul's boredom extended well beyond the array of entertainment choices available to him. Months had passed since the end of his latest failed relationship. With Sophia gone, the house was achingly silent, especially at night, and as a lifelong night owl, he was always up and at loose ends during the loneliest hours of the day. He felt like the walls were closing in on him. He was depressed, which was unusual for him. He'd always been a cheery, upbeat guy, but now the occasional suicidal thought was intruding on his consciousness, which was pretty disturbing.

Something had to give.

And so it was that at just past one in the morning on that night in early June, Paul switched off the TV he'd been staring blankly at for hours, grabbed his keys, and walked out of his house. After locking the door behind him, he stepped down from his porch, strolled out to the street, and took a look around.

The residential street was very quiet at that hour. A streetlight blazed almost directly overhead, illuminating a wide swath of pavement and adjoining yards. The yards were mostly well-tended. His own lawn was the sole exception. The grass was overgrown and should have been mown at least a week ago. A plastic white grocery bag was lodged in a shrub next to his front door. Glancing at it now, it looked like a weird little apparition floating in the darkness, a slightly unsettling impression standing out here in the empty silence.

Paul lived in an area adjacent to the hipster haven of east Nashville. Somewhere out there not too far in the distance was an array of coffee houses, bars, restaurants, and tattoo parlors catering to young douchebags who listened to boring bands, sported excessive amounts of facial hair, and wore stupid nad-squeezing jeans. Paul hated them all.

A turn to the right would take him in the direction of all that commerce. Many of the businesses—if not most of them—would be closed at this hour. Still, he was most likely to encounter other nighttime wanderers by going that way, so Paul went in the opposite direction.

He reached the end of his block in less than a minute, stopping at the intersection of Rosedale and Triumph. Triumph was the crossing street. It was also the name of a band he vaguely remembered from his youth. Well, he remembered the name. He couldn't remember whether they were any good or not. Not that it mattered. Nothing really seemed to matter anymore.

Paul took a right at Triumph and continued his walk. He'd gone two blocks in that direction when he became aware of the footsteps behind him. Right away he detected an attempt at stealth. The footsteps were faint, yet they almost matched his own step-for-step. There was a sense of the deliberate about this, as if the person following him was doing it as a way of masking the sound. He tried telling himself this was just paranoia stirred by the lateness of the hour, the lack of any other visible human presence in the area, and the dead silence that otherwise dominated the night.

Maybe he wasn't even hearing the footsteps of a follower.

Maybe it was just some kind of weird echo.

Paul quickened his pace. The abruptness of this led to a disruption of the pace-matching and immediately made it clear that what he was hearing was no echo. Once the footsteps behind him fell out of rhythm with his own, they became more discernible. Not only could he hear that someone was definitely following him, but his pursuer was closer than he'd first surmised. From the sound of it, the follower might be as little as ten longish paces to his rear.

He was moving through a dark section of Triumph, passing beneath the low-hanging branches of a tree. The tree was on the other side of a tall privacy fence, but the branches extended out over the sidewalk. Paul started to get scared for the first time as he ducked his head to avoid the branches and momentarily moved through an even deeper patch of darkness.

The footsteps of the follower quickened.

Fuck this.

Paul stood erect again as he cleared the branches. There was another streetlight at the end of Triumph, about another block ahead.

A low, insidious voice whispered behind his back, "Come here, you. Come taste my steel."

A sinister chuckle followed.

Paul didn't bother with a backward glance. That voice and the evil chuckle were all the confirmation he needed. He'd unknowingly put himself on a wandering psycho's radar screen.

He took off running.

Paul heard heavier footsteps behind him as the follower gave chase.

At the end of the block, Triumph intersected with a street called Blakemore. Triumph ended here. Paul could only go left or right, not straight ahead. There was no time to think about it or strategize. He turned left simply because it was the opposite of what he'd done last time.

He'd gone less than twenty feet down Blakemore when he decided to finally risk a glance over his shoulder. No one was behind him on this stretch of sidewalk, but he heard the follower coming, the unknown crazy person's shoes slapping hard against the concrete.

Paul made an impulsive decision to dive behind a bush at the front of the small lawn to his left. He peeked through its thin branches as the follower came pounding down the sidewalk. The racing dark figure zipped right by the bush and continued on another dozen paces or so before slowing and then coming to a halt.

The man stood on the sidewalk, turning in a slow circle as he searched the vicinity for signs of Paul. The man was tall and dressed all in black. A knife with a long blade that gleamed in the glow of the streetlight was clutched in his gloved right hand. He wore a black ski mask, but the mask did not obscure how puzzled the man was. Despite his terror—and despite the scary way his heart was slamming in his chest—Paul almost smiled.

In fact, after another moment, he did smile.

He was still scared, of course. The stranger might yet spot the medium-sized bush and deduce the likely location of his quarry. But now another sound had arisen in the night. It was the growing buzz of an engine and not a small one. Paul saw it coming from a block away. A mass transit bus was barreling down Blakemore. Even from this distance, Paul could see it was nearly empty, which was not surprising at this hour.

The psycho was facing the street as the bus approached, scanning the lawns of the houses on the opposite side for signs of his vanished prey. Acting on impulse, Paul slipped out from behind the bush and rushed toward the psycho. At first he moved in a fast crouch. Then he was standing erect and running. He reached the masked predator at just the right moment.

The man let out a sound of surprise audible even over the loud buzz of the engine as Paul rammed the heels of his hands into the man's back and sent him staggering out into the street. There was a loud splat of impact as the man's body met the front of the bus. A louder squelch of brakes followed as the masked man's body went flying down the street, skidding dozens of feet and leaving a wet, red smear on the pavement.

Paul was already running away by the time the driver got out of the bus to check on the dead man. Two days later local news outlets revealed that he was the notorious Nightside Slasher, who'd been intermittently taking victims in east Nashville for several years. This briefly imbued Paul with a glow of civic pride. He'd rid the world of a deadly menace. He was kind of a hero.

There was just one problem—the exhilaration he'd felt in the aftermath of killing the masked man.

It'd been fun. He'd never felt more alive. The ennui that had gripped him vanished immediately. After that night, Paul took many more late-night walks and soon the city had a new villain to fear.

The media called him The Pusher.

DATE NIGHT

HER NAME WAS CLAUDIA AND she was the coolest girl Derek Peterson had met in a long time. Tonight was their first official date and he was nervous as hell as he stood on the sidewalk outside the theater waiting for her.

They'd met at a science fiction convention in Oregon two weeks ago, clicking instantly over drinks at an after-hours room party, each of them decked out in cosplay gear. He was dressed like Captain Mal from *Firefly*, she like Chiana, the blue-skinned alien chick from *Farscape*. Thereafter there had been many extensive getting-to-know-each-other phone conversations and now they were about to start the dating game and see where it went.

Derek liked Claudia a lot. Like always with anyone new, he was afraid of coming across as too much of a dork and blowing it somehow. Right now, though, his nervousness was more about the time rather than any concern over making a bad first date impression.

The movie was set to start in ten minutes and there was no sign of Claudia. The 9:00 PM screening of the latest Avengers movie would be well-attended, but Derek wasn't worried about it selling out, having purchased tickets in advance online. At this point, their planned 8:30 meetup time was more than twenty minutes in the rear-view mirror. This felt like an apt analogy, because the paranoid part of him felt a bit like Claudia was already slipping away from him. He feared he was on the brink of being stood up. They'd last talked less than an hour ago, but it was feeling like a lot longer than that. He was suddenly sure she'd gotten cold feet and had opted to simply not show up rather than bother with the stress and potential drama of an explanatory phone call.

For about the hundredth time that night, he looked at his phone, hoping to see a text from Claudia on the screen. There were no new messages. Seeing the background image of Claudia in her con costume caused a twinge of heartache. He considered calling her, but had a hunch she wouldn't answer. If she was standing him up, why would she? Besides, if some legitimate explanation for her extreme lateness existed, she could easily have called him herself to set his mind at ease. That she hadn't done so spoke volumes as far as Derek was concerned.

Just as he was on the verge of giving up and heading out to his car, he spied a yellow cab pulling into the farthest entrance to the large theater parking lot. The taxi zoomed up the side of the lot fast, swung around as it reached the wide-open space between the front row of cars and the multiplex, and soon screeched to a halt at the curb right in front of Derek.

He saw dark figures moving around inside the cab, dimly visible through the tinted windows. It looked like a single passenger in the middle row of seats was leaning forward, proffering payment to the driver. Derek's heart felt frozen in his chest as he waited for the door to open and reveal the identity of the passenger. He hoped desperately it would be Claudia, but he was prepared for disappointment.

But that didn't happen.

The door slid open and Claudia emerged from the taxi's interior, taking Derek by surprise as she launched herself at him and threw her arms around him. He stood there for a long moment with his arms hanging awkwardly at his sides as she uttered the same words of frantic apology over and over: "I'm so, so sorry. I'm so, so sorry."

Derek watched over her shoulder as the taxi's door slid automatically shut. As the yellow cab drove away, he let out a breath and lifted his arms to embrace her in a tentative way.

"It's okay," he said, whispering the words.

It was okay, he realized.

Right now he didn't care much about explanations. She was here. She hadn't ditched him in the cold and callous way he'd imagined.

Her warm, shapely body was pressed against him. He felt her warm breath on his neck. It was nice and it made everything else irrelevant.

At last, after what felt like at least a couple full minutes, she eased out of the embrace and told him what happened. "My fucking car broke down. And on top of that, my fucking phone died. Can you believe that shit? How much bad luck can one girl have in one fucking night?" She dug her Android phone out of her purse to show him its blank screen. "See?"

Derek nodded.

He didn't really need the visual evidence, but it was clear she felt compelled to provide it. She felt bad about having left him hanging so long without explanation, which in turn made him feel shitty for doubting her.

She shoved the phone back down inside her purse with evident disdain and resumed her story. "So I left my car where it was and started walking. I was in kind of a sketchy area and started getting desperate. Then that cab came along and fucking rescued me. I stepped into the middle of the street to flag it down. I'm sure I looked like some kind of psycho."

Derek chuckled. "Well, that's too bad. Sucks about your car. I'm glad you got here without too much trouble, though. Want to use my phone to call AAA or something?"

She gave a single adamant shake of her head. "I'll worry about it tomorrow. We've got a movie to watch. You can just drop me off at my place after, if that's okay."

Derek smiled.

In what fucked-up, bizarro universe would that not be okay?

"Yeah, no problem," he said, taking her by the hand. "Let's get inside."

Once they were inside the huge lobby of the vast 24-auditorium multiplex, Derek was able to take a moment to appreciate Claudia's appearance. She'd texted him an array of pictures since the con, but this was the first time he was seeing her in person without the blue body paint covering every inch of her flesh. She was absolutely stunning. She had a fit yet exquisitely feminine, busty build. Large breasts strained the fabric of a top that was a dark shade of scarlet. She wore a stylish black leather jacket over this. Tight black jeans and pumps rounded out the ensemble. He was already fantasizing about tearing the outfit off her later in the evening, in the event she invited him into her place.

It was 9:01 as they entered the lobby. Showtime, technically, was at hand. Knowing, however, that trailers and commercials would be playing for at least ten more minutes, they decided they had time for the concessions stand, where they bought large sodas and popcorns.

A short while later, they were inside the auditorium showing their movie. As Derek had suspected, the theater was pretty packed, but they found two adjacent empty seats in a side row near the back. Claudia removed her leather jacket prior to settling into her seat.

Derek spied the white bandage wrapped around her left wrist as he sat down next to her. He glanced at her, arching an eyebrow. "What happened there?"

She dug some popcorn out of the bag in her lap and stared at the screen, where a trailer for a forthcoming horror movie called *The Late Night Horror Show* was playing. An old Bile Lords song blared from the theater's speakers, accentuating the wild action on the screen.

She shrugged. "It's nothing. Just a boo-boo."

The bandage was largish for something described as a "boo-boo". It also looked worn and a bit dirty. Derek had the impression it'd been in place for at least a few days. She'd likely showered with it on, accounting for its degraded appearance. Derek opted against inquiring further. She seemed uninterested in talking about whatever had happened, and he had no interest in pushing her for additional info. They were here to watch a movie and have fun, not discuss minor flesh wounds.

The movie started.

Ten or so minutes in, Claudia set her bag of popcorn on the floor and leaned into him for a kiss. He turned his head in her direction and let her press her lips against his. She surprised him when she pushed her tongue between his lips and cupped his crotch with a soft hand and squeezed. This was no sparsely attended screening of a movie that had been out for a while. The movie was brand new and nearly every surrounding seat was filled. It seemed a bit bold to initiate a groping session in the midst of such a setting. But maybe that turned her on. Maybe she was an exhibitionist.

Fuck it, Derek thought. *If she's cool with it, so am I.*

His left hand went to one of her breasts and squeezed. She whimpered into his mouth and squeezed his crotch harder. Her tongue pushed into his mouth again, probing more insistently than before. He kept groping her breasts as his burgeoning erection strained the front of his jeans in a way that was painful and pleasurable at the same time. Claudia started moaning in a blatantly sexual way after several minutes of this.

And she wasn't quiet about it.

A deep male voice from the row behind them piped up: "If you two don't knock it off, I'm complaining to the manager."

Claudia heaved a breath as she broke the lip-lock with Derek. She turned her head in the direction of the complainer and snarled at him, her face twisting in a way that was at once sexy and frightening. There was a hint of something feral and animalistic in the strained set of her features. And her voice was significantly huskier than before when she said, "Fuck off."

Derek didn't mind going with the flow when the girl he was flowing with was as sexy as Claudia, generally speaking, but there was a limit to how many lines he could cross. He wasn't a rude person and didn't want to cause a scene. Words of apology sprang to his lips, but before he could utter them, something caught his eye and made him frown.

The white bandage around Claudia's wrist was soaked red. A thin line of blood slid to the heel of her hand and dripped to the floor. The so-called "boo-boo" was evidently a wound of much greater significance. He started to say something about it, but Claudia gripped him by the throat and pulled him close. Her hand was tight on his throat, effectively suppressing any further protest as she again pushed her tongue into his mouth.

Blood from the wrist wound pattered on his lap in a thickening stream. Even more alarming, he noted a distinct difference in her teeth as they nipped at his mouth. They were longer now.

And sharper.

One of the nips pierced his bottom lip and drew blood.

Derek whimpered.

What in the name of holy fucking shit is happening?

The deep voice from the next row back piped up again. "That's it. I'm going to the manager."

There was a squeak of springs as the large man rose from his seat.

Claudia again broke the clench and snarled at the complainer. "Sit down and watch, fat man, or I'll tear your head off."

Her voice was even huskier now, barely sounding feminine at all. And her skin tone was darker. Her hair looked fuller and thicker. Longer, too. Also, her eyes were brown now. They'd been blue moments ago, as in all her pictures.

The fat man snorted. "Fuck yourself, whore. I'm getting you and your ugly boyfriend kicked out of here."

He moved to the end of his row and took the first step down.

Before he could get any farther, Claudia sprang out of her seat, leaping over Derek and the couple seated to his left as she intercepted the fat man, who shrieked in alarm, a surprisingly girlish sound that rang out with crystalline clarity in the theater, overwhelming the sounds emanating from the theater's speakers. By then the auditorium was a riot of hushing sounds and irritated voices. The near-capacity crowd wanted quiet for the movie. Within just a few more seconds, though, Derek was sure these people would cease caring about the movie.

Claudia's clothes were bursting at the seams. Hair sprouted from nearly every previously bare patch of flesh. Her hands got bigger, the painted nails lengthening into thick, sharp talons. The fat man's face was a frozen mask of terror as Claudia fulfilled her promise of a few moments ago. She ripped his head off at the shoulders and hurled it away from her with all her might. The severed head hit the movie screen dead-center with an emphatic splat.

Screams erupted all around.

Blood fountained from the fat man's ragged neck stump.

The house lights came up as people began rushing for the exits. Acting on instinct, Derek hurried to join them, but Claudia restrained him with a hand clamped firmly around his throat. She held him in place as she tore out the dead man's stomach with her new snout and devoured a length of pink intestine.

Derek gagged.

Oh, fuck. Oh, fuck, fuck, fuckity, fuck fuck.

Claudia tossed the corpse away and looked at Derek.

"You're mine," she said, her voice barely sounding human now. "You're not going anywhere. We'll be together forever."

Claudia raked a talon across his neck, drawing blood without severing any major arteries. Then she picked him up as easily as one might a light bag of laundry and heaved him over one of her very broad shoulders. His head bobbed as she sprinted down the steps toward the nearest exit. A crowd was gathered there, people desperately trying to push their way out. More screams erupted as Claudia tore into them, pulling off limbs as she pushed fresh victims aside and made her way to the exit.

Moments later, they were outside and running across the parking lot. As Claudia ran off into the night, Derek caught a glimpse of the full moon hanging in the sky overhead and understood.

The bandage.

The "boo-boo".

A werewolf had bitten Claudia and now she was one, too. He felt the hot throb at his throat where she'd scratched him.

He wondered how much that first transformation process would hurt.

THE IMPLANT

AWARENESS OF SOMETHING WRONG DAWNED slowly for John Stark that morning. He awoke with what felt like an ordinary stiff neck, the kind that occasionally resulted from sleeping with his head turned at a bad angle. That he awoke lying flat on his back as his eyes fluttered open didn't matter. He'd been having some restless nights lately and might have shifted sleeping positions any number of times between bedtime and sunrise.

He was groggy at first and felt little motivation to do anything about the discomfort he was feeling as his consciousness continued its slow, lethargic return from dreamland. When his head was a little clearer, he would raise himself up a bit, maybe double-fold the top pillow for added cushioning, and wedge it carefully against the sore area. Then a bit later he'd get up and take some Tylenol. That should take care of things.

In those first moments, though, he was content to simply lie there as he attempted to hold on to fragments of the sex dream he'd been having prior to waking. In the dream, he'd been kidnapped by a gang of beautiful and glamorous female criminals. The babes lived a double life, working as fashion models during the day and committing elaborate heists at night. They took him to their mansion and forced him to be their sex slave. He felt like it'd been probably the most amazing dream of all time, but it was already breaking apart, the few remembered fragments growing fuzzier with each passing moment. Soon, he suspected, he wouldn't remember it at all.

Bummer.

In a few more moments, his eyes opened wider as the grogginess continued to clear. He remembered the basic premise of the amazing dream, but little beyond that, just one or two fleeting images. With the return to full consciousness almost complete, he rose up some, double-folded the pillow beneath his head, and tried to get comfortable.

It was then he began to realize he was dealing with something more than an ordinary stiff neck. Shifting position did nothing to alleviate the ache. Instead, it heightened awareness of the hard center of discomfort. He tried twisting his neck to see if this was some kind of kink that could be worked out, but all this resulted in was a sharp jab of pain he felt all the way down to his toes.

Frowning, he lifted up his head and slipped a hand beneath his neck to probe gingerly at the knot of discomfort. His breath caught in his throat and his heart did a little stutter as his fingertips skidded over the hard, round lump protruding from the flesh just beneath the base of his skull.

John sat bolt upright and probed at the object with a little less delicacy. This resulted in additional jabs of pain, but he couldn't help himself. There was something sticking out of his neck that didn't belong there, an alarming development to say the least. Any pain he was feeling from the stings that resulted from each poke of the object was overridden by other concerns, primary among them being a single basic question—what the fuck is this fucking thing sticking out of my fucking neck!?

It did not feel like a natural object.

This impression was a good thing in the sense that, if accurate, it ruled out the sudden protrusion of a long-developing malignant tumor. The measure of relief this insight afforded him was not insignificant, but it was swept aside by the lingering mystery of what the clearly foreign object embedded in his neck actually was.

He was able to discern the basic shape of the thing with a bit more gentle probing. It was an almost perfectly round knob and felt like it was about half the size of his thumb. He tried pulling at it slightly, but this resulted in a jolt of pain sharper than any of the previous jabs.

He was breathing heavily and his heart was beating faster as he tossed aside the blanket covering his body, got out of bed, and hurried out to the bathroom down the hall. The bathroom door had a tendency to stick in the frame. After shouldering it open, he traipsed across the small space on legs turning more rubbery by the moment. He stopped at the sink and peered at his reflection in the mirror above it.

John knew what he had to do.

But he was reluctant.

There was something in his neck that shouldn't be there. It hadn't been there when he'd gone to bed. That he knew for a fact. He'd gone to bed stone sober, just as he had every night for the last five years, following his fifth (and final) DUI arrest. He'd been in full possession of his senses until lights out, no question about it.

So, again . . . what the fuck?

He lingered there in frozen terror a moment longer, knowing he needed to visually appraise whatever it was. Until he did that, he couldn't even begin to figure out what the thing in his neck really was or how to remove it. And yet a very frightened part of him didn't want to see it, was, in fact, terrified at the very idea. Whatever this thing was, someone else had put it there.

Or something else.

Aliens, maybe.

The idea was ridiculous on the surface. He'd always scoffed at tales of alien abductions and experiments, treating the stories with the same disdain he felt for kooky conspiracy theories. Only now, with this goddamn thing stuck in his neck, it was hard to discount any of the wild possibilities he'd once treated with such contempt.

"I've got to do this," he muttered, his voice too loud in the otherwise empty room. "I've got no choice."

He turned to his side, craned his neck around, and lifted up the little scraggle of dark hair at the nape of his neck. The object protruding from his neck was pretty much as he'd envisioned it from his initial tactile examination, except that the hard knob was a shade of light blue rather than the dark brown or black he'd expected.

Leaning over the sink, he put his head as close as he could to the mirror, his eyes swiveling and straining in their sockets as he tried hard to get the best possible view of the thing. He still couldn't tell whether it was made of metal or some other hard material. With the fingers of his other hand, he pressed down as hard as he could on a patch of flesh adjacent to the protrusion, hoping for a glimpse of the part of the object that was actually inside his flesh. This resulted in a series of minor stings that were bearable and nothing compared to the sharper jabs that came when he applied direct pressure to the object.

By doing this, he was able to catch a brief glimpse of something silver attached to the bottom of the blue knob. He was only able to observe it for a few seconds before the stinging sensations became more than he could tolerate. Though minor at first, they became steadily more intense the longer he pressed down on the flesh adjacent to the object.

He took his hand away from his neck and let out a breath.

A rod or bolt of some sort, apparently made of metal, had been inserted in his neck while he slept. How this had been accomplished without waking him or causing excruciating pain, he did not know. He stared at his reflection and wondered what to do.

Get it out. Now.

Well, that was easier said than done, wasn't it?

The object was deeply and firmly embedded in his flesh. Removing it would require a significant amount of force. Judging by the jabs of pain triggered by simple prods of the exterior knob, any attempt at removal would likely result in waves of mind-bending agony. There was also the issue of the placement of the object to consider. It was lodged dangerously close to critical areas such as his brain stem and spine. By trying to forcibly extract it, he might inadvertently cause some kind of debilitating and irreversible damage.

John nodded, still staring at his reflection.

What he needed was the help of medical professionals.

On the other hand, what if his wildest imaginings were true and the object in his neck was some weird piece of alien technology? Once this was determined to be the case, he might be taken into custody by the military and shipped off to fucking Area 51 or some other secret place from which he might never return. Where once he might have dismissed such a notion as paranoid and absurd, it now seemed all too plausible.

John Stark really didn't want to spend the rest of his life locked away in a secret underground laboratory. He also didn't much relish the prospect of doing nothing and leaving himself at the mercy of whoever had implanted the object, regardless of whether those responsible were actual creatures from somewhere beyond earth or some sinister and equally mysterious earthbound organization.

Several more minutes of thinking it over resulted in no revelatory insights, but he did come to a conclusion about what he needed to do next. He shuffled back to his bedroom, grabbed his phone from the nightstand, and called Mike Carter.

Mike was his oldest and most trusted friend. They'd known each other since elementary school. They'd been through thick and thin together. John had been best man at both of Mike's weddings. Mike had bailed him out of jail a couple times back when he was still drinking and getting into trouble. His old friend might not have a solution for him, but he might be able to steer him in the right direction as far as what course of action to take.

That initial conversation was brief. John didn't want to tell the full story over the phone because it would make him sound crazy. Mike would think he'd suddenly started drinking again, which would be a logical enough deduction to make minus the visual evidence. Instead, John kept it simple, effectively imparting a sense of urgency and direness in just a few terse sentences.

Mike said he'd be right over.

He got to John's house inside of fifteen minutes.

At first he expressed the expected skepticism when John told him what had happened and his suspicions about it. The skepticism faded, however, when John showed his friend the object embedded in his neck and invited him to press down on the flesh adjacent to it in order to glimpse the silver bolt.

They were in John's living room at that point. The morning light spilling in from the sliding glass doors overlooking the patio and large, leaf-scattered backyard was muted, the day overcast and drizzly. Only a single lamp was on in the living room. The semi-gloom imbued the moment with a disquieting sense of the funereal.

Mike drew a hand across his mouth and scratched at his jaw. "Maybe you're not paranoid, after all."

John let out a shuddery breath and nodded in an emphatic way. "Damn right, I'm not. That thing is there. It's weird, but it's real. And I want it the fuck out of me. What the hell do I do?"

Mike took his hand away from his mouth. "There's only one thing you can do."

John's brow furrowed in confusion. "And what would that be?"

Mike smiled.

For the first time, John experienced a mild tingle of trepidation where Mike was concerned. There was something in that tight little smile that was not at all friendly. But surely that was just more paranoia, right?

Mike reached inside his jacket and took out an automatic pistol. "What you need to do, John, is put this gun in your mouth and wedge the sight up against your soft palate. Once it is firmly in place, squeeze the trigger."

John laughed, albeit nervously.

This had to be a joke.

Only it didn't seem like a joke. And that gun was very real. "This isn't funny."

Mike nodded. "Unfortunately for you, John, I'm not attempting to elicit a humorous reaction."

John flinched but did not retreat as Mike approached him and pressed the gun into his right hand, forcing him to curl his fingers around the grip of the pistol. Once the gun was securely within John's grip, Mike moved back several steps, glanced briefly at the smart watch strapped around his hairy wrist, and shifted his gaze back to John.

His tone was stern and devoid of even the slightest trace of mirth as he said, "Put the gun in your mouth, John."

John glanced at the gun. He tried willing his fingers to uncurl and allow the ugly weapon to fall to the floor. Instead the gun came to his mouth. Then it went inside his mouth and in another moment the sight was wedged painfully against his soft palate. He trembled and whimpered and longed to yank the gun away, but he just stood there, powerless, no longer in control of his own actions.

Mike's expression remained mostly emotionless, but there was a small hint of smug satisfaction at the corners of his mouth. "You're probably wondering how this is happening. And you're probably wondering why you're best friend since childhood is compelling you to do this."

John could not nod. He just whimpered some more. His bladder loosened and a flood of piss stained the crotch of his briefs.

Mike's nose crinkled slightly in distaste. "The answer is simple. I'm not your best friend. In fact, before I walked through your front door a few minutes ago, you'd never met me before. Everything you know about our history together is a fiction. It is an elaborate tale woven into the code of the implant in your neck, which was not put there by little green men. Since you're about to die and take the secret to your grave, there's no harm in telling you that it's an experimental mind control device developed by rogue elements of your own government, for whom I work, albeit in a necessarily secret capacity." Now he smiled again, more broadly than before. "Your tax dollars at work."

John couldn't believe any of this. It was crazy. He'd shared so much of his life with this guy, countless things that were an integral part of the fabric of his existence. No way could those things all be products of computer code.

Mike sighed. "You don't believe me."

John managed to mutter the word "no", though it was muffled by the barrel of the gun.

"Device," Mike said, his tone turning more precise as he pitched his voice louder. "Cycle red, directive one, wipe."

The moment the word "wipe" was spoken, John knew he was staring at a stranger. Everything the man had said was true. The truth about his life came back in an instant. He was a lonely, broken-down alcoholic. He had no friends. None that were still alive, anyway.

Tears spilled down his face.

His heart thudded painfully in his chest.

Mike cleared his throat, straightened his tie, and said, "I'll take the device with me when I leave. The angle of the shot about to split your head wide open should erase any evidence of its insertion. The gun is registered in your name. Yes, I know you've never owned a gun before. We've arranged everything, all the paperwork and the suicide note you were compelled to write before device insertion last night."

"Please," John managed, the tears spilling faster and hotter down his face. "Don't."

Mike ignored this plea and said, "Your country thanks you for your service and your contribution to our ongoing mind control studies."

John screamed. He glared at his hand, tried again to regain control over his body and pull out the gun.

To no avail.

"Device," Mike said, again speaking in that loud, clear tone. "End program."

John's forefinger began to squeeze the trigger.

He managed one last muffled scream.

The last thing he saw before the bullet blew out the back of his head were the unforgiving, soulless eyes of the stranger, which were faultlessly observant and appraising to the end.

HIGHWAY STOP

THE FAMILY TRIP TO MYRTLE Beach felt like it was cursed from the beginning. It was a journey marred by setback after setback, a relentless series of unfortunate incidents and countless moments of sheer bad luck. The first thing that happened was a flat tire. The Gruber clan had been on the road maybe five minutes, the rented minivan they were traveling in having just merged into highway traffic.

At that point, John Gruber unleashed an impressive storm of profanities, slamming the heels of his hands against the steering wheel again and again as his puffy face turned red. Mary Gruber, John's wife of thirteen years, became instantly alarmed. John had heart problems. He also had severe anger issues. He took pills for his heart and years of counseling had helped him learn how to better channel his frustrations. A lot of time had passed since either of these things had last truly concerned Mary, so the outburst came as quite a shock. He looked like an overheated human pressure cooker, on the verge of explosion.

To his credit, John seemed embarrassed by his overreaction. He apologized profusely as he pulled the minivan over, smiling and cracking jokes as he took a few moments to reassure his family. Mary and the two Gruber children—Beth and Hunter—all breathed audible sighs of relief.

Then John got out to change the tire.

And got stung by a wasp just above his right eyebrow as he was kneeling next to the car on the highway. The darkness that always lurked within John returned after that and never fully went away again. His foul mood only got worse as the setbacks mounted.

There were more car issues. Personal items belonging to the kids got lost or misplaced and there was considerable related drama, all of which wore on John's nerves. Mary worried each time she saw his face turn scarlet. The first couple times she urged him to calm down, but the sneering looks he gave her soon made her stop. The second day of the journey east occurred mostly in sullen silence. They arrived at their hotel in Myrtle Beach late that day. There was a mix-up at the hotel where they were supposed to be staying. The hotel had no record of their reservation and was booked solid for weeks.

The ensuing scramble for alternate lodging went on for hours. Shortly after they finally found a place and got checked in, John received a call from his brother. Their estranged father had passed away earlier that afternoon. John hated his father and would not be attending the funeral, but news of the man's death turned his dark mood intractable and cast a pall on the rest of the trip.

On top of all that, the relentless march of bad luck continued. Multiple unrelated things went wrong for everyone. It was like the Vacation movies from the 80s, only without the laughs. Mary did her best to grin and bear it and tried to hold everything together for the sake of the kids, but after four days of nonstop tribulations, she begged John to take them all home early for the sake of their sanity. To her relief, John agreed and they decided to make the return journey in one day instead of two. They would be beyond exhausted by the time they got home, but Mary figured it would be worth it just so the ordeal would finally be over.

They had been on the road nearly ten hours when John hit the minivan's blinker and began to slow down for an exit. Mary's eyes fluttered open as she yawned and sat up straighter in the front passenger seat. She'd fallen asleep with her Kindle open in her lap and now it slid to the floor.

"Getting gas?" she asked, glancing at John as she leaned forward to scoop the Kindle off the minivan's floor.

John shrugged. "Might top off, I guess. We've still got three quarters of a tank, but I've gotta piss like a motherfucker thanks to the coffee I got at the last stop."

Mary gave him an admonishing look as she sat up straight again. "John, the kids."

"What about them?"

"You shouldn't curse in front of them."

John grunted. "They're asleep."

Mary glanced over her shoulder. He was right. Both her babies were conked out, slumped down in the back seat, with their heads tilted toward each other, nearly touching. A fleeting smile flickered on her lips, but then she remembered the circumstances and it faded.

She looked at John. "Okay, they're asleep. You still shouldn't talk like that around them."

"Whatever."

Nothing else was said as they pulled up outside a gas station. John parked at the curb in a spot directly facing the entrance to the brightly-lit store. It was almost two in the morning and there was only one other car in the lot, a beat-up old Subaru. The Subaru likely belonged to the sole night clerk on duty, who watched them with a blank expression from the other side of the counter.

John unbuckled his seatbelt and reached for the door handle. "Be right back."

Mary nodded and didn't say anything. She was still unhappy about his rude demeanor. She could also still sort of feel the imprint of his hand on her jaw from where he'd slapped her last night after one too many drinks from the minibar.

John grunted again. "How about you work on your attitude while I'm away, eh? Nobody likes a sourpuss."

He got out of the car and slammed the door shut.

Mary frowned as she watched him go. She was upset and worried about too many things. The slap was the first time John had laid a hand on her in anger in almost five years. She'd thought that unpleasantness at least had been permanently relegated to the past, but apparently she'd been wrong. Her emotions were in wild conflict. She couldn't put up with that kind of behavior, but the thought of doing something about it was too overwhelming in the wake of all that had happened over the last few days. What she needed was some time to think about it all and get some fresh perspective.

But before that she needed rest and a lot of it.

She'd just started dozing again when she heard the deep voice speaking to her left. "Guy's an asshole. I think we can all agree on that."

Though she was on the verge of sleep, Mary understood that this was no voice from a dream. Some stranger was in the car, ensconced behind the steering wheel. Her eyes opened wide in alarm as her head swiveled toward the voice.

She screamed.

The stranger seated behind the steering wheel had skin that looked freshly scalded, pink and blistered all over. His head was twice the size of a normal human head and had an elongated, pointed chin. Horn-like stubs protruded from the sides of his forehead. Large flaps of leathery flesh rested against the creature's broad, muscular shoulder. Their fine, membranous tissue made them look sort of like wings.

The creature chuckled. "I know what you're thinking and you're right. They are wings. I'm a demon, you see. From Hell. For real."

Mary stared at him in open-mouthed disbelief for a moment.

Then she screamed again. Surprisingly, the sleeping children did not stir.

The creature's deep sigh was accompanied by an odor like sulfur. "Please don't do that. It's pointless. I'm not here to harm you or your children."

Mary shrank back against the door. Her whole body was shaking. "You're not real. This is a dream."

The creature shook its head. "Except it isn't. And you know it."

Mary stared at the creature for another long, silent moment. She glanced at the store and saw no sign of John in the brightly-lit interior. He was probably still in the bathroom, either pissing away all the coffee he'd thrown back tonight or asleep on the toilet. Her gaze shifted back to the creature. She'd half-expected it to vanish the moment her gaze was averted, revealed after all as a lingering wisp of something carried over from a nightmare.

But the thing was still there.

"You're real."

The demon scratched a long black talon along the edge of its pointed chin and looked thoughtful. "I am, yes."

"So why are you here? How are you here?"

She was amazed by how calm her voice sounded. By all rights, she should still be screaming and squealing with terror. Whether the thing next to her was real should still be an open question. Demons didn't exist. She'd always believed this. They were mythological things, bits of lore left over from a less enlightened age. A more logical explanation for what she was seeing would be that she'd suffered some kind of psychotic break and was hallucinating.

The creature's thin, blackened lips stretched in a manner suggestive of a smile, revealing black, diseased-looking gums and rows of long, crooked teeth. "I'm able to appear to you here because the area surrounding the interstate exit your husband took tonight happens to be adjacent to an actual, physical portal to Hell, one of only a handful on earth."

"You're kidding."

The creature's sickly smile stretched wider. "I'm not. And you're not hallucinating."

Mary thought about that a moment.

She glanced again at the store. Still no sign of John.

She looked at the creature. Still there.

"What do you want with me?"

The creature scratched his chin with a long talon again. "I'm here to tell you something. A revelation. Information you can use, as they say. And to offer a solution to your problem."

Mary frowned. "What problem?"

The creature indicated the convenience store with a tilt of his chin. "The one squatting on a toilet in there. Your husband. Who, by the way, is taking a while because he's busy jerking off while thinking about your sister."

Mary shook her head. "You can't know that."

The creature chuckled. "Except that I do. He thinks about Karen every time he has sex with you."

Mary flinched at the mention of her sister's name.

The creature sighed. "I'm sorry. I don't mean to upset you. You just seemed to need extra convincing."

Mary glared at the demon, getting angry now. "Is that the information you were talking about?" She laughed harshly, the sound devoid of actual mirth. "Because I don't care what John thinks about when we have sex, which we hardly ever do anymore, by the way. I don't think I even love him anymore."

The creature chuckled. "Be honest, Mary. You know you don't love him anymore."

Mary said nothing to that.

The creature nodded. "As I thought. And to answer your question, no, that's not the information you need."

Mary sighed. "So how about you just spill it? I'm tired and I've got no interest in guessing games."

The creature tilted its head, the twist of its strange mouth now looking more like a smirk than a smile. "Making demands of a creature from Hell, are you? Gosh, you are far ballsier than your husband believes."

Mary groaned in frustration.

The demon chuckled again, but when it next spoke, its tone was unexpectedly somber. "Your husband has fantasies of killing you and your children. Very vivid, very bloody fantasies."

Mary frowned, trying to gauge from the set of the creature's strange, distorted features whether he was telling her something that might be true or was just fucking with her. The latter felt like a distinct possibility. After all, this thing was a demon and thus a servant of the devil, the so-called father of lies.

John was an imperfect man. She wasn't naïve. He'd abused her in the past and now, after a long period of more or less behaving himself, he'd demonstrated a capacity for doing it again. He'd let her have one across the face while he was in his cups and frustrated. There was no denying the wrongness of that, regardless of excuse. But thinking he could go from that to butchering his entire family was quite a leap. Despite his flaws, she thought John loved his children too much to harm them. And she had no good reason to trust this . . . thing.

"Are you wondering why you should trust me?"

Mary arched an eyebrow, mistrust evident in every line of her face. "There's no way I can trust you. You're a demon. By definition, you're evil. And evil things lie."

The creature laughed softly. "You're smart. Far smarter than John knows or deserves. And despite your agnosticism, those old Sunday school lessons have stuck with you. You require proof that I'm telling the truth."

Mary nodded. "Yes. And I don't see how that's possible."

"When you were a child, you went into your sleeping brother's room and held a pillow over his face until he gagged. He mumbled your name in his sleep. You got spooked and ran out of the room. You were five years old and you've barely thought of it since then because the memory understandably troubles you, but if your little brother hadn't uttered your name, you might have suffocated him that night."

Mary's heart pounded in her chest.

She gaped at the demon, unable to breathe for a moment.

The creature nodded. "See? I know things."

Mary sucked in a big breath and blew it right back out. "But . . . how can you know that? Nobody knows that. I've never told a soul."

The creature's smirk deepened. "Hello? Fucking demon over here. I can possess humans who come within range of the portal. This allows me to know things. I briefly possessed you and your husband after you left the interstate. For mere moments, mind you, but it was long enough for me to know all your deepest, darkest secrets. The one about your brush with childhood murder is a doozy, granted, but it's an anomaly in your life. You never did anything like that again. And you were just a small child. You were jealous of the attention your baby brother was getting and you didn't know how to deal with it. John, on the other hand . . ."

The creature shrugged.

A silent beat passed.

Mary huffed an impatient breath. "What about him?"

The creature's smirk faded, giving way to a more serious expression. "He's done things, Mary. Bad things. We don't have time to detail them because John won't be sitting on that toilet much longer, but trust me, I'm talking about some of the worst things you can imagine. They usually happen on his so-called business trips. And he thinks about doing the same things to you and your kids all the time. One day, perhaps not too far in the future, he'll actually do those things. But there's something you can do right now to prevent it. A choice you can make. This is where I come in."

Mary glanced at the store.

Still no sign of John. The bored clerk at the counter was paging slowly through a porn magazine.

She looked at the demon. "What kind of choice?"

And now the creature smiled again. "You can choose to do nothing. I'll vanish before John returns and you and your family can return to your home and await your sadly inevitable fate. Or . . ." And here the demon paused to snap its fingers, a sound that made Mary cringe. It was a skeletal, graveyard rattle. "I can induce a heart attack in your husband right now. He'll be gone and all your problems will be over. John does have a sizeable life insurance policy, you know."

Mary did know that. It was in excess of seven figures.

She looked at the store. Still no John.

The creature frowned. "You have very little time left to decide. John is currently wiping his flabby, flatulent ass. Soon he'll be back in the car and this opportunity will pass. Think about it, Mary. This is your chance for a clean end to things. You won't have to do anything desperate later. It's better this way."

Mary looked at him. "Why are you doing this? It can't be out of the goodness of your heart. You're a demon."

"You're right, of course. My motivation is simple, though. I'm getting my jollies simply by putting you in the position of having to make this decision. And, frankly, I will get to gloat a bit over the initial trauma your children will experience when the ambulance arrives and the EMTs are unable to revive your husband."

It grinned wickedly now.

A cold shiver went down Mary's spine.

She looked at the store. Save for the clerk, the visible part of its interior was still empty.

The demon made a loud throat-clearing sound. "John is washing his hands."

Mary looked at him, her voice quiet as she said, "Do it."

The creature's wicked grin broadened. "There is one other option."

Mary groaned.

She should have known the creature's mind games wouldn't stop there. "And what would that be?"

"Instead of inducing an instantly fatal heart attack, I could engineer another kind of demise for him. Something that would give him the scare of his life before he dies. Before you automatically say no, you should know that John doesn't just fantasize about your sister, he actually has fucked her. Many times."

Mary's hands curled into fists in her lap

She seethed inwardly, her face twitching. The information confirmed a nagging suspicion she'd tried hard to ignore for years. But she was aware of time passing and knew she couldn't afford to brood. She let out a breath and looked at the demon.

"Do it."

"Scare the bastard first?"

Another tightly released breath. "Yes."

The creature laughed, sounding smug. "Excellent. Consider it done. Keep your eye on that clerk. He's about to experience an unexplained psychotic episode."

The demon vanished and the driver's seat was again empty.

Mary's gaze shifted back to the store. John had emerged from the bathroom and was approaching the counter. His face was very red. Evidently the frantic masturbation session had strained his heart. Mary felt contempt when she saw the long piece of dirty toilet paper clinging to his shoe.

John approached the counter, probably intending to buy some cigarettes.

The clerk took a gun out from under the counter, screamed something in a foreign language, took aim at John, and squeezed the trigger. John was too stunned to react. There was no time, anyway. The bullet hit his forehead dead-center and a spectacular rain of blood and brains erupted from the back of his head. As he fell dead to the floor, the clerk put the gun in his own mouth and pulled the trigger again. More blood and brains splashed against the window behind him before his corpse dropped down out of sight behind the counter.

Mary stared in disbelief for a long moment. A part of her thought this might still be some insane dream from which she would soon awake. But that didn't happen. John stayed dead on the floor, an ever-widening pool of blood spreading out around his head.

Mary turned her head and glanced at the backseat.

Her children were still sleeping.

Her gaze went back to the store.

Then she smiled, dug her phone out of her purse, and called 911.

THE DOLL

THE DOLL WAS ON THE dining room table in his two-bedroom apartment when Sam Thorne got home from his security guard job at the local mall that night, but its presence there did not immediately register. He was tired and distracted by stress related to his job. All he cared about was getting changed out of the goddamn security guard uniform, cracking open the first beer from his nightly six-pack of Old Style, and settling into his recliner for a night of mindless entertainment crashed out in front of the TV.

Sam walked right by the table on the way to his bedroom. He saw the doll. It was almost a direct look rather than a fleeting glimpse in his peripheral vision, but there were other objects on the table, familiar things, and their obscuring presence contributed to the delayed recognition. Among the other items were a basket in the center filled with white napkins, salt and pepper shakers, and an 18-inch-tall ministatue of W.C. Fields. He'd inherited the statue from his grandfather. Sam didn't care much about the old-time comedian, but his grandfather had been a big fan so he held on to it for sentimental reasons. The doll, folded into a sitting position, had been wedged in between the legs of the statue.

After passing by the table, Sam shuffled bleary-eyed down the hallway to his bedroom, where he began the process of shucking off his uniform. His face was fixed in a grumpy frown as he tore at the buttons of the shirt, anxious to have the uncomfortable garment off his body. He'd gained considerable weight since starting the job six months ago, causing his pudgy flesh to strain against the fabric. A sigh of relief rolled out of him as he pulled off the shirt and tossed it aside. He'd put in a requisition for larger uniform shirts and slacks several weeks ago, but his bosses had yet to approve it, the penny-pinching bastards. It was just one of many aggravations that had him thinking about looking for some other form of gainful employment. Right now, though, he didn't care much about that. He'd reached the end of a long week. All he wanted to do was get some drinks in him and unwind.

After changing into cotton gym shorts and an XXXL-sized Looney Tunes T-shirt, he walked out of his room and into the bathroom on the other side of the hallway. He pushed his shorts down to his ankles, sat down on the toilet seat, and selected an old issue of *Fortean Times* from the wicker basket on the floor next to the toilet. Midway through an article about a mysterious creature spotted in the woods near York, Pennsylvania, the image of the doll shifted from the foggy outskirts of his subconscious to the forefront of his brain.

The magazine slipped from his suddenly numb fingers to the floor as his eyes opened wide and his mouth fell open. His throat felt constricted and he was unable to swallow for a long moment. The thudding of his heart in his chest felt more labored than usual. Sweat rose on his brow and formed in his armpits. His sphincter opened wide and some good-sized turds plopped loudly into the toilet, a sound that made him wince because he feared it would give away his location to the intruder in his apartment.

Granted, the person who'd put the doll on the table might not still be on the premises, but he couldn't be certain about that. That someone with malicious intent had broken into his apartment and placed the doll there was not in doubt. Not only that, but it had been put where he was sure to see it, a deliberately provocative act. Until proven otherwise, he had to operate on the assumption that the culprit was still here.

At last, he was able to swallow and draw in a deep breath. His heart was still thudding, but not quite in that same scary, laborious way. After sitting there several more moments and listening very carefully for sounds of movement elsewhere in the apartment, he relaxed a little. The situation remained dangerous. He had no doubt his life was in imminent danger. However, he thought there was a decent chance the intruder had left the apartment and was lurking somewhere outside, perhaps waiting for him to show himself, which of course he would have to do at some point.

He couldn't stay here.

Not now.

Not anymore.

But he couldn't quite dismiss the possibility that the intruder was still in the apartment, perhaps lurking in the second bedroom. He used that room for storage and kept its door shut most of the time. He had not peeked inside it upon returning home tonight. If his intruder was still here, that room would be the likeliest hiding place.

Not bothering to wipe his ass, Sam lifted his bulk off the toilet seat and pulled up his gym shorts, taking care to do this as quietly as possible. He didn't want to tip off anyone who might still be here that he was in motion again. He wouldn't be able to manage that indefinitely, of course, but anything he could do to possibly gain even a little bit of an edge was worth trying.

After moving quietly across the bathroom floor in his bare feet, he put his ear to the closed door and listened for a few moments. Again, he detected no hints of movement, hushed voices, or other human activity. His Glock was in the top drawer of the nightstand by his bed. He could get to it within seconds if he could just work up the nerve to open this door and get moving. His right hand went to the doorknob and curled loosely around it, lingering there a few moments longer as he kept his ear to the door and continued to listen.

All he heard was the quiet hum of the air-conditioning.

He let out a breath and made up his mind. No matter what else happened here tonight, time was of the essence. He had to get moving and get out of here to have any hope of living to see the next day. After allowing himself one last moment to psych himself up, he pulled the door open and raced across the hall into his bathroom. In the moment just before he reached his nightstand, he stumbled on a wrinkle in the threadbare old carpet and pitched forward. His forehead smacked the edge of the nightstand, opening a gash in his forehead.

Things went blurry for a long moment as he tumbled to the floor. When his head was clear again, there was blood in his eyes and his head was throbbing. He wiped the blood away and sat up slowly, wincing at the sharper ache this movement provoked. Remembering his predicament, his head snapped up as his gaze went to the open bedroom doorway.

No one had come into the room.

He relaxed a little, deciding the intruder almost certainly wasn't still in the apartment. Otherwise he (or she) would surely have come running at the sound of his tumble, which had been quite dramatic and loud. Pushing his way through the pain, Sam got to his feet, pulled open the top drawer of the nightstand, and took out his Glock. He breathed a ragged sigh of relief upon seeing it. Until just then, the possibility that the intruder might have stolen it had not occurred to him. But it was here and now he was smiling. The predicament facing him remained dire, but a loaded gun in his hand evened the odds nicely.

Time to get down to business, he thought.

An inspection of his bedroom revealed no one lurking under his bed or elsewhere. Not that he'd expected anything else, but the search had to be done for the sake of thoroughness. Next he went down the hall to the second bedroom. After listening at the closed door a moment and detecting no sounds of movement within, he opened the door and went inside.

The room was crowded with junk, but no one was inside it.

Sam then went to the window overlooking the parking lot outside the apartment building. Hardly anyone was moving about out there at this time of night. The one face he did see was familiar. It belonged to Lucy Austin, the good-looking woman who lived in the apartment directly beneath him. As he watched, Lucy got in her silver Sonata, backed out of her space, and drove away, probably heading out for a night of bar-hopping. She did that a lot. Sam knew, because he'd been keeping a close eye on her for a while.

Once Lucy was gone, he more closely scrutinized the other cars in the lot. He saw none that looked unfamiliar or suspicious. There were no dark-clad figures sitting slumped down in the seats, at least none he could discern. It was nighttime, though, and the illumination provided by the pole-mounted sodium lights wasn't as strong as he might have hoped.

Regardless, he knew time was short. Whoever had been here would be back. He had to act now. To that end, he hurried back to his bedroom, dragged a large travel bag out of the closet, unzipped it, and set it down in the center of his bed, laying the Glock down next to it. He then began rapidly filling the bag with as many clothes and necessities as he could manage. Doing this included multiple trips back and forth across the hall to the bathroom and several more to the second bedroom where his most treasured things were stored. There was so much more he wished to take with him, but he just wouldn't be able to do it. It filled him with rage and a burning sense of loss. He wished he could get his hands around the neck of the person who'd put that doll on the table.

At last, he could fit no more items in the bag. It was stuffed to overflowing and he just managed to pull the zipper shut. By then he'd changed into more suitable clothes and was ready to go. He picked up the gun and shoved it into the waistband of his pants. He then grabbed the thick strap of the travel bag, slung it over his shoulder, and walked out to his living room.

Where he froze in his tracks.

They were waiting for him there, the men in the black ski masks. Upon closer inspection, one of the intruders was a slim woman with small breasts. The four intruders were dressed all in black. All appeared unarmed. The door behind them was standing wide open. It stayed that way only another moment, until another ski-mask-wearing intruder came in and shut the door. This fifth person was larger than the rest, bigger even than Sam. Like the others, he appeared unarmed.

Stupid assholes.

Sam dropped the travel bag and aimed the gun at them. "Congratulations. You tracked me down. I hope you got some satisfaction from that, because you're all about to fucking die."

Sam squeezed the trigger multiple times.

Nothing happened.

None of the intruders made a sound. They just stared at him. Sam checked the Glock. The magazine was empty. The fuckers had unloaded his gun. He had some extra ammo in his travel bag, but he knew he'd never have time to get to it. Something shiny glinted in his peripheral vision.

His head turned toward the dining room table.

There were multiple sharp instruments there.

And more dolls.

All at once, he knew what they had in mind. And he couldn't allow it to happen. It was a horrifying, ghastly notion. The thought of enduring it was more than he could bear. There was only one course of action left open to him. He lowered his head, gritted his teeth, and ran right at the main group of intruders, hoping to bull his way through them.

For a fleeting moment, he thought he might actually make it out the door. He'd taken them by surprise. Two intruders got knocked to the floor as he ran into them. Another was staggered by a powerful roundhouse punch he delivered to the man's chin. But there were just too many of them. Soon they recovered and overwhelmed him.

He was dragged kicking and screaming into the kitchen, where he was forced to lie flat on the floor. A rag was stuffed in his mouth to muffle his screaming. The woman knelt next to him and cut open his shirt with a scalpel. Sam struggled harder than ever, putting every bit of his not inconsiderable physical strength into the effort, but he was unable to budge them.

The woman pushed the exquisitely sharp blade of the scalpel into his quivering abdomen and parted his flesh in a straight line down to his waist. The pain was immense as blood gushed out of the deep incision. He bucked harder than ever as the woman—who he now saw was wearing surgical gloves—pushed her hands through the gash in his belly and began sawing away at something else inside him. A disconnected part of him had a feeling she knew what she was doing, that she had the detailed anatomical knowledge of a professional, but it was hard to care much about that as the blood continued to gush and the pain spiraled out of control.

After what seemed like a thousand agonized eternities, one of the intruders moved out of sight for a moment and returned with a handful of the dolls. These were handed one by one to the woman, who pushed them through the gash in his belly and into his open stomach.

There were five in all.

Five Barbie dolls.

One, no doubt, for a dead daughter belonging to each of the five intruders. It was symbolic retribution. Sam knew this because at varying times over the years he'd perpetrated a similar act on the corpses of their children. He didn't need to see their faces or hear verbal verification to know this. He'd thought he'd been so careful with the frequent moving around and changing of his name, but somehow they'd caught up to him.

He ached to say something defiant and hurtful as the life drained out of him, but the pain was just too much.

The Barbie Butcher choked on his own blood on his way down to Hell.

BLOODSUCKING NUNS FOR SATAN

MOSES DICKERSON HAPPENED UPON THE provocative scene purely by chance that warm July evening, those alluring nuns doing things he never would have imagined nuns doing. He'd been on his way back home after a night of sucking down Millers at Reggie's Pub. After arriving at the corner of Dreadmire Street and Impaler Avenue, he made the call to turn left instead of continuing straight ahead to the other side of Dreadmire.

Straight ahead was his usual route home. It was the quickest way back. Tonight, though, he felt like taking his time and walking the streets a bit. There were two main reasons for this, one being that he'd had significantly more than the usual amount to drink and wanted to allow his level of inebriation time to fade a little before he returned home. This wasn't done out of fear of Valerie—his wife of sixteen years—giving him shit for drinking too much. She didn't care. Hell, she drank more than he did. They were happy together and tolerant of each other's vices and bad habits. Moses looked forward to seeing her again in an hour or so. He just didn't like to come home too hammered because of unhappy memories of his bad-tempered father doing the same. He preferred to return home with nothing more than a nice, pleasant buzz.

The bigger reason for taking the long way home was harder to explain. Sometimes, for reasons he would struggle to articulate if asked, he just got a little restless. When these moods struck him, he liked to get away by himself for a bit and just wander. These infrequent urges nearly always came over him without warning and tonight was no exception.

So he continued down Impaler Avenue for a time, moving at an unhurried pace along several blocks, pausing occasionally to peer in at the wares on display behind the windows of closed stores. At one store, Marie's Curios, he spied a necklace that struck his fancy. He thought it would look pretty draped around Valerie's slender neck. The price handwritten on the little tag next to it was more than reasonable, too.

Making a mental note to return to the store the next day, he moved away from the window and continued down Impaler Avenue until it intersected with Delphine Street. On impulse, he checked traffic before crossing Impaler to the other side of Delphine.

It was a nice night. The sky was clear, the stars above little pinpoints blinking on a black velvet canvas. There weren't a lot of pedestrians out and about at this hour. Moses heard a distant sound of cars, but none were in sight and for a moment it was possible to pretend he was alone in the city. It imbued him with a peaceful feeling.

He was a few blocks along down the opposite side of Delphine when St. Seyrig, a very old and very gothic-looking Catholic church replete with spires and carved stone gargoyles on the roof, came into view on his right. The wrought-iron gate to the church's courtyard stood slightly open, which was the norm. It was closed and locked only on rare occasions. The church was just another of the city's many familiar landmarks. Moses had passed by it countless times over the course of his life, and he would have paid it no mind whatsoever tonight if not for the moaning.

His ears detected the sound—faint at first—just as he was walking past the gate. At first he assumed he was hearing sounds made by a drunken homeless person passed out somewhere nearby, perhaps even inside the courtyard. Some of them experienced moments of religious delirium when they were really far gone and found their way in there at night, but he soon realized this was something else altogether. He'd continued on for a few more strides when the sound abruptly rose in volume. It was then that he perceived its lustful quality.

Moses stopped walking and listened a moment longer, frowning as he strove to determine whether he was actually hearing what he thought he was hearing. In any other circumstance, the question would not have been in doubt. Moses knew the sound of a woman in the throes of sexual ecstasy when he heard it. What was baffling was that it did seem as if it was originating from somewhere inside the dark courtyard. Not being a religious man, Moses was not offended by the basic notion of sexual activity occurring on church grounds, so long as it was engaged in by consenting adults rather than pedophile priests taking advantage of altar boys. If two grownups were in there screwing around, more power to them. He didn't consider it sacrilege, a concept that meant little to him anyway.

In all his years of walking past this place, however, he'd never heard anything remotely like this issuing from the premises. This was what puzzled him. Bums doing things to each other in the dark wouldn't have been too surprising, he supposed, but this didn't sound like that either. Though he hadn't yet glimpsed the person doing the moaning, the sound struck him as entirely too healthy-sounding to have emanated from the rotgut-roughened throat of a homeless person.

Not only that, but it was . . . exciting.

After several moments of standing there and listening to the woman's moaning—which was not getting any quieter—Moses realized his dick was getting hard. He glanced down and saw an erection straining the front of his jeans. Another moan issued from inside the courtyard, this one significantly higher in pitch than any of the previous ones. Judging from the sound of it, the mystery woman wasn't far from transitioning from moans to screams. Moses's cock twitched, further straining the crotch of his jeans.

The intense state of arousal surprised him. He'd always found female aural expressions of pleasure stimulating, but hearing such sounds, especially when he hadn't had sex on the brain at all until just a moment ago, didn't tend to produce instantaneous, rigid results. Usually a visual element was required, too. And there was the issue of how much he'd had to drink to consider. This made the painfully swollen state of the organ doubly surprising, as a very high blood alcohol level normally suppressed arousal, at least in his experience. He knew guys who claimed otherwise—that, to the contrary, being hammered made them extra randy—but he was not one of those lucky assholes.

Bottom line, his dick should be pretty limp right now, but it wasn't.

Weird.

Moses was turning around and moving toward the open courtyard gate before he was even consciously aware of having decided to do so. When he did realize what he was doing, he admonished himself against it. He should turn around and hurry on home. Maybe when he got there he could surprise Valerie with one of the hardest fucks she'd enjoyed in some time.

This is what he told himself as he stood there with his right hand curled around one of the wrought-iron bars of the gate. It was what he should do, no doubt about it.

Moses's hand tightened around the wrought-iron bar.

He let out a breath.

Then he pushed the gate open wide enough to slip through the opening and enter the courtyard. The gate's hinges creaked slightly as he did this, making him wince. He feared the fornicators would hear this and lapse into silence. After all, it was possible they were so into what they were doing they simply hadn't considered the possibility of being caught in the act. His intrusion on the scene might change that.

The moaning did not cease, however, nor falter for even a moment.

Moses continued deeper into the courtyard, winding his way along the concrete path and passing by benches, trees, statues of various religious figures, and a water fountain. A very large tree with thick branches and abundant leaves dominated the center of the courtyard. The big tree stood in a circle of grass, around which was a low brick wall. Years had passed since Moses had last ventured inside the courtyard, but memory told him another long bench sat inside near the tree. The moaning seemed to be coming from that general area.

He went into a crouch as he approached the wall. When he reached the wall, he dropped to his knees and peered over the top of it. What he saw then made his cock strain harder than ever and set his heart to pounding. He reached down and fondled himself through the fabric of his jeans.

Two Roman Catholic nuns were inside the wall beneath the low-hanging branches of the tree. A direct stream of moonlight shined through a serendipitously open section of branches, providing ample illumination. One of the nuns was on her back on the bench near the base of the tree. Most of her garments—including the holy habit and its underskirts—were strewn about her on the ground. Of her holy garments, she wore only the wimple that covered her head and framed her lovely face, which was currently sheened in sweat, the mouth open wide in ecstasy. Her legs were spread wide, one propped on the bench, the foot of the other on the ground.

The second nun—also wearing only her wimple—was on her knees between the supine nun's spread legs. Both women had large breasts and lean, toned bodies. This came as a surprise to Moses, who was not accustomed to nuns looking like Playboy models. The kneeling nun had a nice round ass. He gave his crotch a harder squeeze as he stared at it a moment

The nun on the bench moaned again, writhing on the bench and squeezing her breasts as the other nun flicked rapidly at her clitoris with the tip of her tongue. She screamed when the nun pleasuring her pushed three hooked fingers into her vagina and flexed them. The explosion of sound was like a gunshot ringing out in the night. A few moments ago, so dramatic a noise might have scared Moses off, but he was too enthralled by what he was seeing for that to happen now. He opened his pants and reached inside them to grab his dick, gasping as he did it.

A part of him felt bad for what he was doing, like a peeping Tom. This wasn't the kind of thing he did ordinarily. In fact, he'd never done anything like this until now. He wasn't a voyeur. He wasn't a lowdown, creeping predator. In the normal course of things, Valerie was all he ever needed to satiate his needs.

But there was nothing normal about what was happening here. The need driving him consumed him. He felt powerless. It took him a few moments longer to begin to realize just how true that was.

Another sound from inside the brick wall snagged his attention, pulling his gaze toward a man who was lying on his side several feet away from the bench. The man was nude and facing away from Moses, who initially assumed the sound he'd made was just another result of sexual ecstasy. He figured this was some kind of freaky Catholic free-for-all threesome. The guy was masturbating while watching the nuns go at it. But then the man made the sound again and Moses realized what he was hearing was more like an expression of pain.

More of an agonized squeal than a moan.

And he was making the sound repeatedly.

Moses's hand froze around his dick.

He frowned.

Maybe there was something much darker going on here than he'd first suspected. In fact, maybe it would be a good idea to start backing away and get the hell out of here.

While he still could.

But before he could do that, the head of the squatting nun snapped toward him. Yellow eyes flashed in the moonlight. Her mouth opened wide, exposing long fangs at the corners. Her mouth was smeared with blood.

Moses swallowed hard.

"Oh, fuck," he whispered.

Fucking lesbian nun vampires. Didn't see that one coming.

He began to raise up out of his crouch, setting his feet beneath him as he got ready to turn and run.

The nun on the bench sat up straight. Her eyes also flashed yellow in the moonlight. As the moonlight fell across her flat belly, Moses saw that three large, looping numbers had been freshly carved across it, blood dripping from the gashes.

Three sixes.

Moses gulped again.

Fucking Satanic lesbian nun vampires. Fuck me sideways with a rusty pitchfork.

The nun with the numbers on her belly beckoned to him with a crooked finger. "You." Her voice sounded barely human, tinged with the sibilant hissing of a serpent. "Come to us."

Moses shook his head. "Nope. I'm out. Sorry."

He had every intention of bolting from the place as he uttered these defiant words. However, he found he was unable to resist the nun's command. Against his will, he walked into the brick circle, whimpering as he approached the nuns.

More commands were issued.

Moses stripped off his clothes and tossed them aside, again against his will.

The nun on the ground grabbed his still-engorged member and tore it off at the root. Moses screamed. The nun grabbed him and pulled him close, clamping her mouth around the gushing wound. The other nun leered at him as she watched and feverishly fingered herself. The man on the ground—the other victim—rolled onto his back and stared blearily up at Moses. He'd also had his cock ripped away and looked close to dead from blood loss.

Moses stared up through the branches at the moon as the nun kneeling before him continued to suck blood from his ruined nether regions. He thought about Valerie and how much she would miss him. Deep regret overwhelmed him in that moment.

He sighed as things started to turn fuzzy.

Really wish I'd gone home drunk for once. Fuck me with a serrated tent-pole.

He was dead a few minutes later.

Later that night, he and the other castrated man were buried in unmarked graves in the cemetery behind the church, joining hundreds more men who'd fallen victim to the vampire nuns of St. Seyrig.

SOUTH COUNTY MADMAN

Tennessee
1987

THE DOGS WERE BARKING AGAIN. Luke Benson's eyes snapped open in the darkness. He was flat on his back in the little twin bed in his room. A glance at the glowing blue numbers on his Panasonic VCR told him the time was a hair past one in the morning. He remained still a few moments longer, waiting for the last vestiges of unconsciousness to slip away. The dogs kept right on barking. The sound wasn't unusual. Hell, they were dogs. Dogs barked. He lived on an isolated patch of land right on the edge of the woods in his single-wide trailer. Now and then a squirrel would go scampering across the property, never failing to set off Jasper and Harley. The two Dobermans were chained to spikes driven into the ground behind the trailer. They were sweet, loving animals, but the fearsome reputation of the breed effectively kept away anyone who might wish to do him harm. And the sad truth was, there were quite a few folks around who'd like to see him six feet under.

The barking wasn't letting up, the way it usually did after a wandering squirrel or possum had the good sense to get gone from the area. If anything, it was becoming more shrill and strident. That shrillness bugged Luke. It bespoke an unusual, worrying level of agitation, which stirred his paranoia. Years had passed since that business with the dead girls, enough time to start hoping the worst of that ugliness was truly behind him. But deep down he knew better. He thought of Stump Wilhoite, saw the old man's scowling, bitter face in his mind, and remembered the vow of vengeance he had sworn in the wake of Luke's acquittal. It had been an emotional moment and Stump had been speaking from a place of monumental rage. You couldn't blame the guy. Some sick bastard had done quite a number on his teen daughter. She was violated and dismembered prior to being dumped in the woods a scant two miles from Luke's trailer.

One of the dogs—he thought it was Harley—yelped.

Luke rolled onto his side and reached under his bed, curled a hand around the grip of his .357 Magnum, and got out of bed. He pulled on jeans, stepped into shoes he left unlaced, grabbed a flashlight, and hurried out of the trailer.

"Jasper! Harley!"

The dogs were straining at the ends of their leads, continuing to bark in that overly agitated, shrill way as they faced the woods. Luke snapped on the flashlight and aimed the beam at the line of trees bordering the property. Seeing no one there, he swept the beam around the barren yard and still came up empty. Didn't mean there wasn't someone lurking out there deeper in the woods, but he wasn't about to go stumbling around out there at this dark hour. Even if there was a trespasser in the area, Luke was confident the ferocious response of his animals would prevent the skulking son of a bitch from coming any closer.

He approached the dogs and knelt between them, setting the gun and flashlight on the ground in order to reach for the scruffs of their necks. They kept straining and barking a few moments longer, but began to settle down as he cooed at them and kneaded the furry flesh between their shoulders. Jasper was the first to fully relax. He sat next to Luke and lapped happily at his face with his gritty tongue. Harley soon followed suit and within moments he was overwhelmed with canine affection. He laughed softly and tried halfheartedly pushing them away, but they immediately came back for more slavering attention.

The smile died on his face as he spied something on the ground a few feet to his right—it was a hunk of raw meat, what looked like a slice of store-cut steak. His chest tightened and he couldn't breathe for a moment. There was only one possible reason it was there. Someone had attempted to poison his dogs. Thankfully, the sliver of meat looked like it had not been touched, a miracle he could only chalk up to the dogs' agitation at the intrusion of a stranger. The thought of someone trying to harm his animals supplanted the terror he'd felt upon spying the meat, igniting a fury that had him clenching his teeth and reaching for his gun.

He scooped up the hunk of meat, came out of his crouch and aimed the .357 at the woods, squeezing off three quick shots despite the absence of a visible target. The intent was intimidation, though an accidental lethal result wouldn't bother him any. Any asshole willing to hurt his animals to get at him deserved whatever they got. The explosive reports of the gun got the dogs all worked up again, making them bark and strain at their leads some more. After a few moments, the ringing in his ears receded some and he began to perceive another sound just barely audible above the barking of his dogs.

Someone was crying out there in the woods. Whimpering and moaning. Calling out for their mama. Poor dumb bastard. Luke had gotten lucky with one of his shots. He didn't feel good about it, but this was the chance you took when you intruded on a man's property out here in the sticks, especially when that man had ample reason to mistrust intruders.

He carried the hunk of meat over to the steel trash can at the side of the trailer, lifted the lid, and dropped it inside. Then he wedged the lid back down firmly, secure in the knowledge that it was out of the reach of his dogs.

That done, he returned to the rear of the trailer and knelt next to Harley. He unclipped the wired, straining animal from his lead, gripped him by his collar, and pressed his mouth close to the dog's ear. "Harley, find!"

He released his grip on the collar and Harley shot off into the woods.

After retrieving his flashlight, Luke stood and glanced at the other dog. "Jasper, stay! You watch over things here while Harley and I check this out, okay?"

The animal sat and gave him a bright-eyed, doggy grin. Luke scratched him behind the ears and took off after Harley.

Tracking the dog down wasn't difficult. All he had to do was follow the sounds of growling and screaming. Keeping the flashlight aimed ahead of him, he threaded his way through a maze of trees, occasionally having to shoulder his way past vines and low-hanging branches. After just a couple minutes, the flashlight's beam found

Harley's excitedly wiggling rear end. A shift of the beam revealed the tear-streaked face of a young man sitting with his back against the base of a tall tree.

The man held shaking hands in front of him in a pitiful attempt to ward off Harley's snapping teeth. Luke noted that his hands were covered in blood, probably from where he'd been pressing them over the wound in his side. He gibbered insensibly and stared up at Luke with wide, terrified eyes. The guy looked familiar, though he was sure he didn't know the man personally. It was something in the shape of his nose and the set of his eyes. The firm jawline, too. It reminded him strongly of someone else. His brow furrowed as he searched the nooks and crannies of his memory, straining to make a connection.

And then he had it.

He let out a breath.

Shit.

After making Harley heel, he aimed the flashlight's beam right at the man's face and said, "You're Stump's boy, right? Calvin, ain't it?"

The young man grimaced as he sucked in a breath between clenched teeth. Then he glared at Luke. "Yes. I'm Emma's brother."

He was the brother of one of the dead girls. It made sense. Luke figured most folks had let go of their outrage in the years since the trial. It was just the way life worked. People got wrapped up in the drama of a big thing like that, but public indignation over a supposed injustice had a short shelf-life. The furor died down and the general populace moved on with their lives. But it didn't work like that with family. Luke knew that well enough. He was still clinging tight to decades-old grudges of his own. With family, you don't ever forget, especially when it comes to murder.

Luke shook his head. "So what was the plan, Calvin? Kill my dogs, break into my trailer . . . and then what?"

A corner of Calvin's mouth twitched, his eyes burning with defiance in the glare of the flashlight's beam. "Was gonna slit your throat and watch you bleed out like a pig."

Harley growled at the more aggressive tone, prompting Luke to gently nudge one of his hindquarters with the toe of a shoe. "Easy, boy." The dog ceased growling and looked up at him, tongue lolling out as he panted. "Calvin, I didn't kill your sister. Didn't kill any of those girls."

That same corner of the kid's mouth twitched again. "Bullshit."

"It's the stone truth, boy. I don't know who killed Emma or any of the others, but it wasn't me."

The kid grimaced as his hands went to the wound in his side again. "You're a liar."

Luke moved closer and knelt beside him. He set the flashlight on the ground, but kept the .357 clutched in his right hand. "Let's get a look at this. Lift up your shirt."

"Get away from me."

Luke sighed. "Kid, if I was gonna kill you, I would've done it by now. Now lift up the damn shirt."

Calvin's expression remained mistrustful, but he complied with Luke's request, the pain from the wound evidently overwhelming his righteous fury. He was wearing a flannel shirt over a white T-shirt. His blood-stained fingers shook as he worked at the buttons of the flannel shirt. Once it was open, he tugged up the T-shirt, and Luke leaned closer for a better look.

The bullet had carved a pretty nasty groove along the side of his ribcage. Luke didn't doubt it hurt like a bitch, but the kid had been lucky as hell. The bullet hadn't actually entered his body. If it had, the little asshole might be dead already. "All right, let your shirt down."

Calvin winced as he took his own look at the wound. "Oh, shit. Oh, shit, man."

"Relax. You're gonna live." Luke snatched up the flashlight, stood up, and moved back a few steps. "Come on, now, get up."

The kid braced his hands on the ground and tried to push himself up, but his face contorted at a fresh surge of agony and he fell back against the tree. Harley shifted on the ground next to Luke, looking up at him with anxious eyes. The look was one that always got to him. It was the dog's way of asking him if everything was okay. That was one thing people who weren't dog people didn't get. They were actually expressive as hell and had many ways of communicating their feelings. Harley looked and acted like a tough critter, but he and Jasper were more like the kids he'd never had than actual guard dogs. He'd acquired the two of them from the same litter shortly after his acquittal, raising them from puppies. In the wake of his post-acquittal estrangement from damn near everyone he'd ever known, they were practically the only family he had left.

The train of thought effectively killed any sympathy he might have started feeling for Calvin Wilhoite. "Tell me something, kid. What kind of cowardly, sick piece of shit poisons animals?"

Keeping his back against the tree for support, Calvin again tried to get to his feet. This time he was more successful. Once he was upright, he fixed Luke with a sneering glare and said, "You ain't got no right to talk, South County Madman."

Luke pointed the .357 at him.

Calvin's eyes went wide as he sucked in a breath and began to tremble. He extended a shaking hand. "No. No. Please . . ."

Luke couldn't help feeling a primal satisfaction at seeing the fear in the boy's eyes. For years now, he'd lived in the long shadow of that murdering asshole, wrongfully branded with the faceless, mysterious killer's hateful nickname. The South County Madman, aka the middle Tennessee boogeyman. As far as many were concerned, he was the South County Madman, regardless of what the jury had decided. There had never been a shred of physical evidence linking him to the crimes. Other than the fact that all five bodies had been dumped in the woods adjacent to his property, there had been no evidence of any kind against him. But that hadn't mattered to the citizenry, who were scared shitless and wanted desperately to feel safe again. So the law went looking for a scapegoat and found a convenient one in Luke Benson. From the beginning, his court-appointed lawyer told him the slipshod case the prosecution had put together would fall apart at the trial level. No self-respecting jury would ever convict on such flimsy evidence in a capital case. Even so, until the verdict was read, Luke remained convinced he had a rendezvous with the electric chair.

After all he had endured, it felt good—albeit in a deeply bitter way—to get some mileage out of his unjustly earned reputation. "What's the matter, boy? You look like you're about to piss your pants."

Fresh tears spilled down Calvin's trembling face. "Please . . ."

Luke lowered the gun. "Calm down, kid, I ain't—"

His next words died in his throat as Calvin propelled himself away from the tree. The lunge happened too fast for Luke to dodge it, but instinct caused him to bring the gun up again, its barrel digging into the kid's abdomen as he slammed into him. His finger squeezing the trigger was pure reflex. It was the last thing he wanted to happen, but there was nothing he could do to stop it. The gun went off as their entangled bodies began a descent to the ground.

Luke cried out in pain as his back hit the rocky forest floor and the kid's dead weight settled atop him. A sense of helpless, bitter horror engulfed him as the irreversible grim reality of what had happened hit him. Another Wilhoite kid was dead and yet again he would be taking the blame. This time he'd actually done the deed, albeit by accident. But no one else would ever see it that way. The court of public opinion would decree Calvin Wilhoite the latest victim of the evil South County Madman. And this time there would be no calm, rational evaluation of the facts leading to another reprieve. He would be railroaded for sure. Hell, considering how high the blood-fever was likely to run amongst the locals, he might not even make it to trial alive this time. An assassination or a staged "suicide" in a holding cell seemed not just possible, but probable.

Harley was going crazy, yapping his head off and dancing around the bodies prone on the ground. His barking had taken on that shrill, frantic quality again. Back at the trailer, Jasper was actually howling, his anxiety over what was happening out in the woods driving him crazy. Luke pictured him straining against his lead so hard he was nearly choking himself. Coupled with the reports of the gun, it was a lot of noise.

Things were usually dead silent out here this time of night. Fortunately, though, there was little chance anyone would hear the ruckus, much less alert the local law over it. Luke had been a loner much of his life. Even before the bodies of dead girls started showing up around his property, he'd had few close friends, a fact that had cemented the public's image of him as a creepy killer. Guys like that were always loners. But it was his lack of interest in the company of other human beings that had prompted him to acquire this isolated patch of land right on the southernmost tip of Rutherford County. The property's location set it inside the county but outside the city limits of Murfreesboro, the nearest town. His trailer was so remote, in fact, that there was no trash pickup and no mail delivery. He had to burn his own garbage and journey to town once a week to pick up any mail that had accumulated at his P.O. box. These things were mildly inconvenient, but Luke enjoyed the solitude. He had never liked other people much, anyway, seeing most of them as duplicitous, backstabbing assholes only out for themselves.

In the end, though, the isolation worked against him, setting up the circumstances that transformed him from being a typical loner—the kind of guy hardly anyone ever gave a second thought—into an outright social pariah. According to Luke's lawyer, it was common for serial killers to dump their victims in remote wilderness locations. It was just his bad luck that this particular killer had chosen the area right around his trailer as his preferred site for corpse disposal. He understood the logic of this, but a more paranoid part of him wondered if there was something more than just bad luck involved. What if he was being specifically targeted by someone who wanted to pin the blame on him for mysterious reasons? Though the lawyer had assured him this possibility was unlikely, he wasn't able to utterly dismiss it.

Though immediate discovery of what had happened here was unlikely, Luke was anxious to calm his dogs and put an end to the noise. He wouldn't be able to think properly about what to do next until that happened.

So he rolled the corpse off him, sat up, and heaved a big breath. Harley was on him in an instant, slobbering all over him and licking his face incessantly with his sandy tongue. Luke endured the anxious canine attention with quiet stoicism for a few moments, happy that the dog had at least stopped barking. And though Jasper was still barking intermittently, he was no longer howling, another relief. Harley began to calm down after getting his neck scratched some and receiving many whispered reassurances that everything was okay. Everything was not okay, but for now he needed his boys to think it was.

Luke got creakily to his feet and stared down at the dead boy, his face twisting in an expression of disgust. He hadn't been any older than eighteen or nineteen. *Too young to die,* Luke thought. *And too stupid to live.*

He felt sad for the kid and for the loss of his abruptly terminated life. Felt bad for his parents, even that mean old Stump. But these feelings were short-lived, giving way to a fury that surprised him. He was an innocent fucking man. A jury of his goddamn peers had affirmed this. Was it so much to ask that he finally be allowed to put the painful past behind him? All he wanted anymore was to be left alone.

And to have some fucking peace, goddammit.

The force of what he was feeling could not be contained. It had to go outward. He let out a screech of rage and started kicking at the dead boy's body, driving the toe of his shoe into his wounded side again and again. Unused to seeing his owner so enraged, Harley started whining. It was the sound of the dog's distress that eventually brought Luke back to earth, shame displacing his fading anger. He stood there bent over for a few moments, breathing heavily with his hands braced on his knees.

He stood there and stared at the body a few moments longer, his brain abuzz with too many half-formed thoughts and ideas, none of which showed any promise of slowing down and coalescing into something coherent. A temporary change of scenery was needed. He turned away from the body and started back toward his trailer, whistling at Harley to follow him, which he did after a final sniff at the corpse.

Jasper went a little haywire when he saw them emerge from the woods, yelping and jumping at the end of his lead. Despite his manic behavior, the dog was clearly relieved to see his owner and canine buddy again. Luke gave him a little extra attention for a minute, then unclipped the dog from his lead and beckoned for both of them to follow him into the trailer. It would be some time before he would feel safe leaving them outside again. Hell, they might even become permanent indoor residents. They could just as easily alert him to the presence of intruders from in there.

Back in the trailer, he snapped on the lights and grabbed a cold can of Old Milwaukee from the fridge. He took a long swallow from it, heaved a sigh, and sat in a folding chair at the little card table in the tiny kitchen. His dogs plopped down on the linoleum floor and looked up at him with big grins. He smiled at them and felt his eyes water as he thought of how close he had come to losing at least one of them.

The noise in his head began to recede as he sat there and drank more of his beer. The front section of yesterday morning's Tennessean newspaper soon drew his attention. Anxious to distract himself from the crisis at hand—even if just for a few moments—he drew it close and read that day's big story, which was more about the Iran-Contra mess. Reagan's boys had screwed the pooch big time on that one. He hadn't had a chance to get down to town to pick up today's paper, but he knew it would just be more of the same. He didn't actually give a shit one way or the other. The top guys on both sides of the political aisle were always out to screw the little guy, regardless of their stated intentions. This was a point of view he'd inherited from his asshole father. Even now, long after their violent falling out, Luke still thought this was a remarkably sensible way of looking at things.

But reading the story did its job. By the time he pushed the paper away and finished off his beer, he was a lot calmer and was thinking much more clearly. He saw only one way out of the predicament Stump Wilhoite's idiot son had created for him. It meant becoming for real the bad guy everybody thought he was. It was a bitter thing, a very hard thing to accept, but there was no way around it, not if he meant to resume some semblance of his normal life. And he did, by God, he did.

After tossing the empty beer can in the trash, he went to the closet in his bedroom and retrieved the box of ammo for the .357 he kept on the top shelf. With the dogs following him from room to room, he carried the box into the kitchen and filled the gun's empty chambers with fresh slugs. He shoved a few extras into his jeans before returning the box to the closet. While in there, he grabbed a pair of winter gloves. He hadn't imagined he'd be donning them again for months to come, but they were necessary for his purposes tonight. That done, he cleaned Calvin's blood off his torso, put on a shirt, grabbed everything he needed, and departed after giving his boys a final affectionate nuzzle behind the ears.

There was a little creek about ten minutes into the woods. Dragging the body along with him, Luke followed the stream of peacefully trickling water down to a narrow dirt access road primarily used by hunters. That was where he found Calvin's Ford pickup. Huffing and puffing from the exertion, he got the dead kid's body loaded into the back. An examination of his wallet gave him his home address, which luckily was in a part of town Luke knew well. He could get there easily enough. A further search of Calvin's pockets turned up his keys, which was a damn good thing. If the kid had dropped them out there in the woods, Luke's plan would have been dead on arrival.

After covering the body with a dirty plastic tarp, he slid in behind the wheel of the truck and jammed the key in the ignition slot. He had a bad moment where it seemed like the engine wasn't going to turn over, but then it did finally sputter to life. Some kind of heavy metal noise issued from the truck's tinny speakers. Luke didn't recognize it. The only rock and roll he liked was from his own youth in the sixties. The Beatles, the Stones, The Who, Hendrix, etc. Even Jimi's famous six-string histrionics had been very different from all this modern-day screaming and yelling over guitars that sounded like they were being tortured. He was more of a Hank Williams and Merle Haggard kind of guy these days, anyway. After silencing the radio, he got the truck turned around and started toward town.

The access road was a couple of long, curving miles of bumpy, rock-strewn dirt. Luke had to go slow and keep the high beams on to avoid collisions with trees. The narrow road eventually petered out and fed into a stretch of two-lane blacktop. From there it was a mostly uneventful eight-mile ride to the outskirts of Murfreesboro. At about the midway point of the journey there was one briefly tense moment when a patrol car from the sheriff's department went speeding past him in the opposite direction. Luke glanced at the rearview mirror and gulped as he saw the cruiser's brake lights come on. He had been sure the cruiser would turn around and come after him, even though he was observing the speed limit. It was a late hour in a small town and hardly anyone was out driving around. The lawmen around these parts had a deserved reputation for stopping people for no reason other than sheer boredom.

But the brake lights winked out again after a ball-shriveling couple seconds, and the cruiser kept heading away from him. This came as a massive relief to Luke, whose gloved right hand had been curled around the grip of his .357 during those seconds. He let go of the gun and listened to the heavy thumping of his heart, wondering how it would have gone down if the sheriff's deputy had come after him. He saw only two realistic scenarios. Either he would have taken his own life or he would have been forced to kill the deputy. Both possibilities were equally appalling. He didn't want to die and he had no desire to risk a gunfight with a cop. The only other possibility would have been arrest and he had already decided against letting that happen. Hell, it was the whole reason he'd embarked upon this crazy course of action.

A few miles after passing a sign welcoming visitors to Murfreesboro, he took a left at Compton Road, experiencing another brief period of uneasiness as he continued down past the VA hospital, where he'd spent some time after his return from Vietnam in 1972. The building was the site of some deeply unpleasant memories, and he didn't fully appreciate how tense its proximity made him until he had to forcibly unclench his teeth.

But then the facility was behind him and he was fully focused on the present again. Ten minutes later he took a right at Church Street and shortly thereafter found himself in the heart of Murfreesboro. He was jittery and his nerves kept yelling at him to go faster and get this over with, but he kept a lid on his fear and mostly stuck to the posted speed limits. Occasionally he went a little faster than that, especially on side streets, where the posted limits were often absurdly low. The key here was in not doing anything to arouse the suspicion of any law enforcement types. Yeah, speeding was a bad idea, but if you went too slow in certain areas you could get mistaken for an overly cautious drunk driver.

Luke navigated his way through a maze of familiar streets and neighborhoods, bittersweet memories from a lifetime ago assailing him in the process. He had grown up here. Driving through the area in the dead of night—something he hadn't done in a very long time—was a strange experience. It was like traveling through a haunted museum of the past. His mind easily conjured images of his youthful self flying down these streets on his Schwinn. The memory was so vivid he could almost hear the flapping sound made by the baseball cards wedged into the spokes of his bicycle's wheels.

The Wilhoite home was at the end of a quiet street in one of the town's older residential areas. The houses here were mainly one-story ranch-style houses built many decades earlier. Many of the families who lived in the neighborhood had been entrenched here for generations. Luke cut the truck's headlights and slowed down as he neared the house, approaching it with an abundance of caution. He heaved a sigh of relief when he realized there were no lights on inside, making it likely no one was up awaiting young Calvin's return. It also meant Calvin's excursion to his place tonight had probably been a lone-wolf act on his part unsanctioned by Stump or anyone else in the family. It would make doing what he had to do a lot easier.

He pulled into the gravel driveway, eased the door shut after getting out of the truck, and let himself into the house with Calvin's key. Once he was inside, he snapped the flashlight beam on and performed a careful search of the premises. It didn't take long. He found Stump Wilhoite and Wilma, his wife, sound asleep in the master bedroom. They were the only people in the house. Everything was falling into place with such shocking ease it was almost possible to believe it was all preordained. Like it was God's will. It was an idea he seized upon with pathetic desperation. These people had unjustly persecuted him for a thing he hadn't done for a long, long time. Looked at in that light, this was just a regrettably brutal way of setting things right again.

Stump began to stir as Luke came into the room, making sleepy, half-aware sounds without coming to full consciousness. Luke shoved the flashlight into the waistband of his jeans, jerked the pillow out from under Stump's head, and jammed it down over his face. The old man did wake up then, uttering a startled, muffled shriek from beneath the pillow. Luke pressed the barrel of the gun against the pillow and said, "You did this. You made it happen."

He squeezed the trigger.

Stump stopped moving.

Wilma came awake then and sat up with a terrified gasp. Luke climbed onto the bed and drilled a gloved fist straight into the center of her face. Her nose broke with an audible snap and she flopped backward as blood erupted from her nostrils. Luke grabbed her pillow and pressed it down over her face. Rather than firing the gun again, he straddled her and held the pillow down until she stopped moving. He then tossed the pillow aside and checked her pulse. When he was satisfied that she was truly dead, he went back out to the living room and peered out at the front yard through a parted curtain. Nothing was happening out there. He nonetheless stood there an additional several minutes to be certain police weren't on the way.

When he was sure no one had called in a report of the single shot he had fired, Luke went out to the truck and removed Calvin's body from the back. This time he carried the body in his arms. This required a tremendous, back-straining physical effort, but Luke didn't want to leave evidence of a body being dragged into the house. It was a warm summer night and the sweat was rolling off him in rivers and stinging his eyes before he was able to get back inside. Once he was back inside, he carried Calvin into the master bedroom and set about trying to stage the scene.

Like most of his firearms—of which he had several—Luke's .357 was unregistered. He didn't like the idea of anyone in any kind of official capacity having an accurate idea of his self-defense capability. This was a product of the deep paranoia that had taken root within him in the aftermath of his trial. He didn't trust anyone in general, a mindset that absolutely included anyone wearing any kind of uniform. Hell, especially those assholes. After thoroughly wiping it down, he wrapped Calvin's dead fingers around the grip of the gun, threading his forefinger through the trigger guard.

What he had in mind was pretty straightforward. Calvin was obviously a troubled kid. He'd had some kind of heated dispute with his parents. Things got out of hand and he wound up killing them in their sleep. In the wake of this act, the reality of what he had done hit the boy hard and, understandably distraught, he wound up taking his own life with the very gun he'd used to murder his father. No one would bat an eye over the unregistered gun. Such things weren't unusual. There would be nothing at all to connect Luke to any of it.

Satisfied he'd done his best to set the scene, Luke got to his feet and headed out of the bedroom. A sudden thought made him halt in his tracks in the hallway. His face contorted with frustration and disgust as he realized he'd overlooked a potentially crucial detail. He went back into the bedroom, knelt next to Calvin's body, and rolled it onto its side in order to aim the flashlight beam at his back. And there it was—the exit wound.

Fucking hell.

The .357 slug had passed through his body. The damn thing was still out there in the woods behind his trailer. Luke was no forensics expert, but he knew the investigation would need to turn up the bullet that killed the boy.

Or at least the one that had apparently killed him.

Luke curled his hand around Calvin's fingers and used them to press the barrel of the gun against his abdomen, lining it up with the original entry wound. This was risky. He didn't like the idea of having to fire a second shot. Luck had been on his side the first time, but doing it a second time would really be pushing it. And yet, what other choice did he have?

None at all, that's what.

So he did it.

And then he got the hell out of that house.

The house where he had grown up was just three streets over. He kept his head down and walked at a brisk pace in that direction. Along the way, he passed just one house where someone appeared to be awake. There was a single dim light on at a window in the back. He eyed the window carefully as he continued on past the house, but he detected no signs of movement. Dogs on chains or in fenced-in yards barked as he hurriedly passed through their territory. This didn't concern Luke much. A nighttime canine chorus wasn't unusual in this kind of neighborhood. Dogs got bored and started talking to each other. For the most part, no one paid it any mind.

The lights were on at 3366 Montgomery Street. The place was lit up like the fourth of goddamn July. Of course. Josh Benson was a retired union man with a generous pension. He was always up all hours of the night, or at least that was how it'd been back when Luke still came around semi-regularly. At first glance, it looked like nothing had changed. He had been counting on that. Josh was his way back home. They had their differences. Big ones. There had been some violent episodes. But when it came down to it, blood was blood and still meant something. His father would help him, he was sure of it.

Luke climbed the porch steps and rapped hard on the front door. Minutes passed and no one answered, but he knew someone was awake in there because he could hear the faint strains of a scratchy C&W record playing on the turntable. "I'm Walking The Floor Over You" by Ernest Tubb. It was one of his pop's favorites. He played it whenever he was in a particularly maudlin mood, which didn't bode well for any interaction they might have here. The song ended and another Tubb tune—"Drivin' Nails In My Coffin"—began moments later. Maybe he was passed out drunk in there and really couldn't hear him knocking. Much more likely, however, was the possibility that he was opting to ignore the late-night caller at his door.

Luke couldn't blame the man. He hated the ornery old bastard, but this reaction was nothing but plain common sense. An unexpected knock on your door at this hour could only mean bad news or trouble of some kind. Still, Luke was in a hell of a bind and had no choice but to continue pressing the issue.

So he banged harder on the door and pitched his voice above the sound of the music. "Pop! It's me, Luke! I need your help!"

A few more moments passed and Luke was on the verge of giving up when he detected the sound of booted feet approaching from the other side of the door, making the hardwood floor inside the foyer creak. The door came open and Josh Benson stood framed in the doorway, a scowl twisting a face flushed a bright shade of red. "Son? What in blue blazes brings you out here at this hour?"

"I'm in trouble."

The old man's scowl faded and he stared at his son with an unreadable expression for maybe a full minute. His breath reeked of cheap beer. Probably Old Style, his favorite going back at least to the 50s. Finally, he shook his head and stepped away from the door. "Come on in, then."

Luke followed him into the house, shutting the door behind him. The living room was directly adjacent to the little foyer. Stepping into it again triggered that impression of traveling back in time. He hadn't been in this room for going on a decade, but it still looked much as he remembered. The furniture—all of it stuff his late mother had purchased new in the early 60s—was all the same, albeit more weathered-looking now. The same framed family photos still hung from the walls. Younger versions of Luke appeared in several of them. He was even smiling in a few of them. Seeing the mostly black and white images now was weird, like looking at pictures of strangers. No, on further reflection, it was weirder than that. The life depicted in those pictures was completely alien to him now. They were like glimpses of life on another planet. A late-night movie was playing with the sound turned down on a big Zenith television opposite the dusty sofa, some old gangster thing with Peter Lorre and Humphrey Bogart. The TV was one of the boxy old-fashioned kind with legs on the bottom.

Josh walked over to the stereo system and lifted the needle off the record, silencing Ernest Tubb with a nasty scratch of vinyl. "Sit down, son. I'll get us both a beer."

Luke stood there while his father walked out of the room. He was too wound up to sit down so instead he crossed the room to examine more framed photos that lined the shelves of a bookcase. He gnawed on his bottom lip and frowned at more pictures of smiling aliens.

"Here, son."

Luke gasped at the sound of his father's voice. He hadn't known the old drunk could tread so silently. He turned away from the pictures and nodded as he accepted the can of Old Style. "Thanks."

Josh opened his beer and knocked back a big gulp, grimacing as he choked it down. "So tell me about this so-called trouble you're in."

Luke popped the tab on his own can and had a tiny sip. The beer wasn't unappreciated, but he needed to stay sober until he was clear of this mess and safely ensconced back in his own home. He nonetheless had another couple contemplative sips as he mulled over what to tell his father. He wracked his brain for some kind of believable cover story, but nothing came immediately to mind. All he could think of suddenly was the .357 discharging into the pillow he'd held down over Stump Wilhoite's face.

The beer can slipped from his gloved fingers, hit the floor, and rolled, spilling beer across the horrible mustard-colored carpeting. The powerful surge of grief and regret took him by surprise and he was powerless to stem the tide of emotion as he dropped to his knees and covered his face with his hands.

He heard his father heave a sigh of disgust and say, "Ah, hell."

Luke's sobbing continued until Josh Benson knocked him upside his head. This was no love tap. The old man had whacked him a good one. The physical pain shocked Luke out of the emotion of the moment. It was the first time his father had hit him since the year before he got drafted and shipped off to Vietnam. A simmering rage displaced the grief and he got carefully to his feet, his hands curled into shaking fists at his sides.

Josh sneered. "I ain't interested in fighting you, son. Hell, I know you could whoop my ass these days. But if you're really in trouble, you need to pull your shit together and tell me all about it."

Luke heaved a breath and let go of his rage. His father was right. And he knew there was no line of bullshit that would cut it in this situation. "I need a ride home. I . . . I . . ." He grimaced. "I killed Stump Wilhoite tonight. And the rest of his family."

His father's face registered mild surprise, but there was no hint of anything like shock or disgust in his expression. The old man didn't reply right away but instead eyed his son in a curious, contemplative way. Luke had a hard time imagining what was going through the man's head and his anxiety redlined again as he waited for him to say something. When he finally did speak, the words he uttered made no sense to him. "Did you do it for me?"

Luke frowned. "What?"

Josh finished off his beer and crushed the can in his hand. "You heard me, boy. Did you do in ol' Stump on my behalf?"

Luke's frown deepened. "Why in hell would I do it for you?"

His father's features took on that quizzical cast again. "To protect me, of course. Am I wrong?"

Luke could make no sense of the turn the conversation had taken. He stared at his father in open-mouthed confusion for a long moment. Maybe the old man was even drunker than he'd thought and had misunderstood him. But, no, that didn't seem possible based on his actual words. Luke remained at a loss until a disturbing thought took shape in his head. As soon as it occurred to him, he knew it had to be true. It made a perfect, diabolical kind of sense, and he had to wonder why he'd never thought of it before.

"It was you," he said, pushing the words through tightly clenched teeth. "You're the South County Madman."

"Yeah, reckon I am. Hell, son, I figured you finally worked it out and went after Stump for me. Shit, I was almost proud of you there for a second." Josh laughed. "Well, don't stand there looking like a damn simpleton. Don't tell me you're gonna hold a grudge against your pa."

A lot of things went through Luke's mind in the next several moments. Much of it was a This Is Your Life-style review of highlights from his childhood. The one big constant was the way his miserable, abusive, sadistic excuse for a father had delighted in undermining him in every facet of his life. There was all the physical stuff, for one thing.

The savage beatings he'd endured when he'd been too small to fight back. The occasional inappropriate touching he tried very hard to never think about. And then there was the openly derisive way he reacted to anything remotely positive that happened in his son's life, including mockery for exhibiting pride at earning good grades at school rather than excellent grades. But that had been nothing compared to the humiliating way the old man had taunted him in the wake of an especially cruel rejection by the prettiest girl in the neighborhood. Making his son cry had been one of Josh Benson's great joys in life for a long stretch of years. He honed the skill to a fine edge during that time, systematically destroying his son's confidence and generally doing much to turn him into the social recluse he eventually became. Dumping the bodies of the dead girls on Luke's property had simply been the culmination of it all, an ultimate expression of contempt, as well as the most perfect way of fucking with him he'd ever conceived.

Josh laughed again. His face looked redder than ever. "Should see yourself, son. You look like someone knocked you a good one upside the head." He smirked. "You used to look like that a lot in the good old days."

Luke launched himself at the old man, slamming into him and driving him to the floor in a tangle of flailing limbs. The fight was brutal and touch-and-go in those first few moments, with his father landing a few solid blows despite being caught off-guard. But Josh had been right earlier—he was too old to get the better of his son now. Luke absorbed the worst of the blows easily and soon gained the upper hand, winding up atop the old man as he relentlessly battered the bastard's face with his fists. He shattered his nose and pulped his lips, broke his jaw and knocked several of his teeth loose. Blood flowed from several wide gashes and his cheeks turned purple. At some point, the old man stopped moving, a development Luke initially chalked up to surrender. But knowing he had won did nothing to dim his fury at first and for a time he continued to slam his gloved fists into the now virtually unrecognizable face of his father. The rhythm of his punches only began to slow as his arms grew tired.

He let his arms hang limply at his sides when it was over. They each felt like they weighed about a million pounds. For a while he just sat there, breathing heavily and staring at his father's ruined face in a numb state of shock. When he belatedly understood that Josh Benson had died, the numbness went away and he let out a strangled gasp followed by another round of violent sobbing. It went on for a while.

Luke's father had been a worthless piece of shit, but he had also been his last living relative. In those first starkly bleak moments in the aftermath of it all, beating the old man to death felt like the perfect capper to a perfectly crappy life. He had no one left in the world who gave a shit about him, even in a twisted, hateful way. No more family. No more friends. Only his dogs loved him. He cried and cursed the old man, letting out a lifetime's worth of frustration and regret, as well as helpless grief for the life he might have had if he'd been raised by people who were decent.

When the explosion of emotion at last subsided, he got up and commenced a careful search of the house. He hadn't come this far to fail now and damned if he was going to let the old man get the last laugh. He found the first part of what he needed in a lockbox Josh Benson had kept under his bed. Inside it were gruesome Polaroid photographs of his victims, along with other sick mementos of his crimes, including locks of hair, various undergarments, ID cards, and a small piece of rotted flesh wrapped in a clear plastic bag. Luke's face twisted in disgust at the sight of the latter, which he was pretty sure had been someone's nipple.

He carried the box out to the living room, removed some of the items from it, and arranged them carefully on the coffee table. The intent here was to make it look as if the old man had been consumed with nostalgia during his last night on earth. Once he was satisfied with the placement of the items, he went out to the garage, where he found his father's shotgun. Back inside, he fetched a chair from the kitchen and put the old man's corpse on it. The chair had been positioned so that where he'd already bled on the carpet would fit with what was about to happen.

Whether he would get away with what he had in mind was questionable. But Luke figured he'd already staged one crime scene tonight, so why not go for a second one? The odds against things working out in his favor were higher than ever, but he was damn well going to do his best.

He wedged the barrel of the shotgun up under his father's chin and got his hands wrapped around the stock of the weapon. It was tricky and took some doing, but he eventually managed to make it happen. The blast of the gun made him cringe and momentarily deafened him while making a suitably messy wreck of his father's head. The grisly tableau was sickening, but he refused to allow another surge of emotion to paralyze him.

His getaway came courtesy of the old Indian motorcycle Josh Benson had kept in the garage next to his Mustang. The bike was rarely used and its absence wouldn't mean anything to the lawmen investigating the scene. If anyone asked him about it later, he would just claim the old man had given it to him months earlier.

The ride back to his isolated trailer was even more uneventful than the ride into town earlier. He didn't cross paths with even a single vehicle from the sheriff's department. The rush of the warm night air felt good against his face as he left Murfreesboro behind and cranked the bike's engine to a high rev, feeling freer than he ever had as he sped down the dark rural roads en route toward whatever the future held for him.

ACKNOWLEDGEMENTS/AUTHOR'S NOTE:

The author would like to note the title tale of this collection is in no way anti-hippie or anti-counter culture. The title is merely a play on a common pejorative view of people in that scene in conjunction with rotting zombies. A joke, in other words. Thanks to the following for the usual reasons: Jennifer Smith (world's number one rock and roll babe), Jeff Smith, Keith Ashley, Brian Keene, Tod Clark, Paul Goblirsch, Ryan Harding, Matt Hayward, Lashon Miller, Carrie Nicely, and Andersen Prunty. Thanks also to my Patreon "super supporters": Brian Keene, Brian Picard, Sr., Christian Wood, Jordan Lindsey, Joseph Branson, Scott Berke, and Tim Feely.

ACKNOWLEDGMENTS AUTHOR'S NOTE

CREDITS

Some Crazy Fucking Shit That Happened One Day first appeared as an ebook original from Bitter Ale Press. It appeared as bonus material in a limited hardcover from Thunderstorm Books. This is the novelette's first widely available print appearance.

"The Restless Corpse", "Chainsaw Sex Maniacs from Mars", "The Thing in the Woods", and "A Slasher's Dilemma" originally appeared on Bryan Smith's Patreon. This is the first official publication of these stories.

"Pilgrimage" was originally published in the themed anthology *Welcome to the Show* from Crystal Lake Publishing.

"We Are 138 Golden Elm" originally appeared in the themed anthology *Chopping Block Party* from Necro Publications.

"The Barrel" originally appeared in *Cut Corners: Volume 3* from Sinister Grin Press.

Six of the stories in *Seven Deadly Tales of Terror* were originally an ebook only publication from Bitter Ale Press. Their appearance here marks the first widely available print publication for most of the stories. "South County Madman" originally appeared in the collection *Set's Quartet* from Thunderstorm Books. "The Implant" later appeared in *Year's Best Hardcore Horror: Volume 2* from Comet Press.

ABOUT THE AUTHOR

Bryan Smith is the author of numerous novels and novellas, including *68 Kill*, *Slowly We Rot*, *Depraved*, *The Killing Kind*, *Last Day*, *Dead Stripper Storage*, and *Kill For Satan!*. Bestselling horror author Brian Keene described *Slowly We Rot* as, "The best zombie novel I've ever read." A film version of *68 Kill*, directed by Trent Haaga and starring Matthew Gray Gubler from *Criminal Minds*, was released in 2017. Bryan lives in Tennessee with his wife Jennifer and their many pets.

Follow him on Twitter at @Bryan_D_Smith and on Facebook at www.facebook.com/bryansmith

Get access to exclusive Bryan Smith fiction at Patreon. Includes serialized novellas and novels, excerpts, short stories, and behind-the-scenes essays. www.patreon.com/horrorauthorbryansmith

Other Grindhouse Press Titles

www.ingramcontent.com/pod-product-compliance
Lightning Source LLC
Chambersburg PA
CBHW010837250626
47157CB00011B/3302